SHADOW OF THORNS

WICKED FAE
BOOK FOUR

STACEY TROMBLEY

Shadow of Thorns

WICKED FAE

Book 4

STACEY TROMBLEY

I

REV

I flinch when shouts begin down the hall. Panic shoots through my veins, but I swallow it down quickly.

I'm home, I remind myself. *Safe.*

My desk is the same wooden structure my mother had made for me after Reahgan's death. My shelves filled with well-worn books I studied for the last two decades are within arm's reach.

But I can still smell death and smoke and shame. Can still feel the ash and blood between my fingers.

The walls that surround me now are solid, luxurious marble. The bed is the same I've slept in since I was a child with silk sheets and a smooth silver cover. This is my safe place. Bright and clean and familiar.

But I am soiled and scarred. I don't belong here anymore.

Caelynn is in the bathing room down the hall. *She's here, she's alive. She's safe.*

I flex my fingers, remembering what it felt like to hold her lifeless body in my arms. To watch her soul suffocate before me. My skin crawls at just that thought.

I'd come so close to losing her. To killing her.

Now, my fingers itch to reach for her. To hold her. To reassure myself that she's here and okay. That I didn't *fulfill* that terrible vow I'd made to end her.

The shouts continue, bangs and shuffling feet sound through the whole palace. I force myself to stand straight, anxiety stirring in my belly, but numbness fills my limbs.

Something is obviously happening. But what?

I take slow steady steps to the window and stare out at the pristine courtyard. Painfully bright light reflects off every surface of the Luminescent Court grounds. I squint, eyes burning, as I peer out over the gates. It's shocking how bright the world can be. After a week inside fae hell—*my God, it was only a week*—my body and soul had apparently become used to the darkness. Now, my homelands feel excessively bright and harsh.

Guards trot down the silver pebbled roadway toward the shining glass gates. They scurry into a formation, lining the pathway and standing at attention just as a massive golden carriage pulled by two shining black stags with golden antlers rattles around the corner. Two smaller carriages follow behind it.

I blink.

So, that's what has the palace in a buzz.

The High Queen of all fae has decided to pay us a visit. My chest tightens. I hoped to have a little more time to recover from our intense mission before facing the queen but alas, that was a baseless hope.

A gentle knock sounds on the door.

"Yes?" I call. The door cracks and a withered fae leans in, his awkwardly bent antlers appearing first.

"Sir, your parents have called for your presence in the great room to greet the High Queen. You—" His dim eyes examine my ragged appearance. I haven't so much as changed my clothes since escaping the Schorchedlands. I don't want to even think about the source of the muck covering my entire body. "Well, I suppose it's a bit too late to get you presentable. I suppose the queen will understand. If you'd like to head down, I can attend to your—*guest.*"

"No." My response is quick. Perhaps a bit too sharp. Chimmie flinches. He has been my personal servant since I was a child. Though his attention and praise hold less meaning than my parents or even my uncles—he's paid to dote on me, after all—he's been a caring figure in my life.

My mate is in the next room, exhausted and magically drained. Vulnerable in more ways than one. Anyone in this household—other than myself—could be a threat to her.

I eye Chimmie.

He would obey my word to treat Caelynn with respect— I do believe that without a doubt—but he, too, loved my brother. And to him, Caelynn is simply his assassin. His murderer.

"I will speak with Caelynn first. Then, you can take over."

Chimmie purses his lips but then nods. "Very well."

I tap on the bathroom door, stark white against my soiled hands, fingernails near black. There's no response on the other side, so after a moment, I push it open slowly, just peeking in. My stomach twists as she comes into view, dark sunken eyes staring blankly at the brown water.

"Everything okay?" I ask, keeping my stare trained to the wall behind Caelynn. I don't want to make her feel uncomfortable, especially considering the way she sinks deeper in the water like she's hiding. Like she doesn't want me to see her.

"Fine," Caelynn mutters. I bite my lip briefly, not wanting to put any new pressure on her. I want her to be able to rest, clean up, eat fresh food and build her strength.

She's so thin, her face so pale, her eyes so dim.

Our time in fae hell was harsh on both of us. I was held prisoner and tortured by the Night Terror. But to be perfectly honest, I feel like I got the easy end of things. Making our way through the Schorchedlands would have been draining enough—with animated skeletons, man-eating trees, parades of mindless wraiths, and more—but throwing in a plot by not one but two ancient powerful beings, one of whom literally suffocated Caelynn's soul from the inside... well, it's a damn miracle we survived it.

Then again, the game isn't over yet. The Night Bringer and Night Terror are still out there and now at full power.

"I don't mean to rush you, but... we have visitors," I say, now wondering if I should have kept it to myself and let her have the break she obviously needs. She doesn't need to face the queen, at least not right now.

Her eyebrows pull down. "Visitors?"

"The High Queen just arrived on property. She's... going to have some questions for us."

Caelynn's expression shifts only slightly, her muscles still slack.

"Is it all right if I come in for a moment?" I ask sheepishly. "If not, that's—"

She waves me in. "Of course you can come in."

"Okay," I whisper, and I take slow steps toward the white porcelain tub in the middle of the massive bathing room. We have many others in different parts of the palace. A communal tub, as is fae tradition, in the king's quarters and guest hall, and a hot spring in the middle of the courtyard, surrounded by green and white lumitrees.

But here, there are more basic bathing quarters. I squat down beside her. "Listen," I begin, unsure what I even want to say. "There's a lot happening. A lot we still have to do. But you can stay here as long as you need." I look down at the murky brown water. Her face is still streaked with blood and muck. "I'll have them draw a second bath. I'll have food brought to the room. I'll talk with the queen for now. You don't have to come."

Her eyebrows pull down. "You sure? You said she'd have questions for the both of us."

"She will. But I can take care of it for now. If she insists or there's some decision that needs to be made, I'll come and talk with you."

Her expression turns sad suddenly, eyes cast down.

"What?" I breathe.

"Will you leave? If she asks you to."

My lips part, heart picking up speed. "No. Not without you."

2

CAELYNN

I stare at the door for minutes after Rev leaves, my mind still. A few hours ago, I was certain I would die. Well, perhaps a bit more than a few hours now, but still less than a day.

My breathing speeds up as I picture that moment. The Night Bringer took over my body. My soul was suffocating. I thought I'd lost. But Rev... he somehow brought me back. He somehow set us free from the prison I'd condemned myself to.

How?

To be honest, I don't even want to know. I don't want to think about what that means. For us. For the world.

I press my eyes closed, pushing down the nausea stirring low in my stomach. After a few deep breaths, I push the thoughts from my mind and force my body out of the cooling water. It was a pleasant feeling, cocooned in warmth, but like anything good in my life, it was short-lived.

Knowing Rev is now preoccupied with the queen, I feel more confident with my nakedness and I cross the room to find a fluffy white towel and rub it over my body. It comes away streaked with brown. Well, I hope they don't mind a ruined towel or two. Even the tub will require a deep cleaning after my time in it.

I rub every inch of my skin with the now-damp towel until my skin is raw and red and the towel nearly covered with brown and red streaks.

A small tap-tap sound makes me flinch. I clench the towel over my chest awkwardly and whirl toward the door on the opposite side of the room where a set of grayed antlers appears through a crack in a door I hadn't paid any attention to. The elderly fae with sagging skin steps the rest of the way into the room, his head bowed. I blink.

"Hello, dear." His gravelly voice has a kind lilt to it, but it sounds forced. Unsurprising. He probably wants me dead.

I swallow, pulling my fist higher up my neck even while knowing it does nothing to cover me. The towel hangs limply over the most important bits, but my hips and waist are bare.

"We have a second bath awaiting you. If you'd follow me."

"A second?" Rev mentioned he'd have a second drawn, and I understand why. The muck we'd acquired over the last week is... inconceivable. But I'm not sure I want to remain idle for much longer. Not now that I know Rev is dealing with the High Queen.

The wheels in my brain have begun to turn again, slowly but surely. And there's a lot I'd like to know. Like what will happen with the spellbook and the scourge? My banishment?

My lips part, and I pause. "Would it be rude if I were to decline?"

His eyebrows rise. I remember him, I realize. His name escapes me, but he... he was here, waiting on Rev and his brother so long ago.

"Not at all, miss. Of course—" His nose wrinkles and he scoots a bit farther into the room. "If I may..."

I nod, permitting him to say whatever is on his mind.

He steps forward, his gaze scrutinizing. I resist the urge to cower, knowing that whatever he is looking for, I will be found lacking. "You've cleaned your skin well enough, though only time will tell if the smell will linger."

My lips part in surprise.

"My apologies, miss. I do suppose that could sound offensive, but whatever you'd done to become soiled as you have—the both of you—"

I wave my right hand. "No need for niceties. I was a wreck, I understand."

He bows his head, and I squirm at the submissive motion.

"I have never been treated as a royal, and I don't expect to begin now." I purse my lips. "Not here," I whisper.

A flicker of emotion crosses the fae's face, but he locks it down behind a carefully-trained expression only a moment later. "Prince Reveln expects you to be treated well. I will make sure that is the case."

I freeze, holding back any possible emotion. I'm not sure what to feel about that, and so I won't dwell on it.

"As I was saying, your body is cleaned well enough for the time being, but... your hair."

The fingers of my free hand instantly reach for my head, finding straw-like strands. Dust and dirt rain down on my shoulders with even just that small motion.

"If you intend to see the queen at any particular point, I'd suggest doing something about that."

My laugh is sharp and bitter. "Yes, I agree."

"I expect her to be forgiving of Prince Reveln's state of dishevelment but you, less so. Of course, I don't know if you'll want to see the queen, but if—"

"Why wouldn't I?"

"Oh!" he says, straightening. "Well, I don't know exactly

what happened out there, miss, but it was rather unexpected to see you both return in the state you were in. I—I don't know if you want the queen to know you... followed the prince... and returned."

I swallow. It was that obvious, wasn't it?

He's totally right, I hadn't thought much of it, but we'll have some serious explaining to do about my role in all of this. I wasn't meant to enter through the Wicked Gates. Only one was allowed to enter and return. It should have been impossible.

So, if she knew we both entered and both returned...

I'm certain the reports about damage to the Wicked Gates will begin soon if they haven't already. And those wraiths went somewhere.

She'll blame me, I realize.

They'll all assume I allowed those monsters to be freed to save myself. And if I don't come forward, they'll just blame Rev instead. I suppose I know which is the better of the two options.

I nod quickly. "You're right. A second bath is necessary. But after, I'll head straight down to greet the queen."

The fae coughs. "Very well. I'll have clothes laid out for you in our guest chambers. Would you like me to show you where they—"

"I'm familiar," I answer automatically, and it's only after the servant freezes, every muscle tense, his face pale, that I realize I *shouldn't* be familiar with this palace. I've been here secretly on two separate occasions now. "I..." I fumble over my words. "I'm sorry. I stayed here one night before we traveled to the Crumbling Court a few weeks ago. I spent some of the night in the room adjacent to Rev's. I assume that's the room you mean?"

He blinks, his body resuming its stiff movements as he crosses the room. "I remember." His voice is hoarse.

"Oh," I mutter, unsure who all knew I'd remained in the palace that night. The guards had spotted me from the window and came storming in. It had seemed that only the king had figured out I was staying by Rev's permission, but perhaps I was wrong about that.

Or perhaps he means an entirely different time I was here.

"I trust Prince Reveln's judgment," he says, hands clenched behind his back, face slack. "And it seems... it does seem as though you have helped him. I..." He pauses. His brows pinch.

"I understand," I whisper. "I am under no illusions of what I am. Who I am. Here, most of all."

He closes his eyes for one brief moment and then turns on his heel to march from the room. I wrap the towel firmer around my body and follow him through a set of doors to find another identical bathroom with a steaming tub that smells of lavender.

The elderly fae rolls a tray overfilled with oils and creams and soaps, brushes, and combs.

"Thank you," I whisper.

He says no more and backs out of the room.

3

REV

I hold my breath as nearly a dozen High Court Guards march into the grand hall in full black armor. They halt in a line, faces obscure beneath their masks. The High Court crest glows in gold over their chests.

The High Queen of all the fae strides in after them, her bronze dress swishing. Her arms and fingers, usually bedecked in jewelry, are bare. Her determination is as clear as the daylight streaming through the skylights and bouncing off the mirrored walls of the grand hall.

I stand beside my mother, equally stiff and dressed as eloquently as the queen herself in a bright white ballgown studded with silver gemstones. Beside her, the Luminescent Court King appears particularly displeased. Though I don't suspect he's displeased by the queen—he's a kiss ass if I ever met one—but he's yet to even look in my direction.

He hates me.

Has hated me since... well, for as long as I can remember. Did he know I wasn't his blood relation from the moment I was born? Or did I have a loving father for a few weeks, months, or years, before he learned the truth and turned on me?

I myself didn't know I wasn't his true heir until the trials only months ago.

I blink as another familiar face rounds the bend at the end of the hall. My stomach sinks as I take in her body language and expression. Kari is beautiful in her purple gown, complimenting her dark brown skin, but her expression is more than grim. Very out of the ordinary for her.

Her eyes dart around the room expectantly. Nearly—panicked. Her pained eyes meet mine, and they grow large.

My heart rate picks up. What's happened?

"Prince Reveln of the Luminescent Court!" the queen projects. "I am surprised I had to learn of your arrival from *my guards.*"

I swallow but resist the urge to wince beneath her withering stare. "My apologies, your Highness. I only arrived last night, and w—I was nearly on the edge of collapse when I did. I do suppose—" I pause, realizing the issue. "I should have come straight to the High Court." That's true. But with Caelynn in my arms and the unexpected way we'd escaped—there was no way that was going to happen.

Her jaw clenches. "What do you have to say for yourself?"

I press my lips into a thin line. I hadn't given myself time to practice what I'd say to her. The journey was nothing like I'd expected. She takes in the state of my soiled boots and blood-splattered tunic.

"Did you complete your mission?" she nearly shrieks.

I blink as the image of the Wicked Gates crumbling, and the wraiths scattering to the wind blast through my mind. "Yes," I blurt out, stress lacing my words as I remember the true mission. "I... retrieved the spell book." That was my mission so, technically, I did complete it. But I know in my heart that I failed the realm.

My mind jumps to Caelynn, and I resolve that it was all worth it.

Kari's hand flies to her mouth, her shoulders slumping into what I have to assume is near a sob. My eyes widen.

"Well?" The queen's voice rises.

I return my gaze to her. Her muscles are still tense.

She knew I'd returned because of her guards watching the Schorchedlands. That means she must know that the Wicked Gates have been destroyed. She must know the wraiths—and more—have been set free.

"Things," I begin, "did not exactly go as planned. But yes." I squat and reach inside the backpack at my feet, nearly as soiled and ripped up as I am. I swear the leather-bound book hisses as my fingers clamp over it and I lift it out for all to see.

A collective gasp rings out across the room. Royals and guards alike lean in, eyes large. They are awed by a book that seemed only a legend.

The binding burns against my palms, but the incoherent whispering I'd heard from it just moments before is missing now. Slowly, I approach the queen.

Her eyes narrow as she looks upon the leather. "I do not wish to touch it."

I clench my teeth against the burn. "Likely a wise choice," I bite out.

"Does it pain you?" Kari whispers between her fingers.

"Yes. I'm... not sure why."

"But you can use it?" she asks, pulling her hand down and leaning over the book.

"Yes," I whisper.

The queen's eyes darken as she narrows in on the book.

"It's been used once already," she states plainly, but her eyes meet mine.

I frown but then nod, and her shoulders relax. Then, she grips her wrist, rubbing it. Just as quickly, she drops it and rolls her shoulders as if releasing stress. I don't dare ask what that means. But I suspect she knows exactly what I did. And somehow—that is the source of her relief.

I pull in a massively long breath just as a final fae joins us in the great hall, and the breath leaves my lungs in a rush.

We all spin to face the beautiful fae standing at the back entrance. Caelynn.

Her hair appears damp, in loose waves over her shoulder. Her face is now clean of muck, and she wears a silver tunic that flows loosely down her body.

My father stumbles forward and points in her direction. "Arrest her!" he shouts. There is not even a beat of pause before the Luminescent Guards leap toward Caelynn.

An arrow is loosened with a pop, streaking toward her. I hadn't even realized there were archers in the hall.

Caelynn simply smiles at the projectile streaking her way.

One quick bend of her knees and shadows whip around her. The arrow slams into the stone wall and, with a clatter, falls to the floor. Her shadows dissipate leaving only the empty place she'd once stood.

Gasps sound and I spin to find Caelynn casually reclining against the royal table behind my father. "Now, that's not a way to treat a treasured guest," Caelynn chides, one brow flicking up.

A roar of rage rips from King of the Luminescent Court. His arm swings out and with it, blinding light that forms the whip that snaps only barely louder than the gasps. But Caelynn is gone.

The royal guards move for the first time, shifting in front

of the queen whose expression and body language show only minor annoyance.

Caelynn appears in the corner of the room with a smirk across her lips, one hand on her hip. I resist the urge to laugh.

"You bitch! I warned you that if you ever came back here…"

"Oh!" Caelynn purrs. "We're telling the queen about that conflict now, are we?"

The queen's eyebrows rise.

My father's face grows deep red. His palm glows brightly.

"That's enough!" the queen finally barks, and he freezes, his lip curled in disgust. "You will deal with your useless feud on your own time. I am not here to endure your bickering. I have more important issues to tend to."

"Agreed, your Highness," I say, unable to hide the smirk on my lips. "Perhaps, we should meet in private to discuss our next steps."

4

CAELYNN

I knew walking into the great hall would be a disaster, but it turned out to be even worse than I'd expected. And significantly more fun.

My heart fills with sick joy as my blood pumps hard and fast through my veins. It probably makes me a bad person that I am so amused, witnessing the hatred pulsing from the king. Maybe if I didn't know how he treated Rev as a child, or that he tried to have him killed in the trials, I would feel more guilt. I did kill his son and true heir, after all.

But he also came for Raven in the human world. He sent fae assassins after an innocent and beautiful human girl just to get to me. So no, I will not feel bad for taunting him. I allow myself to enjoy watching him squirm.

I enjoy the hatred on the faces of many of the Luminescent Guards less, but that's an issue for another day.

Rev stands before the queen, his shoulders relaxed, a small smile hidden at his lips.

Perhaps that's another source of my joy.

"Very good suggestion, Prince Reveln." The queen places a

hand on the shoulder of the guard in front of her, and the lot shifts to allow her room. She steps toward Rev.

For the first time, I notice the book clenched between his fingers. How had I not noticed the power pulsing from it? The gentle whispering cascading through the room.

I swallow and clench my hands into fists as strange territorial urges rush over me. *The book belongs to me.*

Yeeesss, it whispers back.

My eyes grow large, but no one else reacts to the voice. Not even Rev.

I bite my lip, controlling my emotions. *Rev can be trusted.*

Can he? Those words shudder through me and I blink, this time unsure of the source. The book? My own mind? The hair on my arms stand up as I remember the Night Bringer's claws in my mind. That was less than a day ago.

Less than twenty-four hours ago, his talons had carved me up from the inside out.

I push those concerns away and focus on the current obstacle in front of me. The High Queen of the fae realm.

"How?" someone beside the queen whispers. For the first time, I notice Kari, my fae friend. My only female fae friend, to be precise. Her skin is darker than the other royals currently in the room and her dress is a lovely lavender, but that is where her poise ends today.

Her hair is braided but more disheveled than I'd ever seen it, even during the trials. Her usually bright purple eyes are dim and wide as the full moon.

Shit.

Kari is one of the few souls that knew I entered the Schorchedlands after Rev. Not that I'd intended to keep it a secret from the queen, but I hadn't intended to tell *everyone.* Especially considering my lack of appreciation from this court in particular.

"What the hell happened?" she whispers. Her expression is full of panicked awe.

"Privacy is an apt suggestion," the queen announces quickly. "Lead the way."

Rev nods, letting out a relieved breath. He deposits the book back into his bag, which he then slings over his shoulder. "This way," he says to the queen.

Kari and the High Queen follow Rev through a side door and down a brightly lit hall. The queen's personal guards begin to follow, but she holds up a palm and they freeze. Then, she waves me forward.

One of the Luminescent Guards growls, and the High Court Guards clench their jaws.

"Come, Caelynn," she purrs, and I begin forward.

Whispering scatters across the room and I smirk, one part because of their collective bewilderment and one part because their murmurs remind me of the Whisperwood.

I could go back, I try to tell myself, *to my beloved lands.* To the shadow sprites. To my heritage. But can I? My banishment was only rescinded until the mission was complete—and now it is.

Will I be immediately kicked out of the fae realm?

"Your Highness," the gruff voice of a guard sounds through the hall, a demand.

She only sneers in response.

"No!" one of the Luminescent Guards spits out. "You cannot be alone with her. She's the betrayer!"

The room hushes with one glaring look from the queen. "Do you think I do not know exactly who she is? Do you really question your queen?"

The following silence stretches for several achingly long moments.

"As I said. *Come,* Caelynn."

My lips curl into a smile as I cross the room, passing all of those who hate me so deeply, to meet with the High Queen of the fae realm.

"No need to be so smug, girl," the queen comments as I enter the meeting room and the door clicks softly behind me.

I let out a low chuckle. "Apologies. I have few pleasantries in my life. Shocking those who hate me is one of them."

The queen rolls her amber eyes.

I let my smile fall—an easier feat than it should have been given my amusement, but the weight, so heavy on my soul, remains hooked deep. It's easy to revert back.

I look up at the domed ceiling bordered with glistening marble. I've been to many places in this palace, but this is new. The walls are decorated with framed, shattered glass artwork. It's surprisingly lovely.

"Caelynn, what the hell?" Kari squeaks out the moment the door is securely shut behind the four of us. She rushes forward, throwing her arms around my neck.

Warmth spreads over my chest, and I return her embrace. Her limbs tremble in my arms, and I squeeze her tighter.

"You... how... I thought you entered the Schorchedlands? I thought you both did. What the hell happened?"

She pulls back, and I notice the red in her eyes and the bags beneath them.

I narrow my eyes, ignoring her question and asking one of my own, "What's happened?"

"You ask me that?" she hollers. She wrings her hands raggedly and sucks in each breath like it will be her last.

"Shhhh," the queen murmurs, the lines on her mouth

becoming more prominent. "Settle, child. We'll get answers. We'll get what we need."

"What do you need?" I ask.

"The cure!" Kari nearly shouts and then slaps her hand over her mouth, tears welling in her frustrated eyes. My stomach sinks, and then I remember. She'd confided in me at the High Court ball, the same night Rev and I entered the Schorchedlands, that the scourge had stopped just outside a Crystal Court village. She was desperate for the cure to save her people.

We'd been gone a week. I'd wager that the scourge is no longer frozen.

My eyes lock with Rev's, but I don't let them linger. I turn back to Kari. "We can depart immediately," I rush out. "We have the spell book, and Rev—he can..."

A gentle hand grips the back of my upper arm. "Caelynn," he says. His breath on my neck sends a shiver over my whole body. Dizzying delight at just that small touch. At my name on his lips.

The queen narrows her eyes. "My, my. Much has happened, I see."

"What's going on?" Rev asks, his voice deeper now, determined.

"When we entered the Schorchedlands," I say, "the scourge had paused—just outside a Crystal Court village."

"It's not idle any longer," Kari confirms.

My stomach sinks, but my heart swells at the clear depth of devotion Kari has for her court. I couldn't admire her more than in this moment, even as I pity her.

"I see." Rev blinks at the smooth silver tile on the floor. "Yes, we'll... we'll prepare to leave immediately." His eyes flick up to the High Queen. "After we discuss a few details."

I swallow, and Kari's tear-filled eyes flick between us.

"How did you get out?" she asks, as if just now remembering her initial question.

I lift my chin, eyes going hard as I prepare to take the fall. To take the blame.

"It doesn't matter," the queen barks. "We have the book. That is what matters."

I flinch. Then, an uncomfortable calm takes hold over my body as I examine the queen.

She knows.

She's always known what needed to be done. Maybe... maybe she's even relieved that monster is free. Because the game is over.

My wraith—Darren—had implied the queen had been in on all of it. She knew the real goal of the trials. She knew... *She knew.*

Maybe she'd been forced into a bargain like me. I don't know. Her wrist is bare of the mark. The mark the Luminescent Court King wore the night of the High Court ball when he convinced me to follow Rev into the Schorchedlands. The mark I'd borne when the Night Bringer sent me to kill Rev.

I may never know to what extent the queen was involved. But as she said, it doesn't matter. It's clear she knows what we did inside the Schorchedlands, and she doesn't care.

Now, we just have to wait and see what the consequences of our choices will be.

"The book," Rev says. "The book is Caelynn's. The glory belongs to her."

The queen narrows her eyes. "*Only* her?"

He nods.

I almost respond, I almost defend that Rev is able to use the book as well, but I clamp my mouth shut, remembering it's best to take the brunt of the blame. The Night Terror has been released, and the book was the key to that spell. The

Night Bringer will be at his full power soon enough. If he's not already.

"You used it once before," she repeats.

"Well, yes. But that's complicated. Using it again would be—challenging."

"I don't understand." Kari's gaze flickers between us.

"It burns when you touch it," the queen says in answer.

Rev's lips part, but he pauses. "Yes. Caelynn retrieved the spell book. She is the only one meant to use it."

The queen's eyes narrow. "Kari, retrieve the spell book."

My gut twists, urging me forward. I clench every muscle, only barely resisting the urge.

Kari hesitantly shuffles forward and bends down to pull back the ragged canvas of the backpack, revealing the shimmering leather-bound book.

No, the voice hisses. I wince as Kari grips the binding tightly but then seethes and rips her hands away. "Ahh!" she yells, shaking her hands. "What the hell?"

You are not worthy, the book hisses again.

I roll my eyes. "So dramatic."

"What?" Kari's voice spikes.

"Oh, not you." I shake my head quickly. "The book, I mean."

"The book?" The queen leans forward.

"It... speaks to me."

Three sets of eyes bore into me. "You can't hear it?" I mutter uncomfortably and look up at Rev.

He shakes his head slowly. "I... heard incoherent whispers once before, but... nothing now."

I belong only to the Shadow Heir.

My eyebrows rise. "It belongs to me."

"Belongs?"

I shrug. "That's what it said."

"Caelynn retrieved the book," Kari murmurs in awe, "so now it only obeys her command."

My lips part, but it's Rev who responds. "I'm fairly confident I *couldn't* have retrieved it. There—" He shakes his head. "It's complicated."

"I'm sure it is," the queen says. "And again, it doesn't matter who is responsible. It only matters that we have the book and we are able to use it to save our world."

She doesn't want Kari to know only I could retrieve the book because that would unravel all of the untruths she'd told. The trials were all a farce. A trick to get me into the Schorchedlands to reverse a curse that should have never been undone.

The Night Bringer didn't want me to know what I was doing until after the book was retrieved. Then, he planned to force me to complete the spell to release his mate from her eternal prison by using my love for Rev against me.

Things didn't go exactly as they had planned, but they found a way regardless.

It was a chess game I didn't even know I was playing until far too late.

Those monsters succeeded. They're free now.

But it wasn't me that completed the spell. I wouldn't have.

Those monsters had banked on me being willing to do anything to save Rev. Back when I was seventeen? I would have done it. But now? No, I knew better than to think playing along with them would earn me anything.

Death is the only release from their clutches. I would have let us both die to keep them caged. But it turned out it wasn't me that was willing to sacrifice anything to save my mate.

It was Rev.

"But Caelynn retrieved it," Kari says, voice full of awe. "Caelynn is the savior."

"No," the queen and I say in unison.

"I am anything but that."

"Unfortunately," the queen says, casually intertwining her fingers, tipped with sharp red nails, "no one outside of this room should know this tricky bit of truth."

"But she—"

The queen holds up her hand. I meet Kari's eye and shake my head. "She's right."

"But," Rev adds coolly, "she *should* be rewarded."

The queen jerks her head, swinging around to meet his gaze. "What?"

"Pardon her," he demands, his eyes dark and determined, his jaw set.

"You think..."

"I think reinstating her banishment would be the most unfair thing the courts have ever done."

Kari's lips twist into a surprised O shape, the color returning to her eyes as she stares at me.

"No, not the most," I disagree, but my interjection is ignored.

"Ah," the queen draws. "Is that what you really wanted so badly to discuss alone?"

"Among other things."

"It would be rather suspicious, wouldn't it?" the queen murmurs uncertainly. "Many in your court saw her chasing after you toward the Schorchedlands. And how many saw your return together? If I were to then immediately pardon her, the rumors would be unsatiable."

"Sacrifices often have to be made to do what is right," Rev says, his voice poised and determined. The voice of a ruler. "Tell the people it is my wish. I will take whatever backlash comes from it. I can not—I will not—continue on as if none of this happened while Caelynn is banished to the human realm."

The queen rolls her eyes. "Now who is dramatic?"

I snicker. Kari's large eyes find mine, some of the tension has drained from her, but there are still clear lines on her forehead. Even so, she's clearly fascinated by Rev's determination that I be pardoned.

The queen sighs. "It's more complicated than you make it seem, Reveln. I cannot..." She narrows her eyes as she pauses. "We will discuss this further at another time. For now, we have a plague to end."

5

REV

My stomach aches as I follow the three powerful females from the meeting chamber. My chest is tight, my mind buzzing. Nothing is wrong per se, but there is much to do.

I didn't know what I'd need to demand from the queen until the moment I saw her. Saw both of them in the room together. When a guard behind me mumbled about Caelynn's banishment being reinstated.

That bitch oughta be shipped back to the human world now, ya think? Those words burned through me, and it took every ounce of control I had to stop myself from throttling him then and there.

The truth is, I understand their hatred. I'd felt those same things, I'd thought those thoughts— and worse.

So, the anger, I could dismiss. For now. But those words left a deeper sting.

The thought of her leaving is a dagger to my heart.

I meant what I said to the queen. Just as I wouldn't leave her behind in the Schorchedlands, I wouldn't continue on with my life if hers is dismantled.

I *know* I can get her freed, and I'll keep fighting until that's a reality.

What will it mean, Caelynn living a free life in the fae realm? Where will it leave us? I don't know. I don't have the energy to think that far.

I can't... I press my eyes together, quickly shaking the pain from my chest. Caelynn is mine. Maybe not in all the ways I'd like, but in the most important.

I will protect her. I will do what I must to make sure she is not only okay but happy. Whatever that means. I chose her inside the Schorchedlands, and while the world is still against us, that choice will not change.

Not ever.

The queen may not have refused my request, but she didn't agree to it either. Not yet. And until it's official, until I know I've given this back to Caelynn, it will eat at me.

She deserves, more than anyone else, to live in the land she loves. She deserves the chance to walk through the Whisperwood and commune with the Shadow Sprites. She deserves to be seen as the hero she truly is.

Even if they'll never know the full truth.

I'd shout it from the rooftops, all the things she has done if it wasn't for the Night Terror's freedom. Those creatures are out there together and now at full strength. That truth is on us.

Well, it's on me.

I know that, but the world shouldn't know what I've done.

My stomach twists again. *Is that selfish?* I wonder.

Should I accept the hatred that would come along with the truth?

I grew up in the court of light. A place where secrets were rare—at least, I thought they were.

But my mate is from the court of shadows. A place born of secrets and enigma.

I will take a page from her book, for now. *The world shouldn't know the truth.*

I know that's true, even if it's doesn't feel right. It would cause panic and unnecessary conflict. We don't yet know what it will mean for those beasts to be free. Until then, I will keep our secret.

And I'll let the world begin to see Caelynn for who she really is one step at a time, instead of all at once. After all, I'd needed time to open up to her too. To believe that she's a hero instead of a villain.

And it will become my life's mission to show what I know to be irrefutably true.

Caelynn of the Shadow Court is the most wonderful being I've ever met.

I'm so lost in my own thoughts I only notice that Caelynn has disappeared into the shadows when we reach the great hall and she's nowhere to be seen. *Dammit.* Why does she always do that?

The guards straighten, muscles tense, eyes darting around as we enter, and I remind myself that I know exactly why she hides. They hate her.

"We will set out for the Crystal Court in exactly one hour," the queen announces to the room. My eyebrows pull low. She gives me a knowing look and says, "Use that time wisely," and at first, I think she's telling me to go find Caelynn. Then, I follow her gaze to my feet.

To my mud-caked boots.

My lips curl into a wry smile. I'd forgotten how disgusting I must be.

The queen spins to face my father whose harsh expression softens in an instant. She nods, and my father marches back toward the hall, toward the meeting room. The queen follows.

More business, apparently.

The Luminescent Guards examine me with narrowed eyes like I'm a puzzle they're desperate to figure out. These men have followed me, adored me, respected me, for a decade or more. Most have personally heard me discuss all the ways I'd like to punish my brother's murderer.

And so, now, they cannot understand how and why I'd not only align with Caelynn but befriend her.

If only they knew where I'd like to take the relationship next.

My people hate her.

Even while I love her.

~

I heave a huge sigh the moment I reach my room, and I search the shadowed corners for any sigh of Caelynn. Nothing.

"Master Reveln?"

I blink rapidly and turn to Chimmie.

His smile is sad, his eyes knowing. "Would you like a bath prepared?"

I purse my lips. "I'll take care of it." Baths have never really been my thing anyway, and I'm too tense and eager to soak today.

He nods and backs out of the room.

After dropping the backpack onto the bed, I march into the bathing hall, passing the tub. On the other side of a glass wall, there is a stall surrounded by silver tiles on three sides. I enter and pull the wooden lever. Steaming hot water pours from the spout like rain.

I undress quickly, tossing my ragged clothing into the

corner of the room, and let the burning water wash away the muck and pain and fear.

The tension in my muscles eases quickly, and when I close my eyes and picture my future, it's her I see.

6

CAELYNN

"If you pardon that whore, *I swear, Zanterleisha.*" The Luminescent Court King's face is ruby red, and I allow a sweet smile to spread across my face. It's not like anyone can see me anyway.

"What? What do you swear? What will you do?" The queen's voice carries through the room. I shift, carefully eyeing the shadows that hide me, cocoon me.

Okay, using my shadows to spy on the High Queen's next meeting wasn't my wisest of decisions but it was simply too tempting.

I knew I had an hour to waste. I could wander the halls of the palace for the next hour. I could hide away in Rev's room with the shadows of all my haunting memories, or I could come here just on the off chance I'd discover something of interest.

So far, the only interesting tidbit I've uncovered has been that the queen brought her guards into this meeting. Does she trust Rev and I more than the Luminescent Court King?

Shadows tickle my ears, and I shiver pleasantly.

It's quite nice to be able to use my power without the

jagged, painful edges digging deep into my soul. Was that just the Schorchedlands? Or was it the Night Bringer? And if the latter, what does it say that he's leaving me alone now?

The king's jaw clenches, his cheeks burn red, and I wish I could allow the laugh bubbling in my chest to release into the world. I live for his discomfort.

Does that make me a bad person? I don't know. I don't care.

He mumbles some apology but continues to express his displeasure at my involvement and continued permission to remain in the fae realm. Yada yada yada. He hates me; we all know it. We get it.

"She still has a part to play," is the queen's only response. And I am certain that every soul in the room knows he has no power here.

If the queen intends to pardon me, his words will do nothing to change it.

I slip to the other side of the room as the conversation continues on into thoroughly boring territory. Unsure how to get out of the room without making myself known, I come up with a quick plan.

I knock lightly on the door. There's a pause in the conversation as all attention shifts to the door. The queen's eyes are narrow, then her chin lifts in a sharp motion—a signal for the guard to open it. I could almost convince myself that she rolls her eyes as I slip out silently.

The guard pauses for a moment, then the door clicks shut behind me.

I shrug it off. If she knew I was there, it must not bother her too deeply. Likely, she too was just wasting time until we leave for our next mission. I only wasted a quarter of my wait, so I sneak up to Rev's bedroom, only pausing at the top of the stairs to consider the guards.

The marble landing is the same as the last two times I've been here, and my predicament the same. Two guards stand astride a narrow hall I know leads to Rev's bedroom. And once upon a time, Reahgan's.

These two guards, I know, will only allow a fae to pass if they have Rev's personal password.

The first time I passed through here, I snuck by using my magic. But when I was here only two weeks ago, these guards were the few in the palace able to see through my magic. Whether because they're some of the most elite guards in the court or because Rev personally trained them, I don't know. But I assume today will be the same. They'll see me if I try to use shadow magic.

I could expose myself and hope the previous password still stands.

Except, I remember the clear message from the king—I am not welcome, no matter what Reveln says. Does an order from the Luminescent Court King override Rev, even for his personal guards?

Even if I had the password, would they allow me to pass?

I step forward slowly, toward the two soldiers holding spears and swords, still as statues. I remain hidden by my shadows and wait for a reaction.

One of the guard's eyes flash in my direction, but without even a beat of hesitation, his gaze flickers back straight ahead. I frown.

He sees me... but is pretending he doesn't? Is that how this will go? I debate my options here. Give my password and hope for the best. Sneak by slowly and hope I'm not suddenly attacked.

Or shadow leap.

If they can't see me now, they won't see me then.

If they see me but are pretending not to as I suspect, then a leap won't change their minds.

In one heartbeat, I make my decision. My shadows suck at my very being, and without hardly any effort at all, I leap. My eyes open to find myself halfway down the hallway.

The guards haven't so much as flinched.

I continue down the hall and slip into Rev's room without sound or disturbance.

Rev's room is still and quiet, and I finally allow my shadows to fall. I roll my shoulders, feeling stronger than I'd ever have expected given my current circumstances. I hadn't thought I could recharge that quickly after the Schorched-lands drained me bare, but I feel... good.

I haven't eaten much at all. I shoved a banana and a few nuts down my throat before heading down to meet with the queen, but that's all since the Schorchedlands. There is a platter of cheese and fruits sitting on the table by the window. Just one glance and my stomach growls.

You are stronger than you think, a voice leaks from the air around me, and I spin to face the pulsing power coming from the bag on Rev's bed. *But then again, you have me.*

The book.

The plate of food in my grip, I tote it back to Rev's ridicu-lously comfortable bed, sinking into the cushions.

Have you forgotten me already? the book hisses.

I roll my eyes. "Needy much?"

A low hum comes from the bag. I begin plopping fruits into my mouth and chomping down, and before I think about what I'm doing, the canvas is pulled away to reveal the thick brown binding.

I have all you need, shadow fae.

"Lies," I tell it, and my mind flickers to Rev. To the

Shadow Court fountain that fuels the kingdom, where my magic will begin the rejuvenation of my homelands.

I have all the information you need, it corrects.

"Better." I grip the book and pull it into my lap. It buzzes over my skin. "Yeah, yeah, I get it. You belong to me. Yada yada."

The book doesn't respond to that. Carefully, I fold open the cover and run my fingers over the blank yellowed pages.

"Do you only speak audibly?" I ask the book. "You have no written words at all?"

"I can show you what you seek if you'd prefer. Or I can speak it."

"Show me the spell used to curse the Night Terror," I command. The book purrs beneath my fingers, nearly vibrating until ink sinks into the pages before me. I pull in a breath, taking in the complex spell in front of me. There are symbols and arrays, followed by full written paragraphs.

"The spell was made for both of them. They were meant to be imprisoned together but apart."

"How?"

"One inside the flames of justice. One outside."

I purse my lips. I suppose I can see that. "One of the wraiths told me the Night Terror could destroy the flame wall if she pleased."

"A lie."

I swallow. Okay. "So, she was doubly imprisoned. But when we—" I shake my head. "When the spell was undone, it released her from both."

"Precisely."

"Why was the spell book hidden in her prison? Why not somewhere else entirely?" That seemed like such a foolish choice for fae who desired to make the prison permanent.

"Another mistake. I was meant to be taken far from there, to a

place neither night ancient knew. But all did not go as planned, and Sanjaria hid me in the mountain before sealing her soul in the gates. It was a panicked decision.”

Breathing through my nose, continuing to chomp on my snacks as I ponder all of this.

I bite my lip. “Are there ways to kill them?”

“Yes. But it would require like power.”

“Like power. You mean a being like them. Like you?”

“Yes.”

“How about trapping them, like before?” It’s a temporary fix, but it did work before, for a few hundred years. It’s better than nothing.

“You could replicate the spell with my help, but the amount of power it would require is still beyond your capabilities.”

I still need a being of immense power. “Are there more ancients? Now? Beings in our world capable of trapping the Night Bringer and Terror?”

“Yes, but they slumber under protections of their own making. Even if woken, there is no telling they’d be willing to aid mortal beings in order to destroy their own.”

I have more questions to ask, more things to ponder, but right now I have another obstacle to focus on. Healing the lands of the scourge. Once that is done, I’ll dig deeper into how to handle my monsters.

A few more minutes and my stomach feels full. My eyelids grow heavy, but I know I can’t rest now. I’ll have to distract myself elsewhere until after the Crystal Court is saved. Then, I’ll allow myself to rest.

My gaze flickers to the door to the next room. The door that I know leads to the bathing chambers.

“Prince Reveln is there,” the book answers the question I didn’t ask.

“I didn’t ask that,” I hiss. “Don’t go reading my thoughts

and answering embarrassing questions in front of other people."

The book rumbles beneath my fingers. Was that a laugh? *"I cannot hear your thoughts, child. Mortals are simply easy to predict. And no one can hear my voice but you. Others can read what appears on my pages by your bequest, however."*

I purse my lips. Good to know.

I'm tempted to shut the book now and get moving. I'm restless. Uneasy. Many of my most pressing questions are not ones even this all-knowing book can answer. "I need to know the future." I sigh.

"I cannot answer that, shadow fae."

"I know," I mutter. But there is one thing I'd like to know before I move on. "What happened to Darren Shadowspell?"

There is a pause, one beat that feels like an eternity. I'd never known him as anything other than a wraith, but I know he was once the King of the Shadow Court. And now, apparently, he is gone for good. I just want to understand how and why. I have a guess, but until I know for sure...

"Darren Shadowspell spent five hundred and twenty-six years as a wraith before finally completing his soul's mission and finding redemption."

I gasp, those words hit me hard. "He loved me," I whisper.

"Yes," the book whispers in return. *"His redemption came because he chose the adoration for his descendant over his deepest personal desires."*

"He chose me. Over the Shadow Court." Tears well in my eyes. "What happens to a soul when it's redeemed?"

"It passes on to a place even my knowledge cannot reach. I know everything that has ever happened in this world. But I will never know what lies beyond it."

"What did he look like?"

A sketched image appears on the pages before me of a dark-haired, severe-looking male. I blink.

"That's him?" I whisper.

The book rumbles gently under my fingers but says no more. It doesn't look like him. The man in the image is glancing off to the side, his eyes dark but rimmed in gold. He's... *scary* if I'm honest.

I shut the book quickly before I can get lost in the rabbit hole of what-ifs and history that is irrelevant to me now. Maybe one day, if I'm allowed to keep the book that belongs to me and my ancestors, I'll spend hours and hours, days and days, even weeks, learning of all the missing histories of our world. But I cannot lose myself in this now.

Not yet.

Displeasure simmers around the book, but I ignore it and march toward the spare room just to run away from the thoughts and emotions rolling through me.

I should be happy that Darren was redeemed. It's a happy ending for him. But the selfish part of me wishes he were here now. I... trusted him. And there are things I must do now that he could help me with.

My father is gone. And now my ancestor is gone too.

The gentle rush of movement across the room catches my attention. Steam billows from the door at the end of the brightly lit room. The door is slightly ajar. The crack is only an inch or two but enough to hear the faint sounds of running water.

I inch forward, curiosity getting the best of me for only a moment. The splattering of water sounds like... a shower. My experience with the fae realm is still somewhat limited despite growing up here. After all, I grew up in a very poor village.

Bathing here is different than the human world. Mostly

large communal baths, some outdoors, some in. Some are magically heated and cleaned. But never a shower. I'd assume that to be exclusively a human thing.

I step up to the open door and press my fingers to the smooth structure, but I stop myself from going any farther.

"Caelynn?" Rev's voice calls from inside.

My breath catches, muscles tensing, and apparently, that pressure is just enough to push the door in even farther. Steam rushes out, tickling my neck, and then clears.

Rev's eyes lock with mine from across the room, and I freeze. Blood pumps heavy in my skin, ears burning. Steam billows from the stall, but it does little to obscure the view.

He's naked. Entirely.

And I might spontaneously combust right here and now.

He doesn't move for what feels like an eternity, and I couldn't move an inch even if I wanted to. And I do want to. I want desperately to run away, hide, fade into shadow and live there the rest of my life.

There's intensity in his gaze, his chest rising and falling in long labored movements.

Then, his hand slides up the side of the glass stall, and he leans forward ever so slightly—and my God, what that subtle movement does to his muscles.

His thorn tattoos twist from wrist to shoulder and then fade into three blackbirds flying toward his neck.

"You're welcome to join me," he says, voice husky.

I suck in a breath, eyes flashing back to his. His dark locks fall into his eyes dripping water down his cheeks. I imagine a smug tone and expression to go along with those words, but I receive neither. He sounds *sincere*. His eyes are once again that fierce silver that does all kinds of things to me that I don't dare name.

Like an idiot, I freeze again because I have no idea what to do now.

"Caelynn?" His smile fades, and his brows pinch.

"Sorry," I whisper and shift from the doorway, shutting the door behind me.

My eyes close against a storm of emotions. Desire and pain and embarrassment and bone-deep helplessness.

Because this, Rev and I, is so right it's hard to deny. But at the same exact time, it's wrong and impossible and so very, very stupid.

There can never be more than this. I press my palm to my chest, willing the air to settle in my lungs. Willing my soul to stop that incessant nagging.

Mine, it whispers through me.

In another world, yes. Rev would be mine. But the world we live in—the both of us—it will never be true. Not in the ways I want. The ways I need.

I stumble forward a few feet toward the bed.

"Caelynn?"

I grip the bedpost to steady myself, my heart stopping mid-beat.

Turn around, I tell myself. *Face him. Don't be a damn coward.*

"Are you okay?"

I force myself to face Rev, trying with all my might to remain calm, but I can feel my cheeks burning.

Water drips down his bare chest until it reaches the gray towel slung low on his waist. Low enough to reveal that ridiculous V human girls always raved about.

All right, I guess I can see the draw now.

I swallow and meet his eye. He smiles, but there is still concern—and heat—in his gaze. "Didn't peg you for a creep, Caelynn."

I groan and cover my eyes with my palm then push it back

until my fingers tangle in my newly clean hair. "I didn't mean…"

He dismisses my mumbled excuse with the wave of his hand. "I walked in on you bathing. I figure we're even." He takes a few casual steps forward.

I drop my hands, and for the life of me, I can't stop my eyes from roaming over his body. His black thorn tattoos twist intricately up his muscled arms. At the tops of his shoulders, thorns twist into towering trees with branches reaching up. Three birds soar from the trees, toward his neck.

"I've never seen your full tattoo," I comment quietly, knowing full well he knows that my eyes are all over him.

"I see," he says, watching me silently. Allowing me to take him in. His muscled arms and chest, his stomach of chiseled abs. Finally, I swallow and force my eyes away from his beautifully sculpted body.

"How does it feel to finally be clean?" I ask and plop a grape-like fruit into my mouth just to create something other than *this* between us. He doesn't respond immediately, and I finally meet his stare. His chest rises and falls with deep breaths.

"Good." His jaw clenches.

I lick my dry lips, and his gaze snags there.

"Caelynn," he practically croaks, and my whole body aches from it. Panic rushes through my chest, and I know I have to leave. Because we might be mates, and that is an easy explanation for what's happening here, but that doesn't mean it can be allowed.

Rev and I may have survived the unsurvivable, but here, in the fae world, it's a whole other hell. One where I do not have a place beside him. And so, when Rev's fingers reach toward me, I wrap my shadows around myself and I leap to the doorway and disappear into the hall.

7
REV

My whole body is tense, muscles clenching painfully as I enter the carriage without Caelynn.

The shower felt wonderful. Not only was I able to wash away so much of the darkness clinging to me from the Schorchedlands, but I was able to relax for a short time. Something I desperately needed.

But then Caelynn was there. Watching me. The look on her face had me winding up for entirely different reasons. And then, she ran. Fled from me like I was a monster there to take away her virtue.

I haven't seen her since, and it's eating me up inside.

Why did she run? Why isn't she here now?

Does she not want me the way I want her? I mean, I know things are complicated but... I run my fingers through my damp hair.

Kari and the queen climb into the carriage and sit on the velvet-covered bench across from me.

"We should wait for Caelynn," I mutter, wringing my hands because the truth is, I'm not certain she's even coming. Maybe she ran from more than my bed chambers.

"The shadow fae will not be traveling with us," the queen says. "She may be your ally, but she is not trusted by the realm at large. We must be careful of the image we project."

I clench my teeth. "They can learn to trust her, as I have."

"That will take time," Kari reassures me.

"I need her."

The queen and Kari both freeze, eyes wide.

"We may need her to use the spell book."

The queen's mouth opens, then she clamps it shut. A moment passes before she speaks, just as the carriage rattles into motion. "But you used it once before. You, not her."

I continue to be surprised at how much the queen knows. How much she hides. "I did. But I used some of Caelynn's power to do it. I don't know if I'll be able to repeat that feat or if her proximity affects it."

Kari doesn't respond to that, just continues gazing out the window. The queen, however, shifts dramatically. Eyes large brows high, lips parted.

"You used *her* power," she comments.

My stomach sinks again, knowing I'd given away a truth that was perhaps better kept hidden for now. The queen had obviously noticed our *familiarity*. She knows we've grown close. Maybe she assumes we've become lovers. Something that is—sadly—untrue.

But she didn't know we were mates.

Until right now, I suspect.

"That is most illuminating," she mutters.

I bite the inside of my lip and join Kari in staring out the window.

"I suspect she'll be right behind us," Kari says.

The queen quirks her head.

"Caelynn has very few allies." She smiles at me. "But I

know of one other that will help her get where she needs to go."

I follow Kari's gaze out the carriage window, to a set of stags standing before the High Court portal, each with a hooded rider. One is thin, the other broad. I let out a relieved breath, even as so many more questions unearth inside of me.

"Let me ask one thing, Prince Reveln," the queen says without making eye contact. "Have your ambitions changed?"

Her question is simple, but the meaning is loaded. Do I still hope to be named High Heir? Do I still want to become the king of all fae when her time is through?

"No, they have not changed." My heart aches as soon as the words escape my lips.

She nods curtly. "You said today that sacrifices often need to be made in order to do what is right. As High King, as you so aspire to become, your choice of companions... would be limited."

The breath leaves my lungs, but I manage to force a response. "I know. I've always known that truth."

She nods again. "Good."

My hands curl into fists, fighting back the intense frustration because I know exactly what she's telling me.

If I ever wish to be High King, Caelynn can never rule beside me. She may be strong and capable and wonderful, but my job as the king would be to keep unity within our realm. And that will never happen with a dissenter, a prince's assassin, standing beside me.

"But allies," the queen adds softly. "Allies can be found anywhere."

"And friends," Kari says. I swallow, willing my heart to

remain whole. Willing fate to find a way for me to have her. In some way, big or small.

If for only a moment. I'll take it.

8

CAELYNN

I stand at the edge of the Luminescent Court entryway, watching Rev and the queen board the carriage. Off to complete Rev's destiny.

Will he be named High Heir today? Tomorrow? I'm certain it's inevitable. He'll heal the scourge at the Crystal Court. And while there's little we know about how that will happen and how easy it will be to heal the entirety of the lands the scourge has touched, I know that by the end of today, the world will see Rev as a hero.

The savior of the realm.

He'll have it all. And I honestly couldn't be happier for him, but there is still a sting, deep down.

His life will be complete.

Without me.

I swallow. I know there isn't another option. I have my own destiny to complete, and I fully intend to do just that. It's just... going to be a bit harder for me than it is for him.

And then, there's the matter that my monster is still out there. The Night Bringer is alive and well, and now, thanks to Rev and me, reunited with his mate.

Something I'll never have.

Maybe that's what kills me the most. The Night Bringer, the being that ripped me from my childhood home, destroying my innocence, my relationship with my mate, my family, my legacy, has achieved everything he fought for.

The reason he kidnapped me in the first place. The reason he tortured me and tricked me into a bargain. It was all to get the spell book, to release his mate from the prison my ancestors put her in.

And he got it.

He fucking won.

I bite the inside of my lip—hard. If it had been up to me, I'd have let myself die to stop those ancient monsters. I'd have shoved the dagger in my own heart if I had been able. Anything to stop him from winning. Anything to stop him from gaining the rewards he destroyed me to obtain.

We haven't seen even a hint from those beings since we fled the Schorchedlands. And I know Rev made some kind of deal he thinks protected us from them, but not for one single second do I believe that's all there is to it.

And to be honest, even if the Night Bringer would leave us alone forever, this wouldn't be over for me.

His evil cannot go unpaid.

But I know he will act. Somehow, someway, he'll find a way to get to me and Rev. Because that's what he gets off on. He desires fears of the deepest kind.

"You all right?"

I jump at the voice. I'd thought I was hidden well and no one had paid me any mind, but apparently, I was wrong.

I gasp as my mind works to catch up to the view before me. A dwarfish fae, short in stature but wide in girth and muscle, smiles at me.

"Tyadin?" I throw my arms around him. His large arms

wrap around me and squeeze me tight. His thick beard tickles at my ear.

"I heard you were back, and I couldn't believe it." He laughs, pure joy pouring from the sound. My heart swells.

The friend I never thought I'd see again is here, laughing in joy because I am alive and free. Like it isn't incredibly concerning that I'm not trapped in the Schorchedlands. He pulls back, hands still gripping my arms.

His eyes are red and his beard unkempt.

"What are you even doing here?" I ask him. "I thought you had some grand adventure planned to take back the dwarfish kingdom across the sea?"

His lips curve into a smile, but his eyes are sad. "That didn't work out."

"Why? You were so excited about it."

"I was, but... that was before you went into the Schorchedlands. I had a hard time dealing with everything. The helplessness, you know? I couldn't do anything to help, but I couldn't leave either without knowing. One way or another."

"I planned to stay there."

"I know," he assures me. "I know you would have, but I had to know. If Rev came out alone, I'd have mourned with him. If you made it out instead of him, I'd have made sure you didn't destroy yourself from the grief and guilt I know you'd wear like a millstone around your neck."

I don't think anyone could have stopped me from destroying myself if Rev hadn't made it. Even still, the fact that he'd try? It means everything. "Thank you," I finally say. "But you really didn't have to sacrifice your dream for us."

"In the end, I made a choice. I chose my relationships over my dreams."

I don't suspect he's telling me the whole story, but I also

get the feeling he doesn't want to rehash what I'm certain was a painful experience for him.

"I'm sorry. If my actions took away your chance—"

"Stop, Caelynn. You made a very brave choice, and my reaction to that choice is not your responsibility. I stayed because I care about you."

I squeeze his arms. "I don't have many friends," I tell him. "Your friendship means the absolute world to me, you know?"

He nods. "Strange to think a competition made to tear us apart instead gave us some of the strongest relationships we've ever had."

I pull him back into my arms, and I fight the emotion swelling in my chest because if I give into it, I'll begin sobbing uncontrollably. The last week has been more than I could handle in so many ways. Just having him here, caring about me in such an unconditional way, is everything I need.

"Thank you, Ty," I say, and my voice hitches, betraying my emotion. Tears well in my eyes, but I take in a few quick breaths and force it back down. I can't do that now.

There is still so much work to be done.

"So, are you following the savior as he heals the world?"

I fight a bitter bark of laughter, even as my lips still tremble with welling emotions. Then, I take a long breath and nod. "I don't think I'm welcome with the High Queen, though." I think back to just minutes ago when I was blocked from approaching the queen and her party by sneering guards. Was that a punishment for spying earlier? Or has my welcome officially been revoked for good?

"I have an extra mount. Bet we can beat them there." Ty winks and nods to two stags, waiting near the portal to the High Court, saddled and ready to go.

"I thought you preferred ponies."

"Prefer? No. The Crumbling Court simply doesn't have the means for more magically powerful beasts," he admits.

"But that's changed?" I ask, running my fingers along the velvety fur of the gray stags. Their coat isn't nearly as shiny as Rev's had been, but even so, a stag is a highly sought-after mount usually reserved for the wealthy.

"Yes, in fact, you helped me to earn a new ally." I follow his gaze to the royal carriage.

"Let me guess? A beautiful purple-eyed fae princess?"

Ty simply smiles and mounts his steed.

9

REV

When I step out of the carriage, my breath catches in my throat.

I've seen the plague before—the black rot that has swept over the land, leaving only death and decay in its place—but even so, it's shocking.

And this time, even more so because this isn't just a forest or plains. This is a village.

There is a pathway, broken and uneven, black liquid oozing from between the cobblestones. Remnants of crumbled buildings line the street. I can hardly tell the difference between stones and bones.

This village is little, tucked between three large mountains streaked with smooth black stone, like a knife cut clean through the slope, leaving only a sharp cliff.

Kari groans and throws a hand over her nose. I raise my eyebrows.

"You don't smell that?" she inquires, eyeing my slack expression.

The smell is unpleasant, but... "I've smelled worse," I admit.

I swallow and step forward into the broken lands. The plants beside the open pathway drip with black slime. The smell grows stronger the farther I venture into ruins covered in rotting flesh and acidic magic.

This time, I cover my mouth, not because the smell is overpowering but because I can feel the pain. The loss was immense.

"How many died?" I whisper.

"A few dozen. Many knew the scourge was close and left before it moved in. Anyone left behind..."

"Children?"

"Thankfully no. Any children were moved to the capital. Only those who *chose* to stay were taken. Still too many."

We reach a tiny forest in the middle of the town. There's a broken bench and several trees bent and twisted, almost like they thrashed in pain before their death. Their branches hang low with brown, putrid leaves.

The hair on my arms stands up straight as we walk slowly through the damage.

"Is there anyone affected but still living?"

She shakes her head. "Not here. People are too afraid of anyone with the sickness. Most of those that try to aid are then taken as well."

I nod. "That will change. Starting now. I can heal them." Determination and confidence swell in me. My magic stirs inside of me, eager to be used. Eager to help.

She bites her lip. She's not as confident, but hopefully, that will change.

"We need to stop the spread first, Prince Reveln," the queen's haughty voice calls from behind me. "If we can kill the sickness before it reaches more fae, that will never need be a concern of yours." She nods toward the forest. "You will complete your first spell five miles north of here and then continue on to Hynetaesi where we will meet you."

I frown, several questions forming in my mind. "I won't perform the spell here?"

"No," the queen answers. "You will destroy the active infection first."

I stare at the ruins of the village. Sadness wells up in me, realizing that I cannot undo what's been done.

"This town was a loss because any deaths are a loss," Kari says, the stress in her voice obvious. "But on the other side of these mountains, only a few miles north, is a large city—a central trading center. The scourge has nearly reached it. This morning, it was moving ever closer. We've tried to evacuate as much as possible, but even just the structural magical losses in that city would be detrimental to our court. We'll run a high risk of severe poverty and starving families come winter if we lose it."

"We don't know what kind of limitations we'll face," the queen says. "So, to be safe, we will first heal the active scourge that reaches toward new towns. This village contains no actively-spreading curse. It will remain this way until we know the spread has been halted. If we never heal the natural magic of places like this, where the scourge has ravaged, that is fine. So long as we stop it from *spreading.*"

I nod, understanding. There isn't anything left to save here. But if we can stop the scourge from reaching the next city, we'll save countless lives. Perhaps even an entire court.

I follow the queen and a set of guards through the rotting ruins toward the only mountain without the streaks of black. We reach a plain of slimy black grass and the ooze sticks to my boots.

"Is this what the Schorchedlands were like?" Kari asks quietly.

"Not exactly. But... well, if I'd come across an area like this in that place, it wouldn't have surprised me."

"What was it like?"

I shiver and shake my head as so many images flash through my mind. "Indescribable."

She doesn't respond to that. We stand there, staring at the quiet horror of this place for another few moments before footsteps sound behind us.

"She loves you, you know," Kari whispers. I don't need to turn to know who is approaching.

A huff leaves my chest. Pain and uncertainty press down on me. I'm sure she's right, in some way. Caelynn does love me. But I'm still reminded of the way she ran from me. How she hides from any intimacy.

Maybe she just needs me to make my feelings undeniably clear so she can overcome her pain and distrust. Or maybe she knows how impossible our relationship will be, and so she thinks it would be easier to ignore our feelings altogether.

I don't know where she stands with all of this. She cares about me, deeply. But does she desperately desire me the way I do her?

"I hope you're right," I say.

My body is heavy as Caelynn and Tyadin approach. I barely have enough happiness left to give Ty a smile. We'll have to reunite later when this mess is through.

"We're going to travel through the mountains a few miles to reach the edge of the scourge," I tell them both. "Ty, you should stay here."

Ty's thick brow furrows in question.

"Because there is risk in going through the forest. The scourge here is active and can be spread to any who enters. Only Caelynn and I will go."

I meet Caelynn's dark eyes, just to be sure she's on board with this plan.

"I should come too," Kari says quickly but Caelynn reaches out and gently squeezes her arm.

"There is no need for the extra risk. You're important."

"And you're not?"

Cae's smile is bitter.

"She's the most important of all," I say. All eyes shift to me, but I don't back down from my claim. "No harm will come to Caelynn. I won't let it."

Caelynn sucks in a breath.

No one argues further, and I motion for Cae to come with me.

"Travel five miles due north," the queen instructs. "Find the edge of black sludge. You'll know when you've reached the actively-moving sickness."

I nod and motion for Caelynn to follow me as I march into the rotting wilderness behind the ruined village.

IO

CAELYNN

The way Rev looks at me now—like I'm the most precious thing in his life—should make me feel good. But the way my heart pounds eagerly and butterflies soar through my stomach terrifies me.

My boots stick to the black muck covering the ground. I shiver at the sound of our boots sloshing with each step, the smell of death coating everything. I welcome the terror that comes with this place because at least it's a distraction from my thoughts about Rev.

But then... maybe this is worse.

It feels like we're back in the Schorchedlands. Adrenaline and quiet determination fill me. And panic—there's definitely a bit of that on the edge of my mind.

I can feel it now. The being behind this. *It's him.* I should have recognized it the first time I saw the Scourge.

The Night Bringer did this. He set loose this curse on the land, slowly eating away at it, destroying entire villages, and killing children—all to get to me.

More reasons to add to my list of why I cannot let him get

away with it. I cannot let him win this game, even if he'd leave me alone personally.

"Ready to run?" Rev asks before the others are even out of view. I shake my head from my morbid thoughts, and together we pick up speed until we're flying through the trees, around the mountain.

Our rhythm is perfect, our pacing exact. We've been to hell and back—literally. And there is nothing that we couldn't do together.

Well, except have an open and healthy relationship. That's not in the cards for us.

High above the treetops the sun just peaks through the dark, sludge-covered leaves. It's the only reminder that we aren't back there, trapped.

Twenty-four hours.

That's how long I've been free. The time in the Luminescent Court feels like a dream, and I've just woken to find my reality. The horror of fae hell—where I belong.

My eyelids flutter. Do I still believe that? My heart feels more solid, more whole, somehow. Ironic, considering how close I'd gotten to my soul dying entirely.

"Are you all right?" Rev asks.

I slow to a walk, my chest heaving. "It feels so much like the Schorchedlands."

"I know." His voice is low.

"It's hard for me to convince my mind that I'm not back there. But I'm good. Not like before."

Rev spins, halting our movement entirely as we face each other. His fingers reach out and glide down my cheek. My breathing becomes labored, even more than before.

Running miles in minutes is way easier than coping with all the things Rev does to my body just by looking at me. His touch? Forget it.

He searches my expression. "He can't get to you now. I made sure of it."

I narrow my eyes, unsure what that means exactly. Then, my gaze drifts to his wrist, and my soul cracks as I realize what I'm seeing. My hand flies to grab his, turning it over to see the thorn tattoo.

He's had full sleeves of thorn tattoos since before the trials, so I didn't even notice the addition. A bargain tattoo.

Rev made a bargain with the Night Bringer. Well, the Night Terror, I guess?

"What did you do?" I whisper.

"You knew, didn't you?" he asks softly, sincere concern in his tone.

I shake my head. "I knew... I know what you did. But... a *bargain*?"

"It was the best way to keep us safe, Cae. They can't touch us now. Neither of us. Or our courts. Or our children."

My jaw is so tight it hurts, sending pulses of pain throbbing over my temple.

"You know I couldn't trust their word. I had to make a deal or..."

"I can't believe you did it," I admit. I wouldn't have.

"It was that or stab you in the heart myself." He spits the words, angry. Defensive. "And I couldn't do it. I wasn't strong enough for that."

My breath is shaky.

"If I didn't kill you, or take the bargain, they'd have taken your soul again. *Again, Caelynn.* He had you. Do you remember that?" His hands are on me now, fingers digging into my upper arms. "Because I can't get it out of my head. I'd make the same choice even now. Easily. No question. Because I couldn't kill you. And I couldn't allow that to happen to you again. I saved you. And if that choice dooms the world, then so be it."

II

REV

Inky black sludge writhes on the forest floor, twisting and hissing. Puffs of smoke release from the tar-like substance that covers everything within sight.

It crawls over the rocks and up the tree bark.

I shiver and hold my hand over my nose. "This is awful," I breathe.

Caelynn steps farther into the forest opening, closer to the living magic actively eating away our surroundings.

"Cae," I whisper. "Don't get too close."

"If it moves this slowly, how does it kill so many people? Can't they run once they see it coming?"

"I've heard it seeps up from the ground, even through tile and stone flooring. Also, that there's a poison in the air that immobilizes some fae."

She takes another step, her boot toe inches from where the tar wiggles eagerly.

"Cae, stop moving toward it, *please*."

"I want to kill it."

"We will. But I don't want you to get sick before we get started."

She spins away from the crawling scourge and takes a step toward me. "Worried you won't be able to heal me?" She smirks.

"There's no doubt I'd find a way, but I'd rather not have to. That may stop me from being able to heal the rest of the land and therefore the huge metropolitan city," I nod past the inky sludge, "just a few miles that way, from being destroyed by this plight."

Her expression slackens. "It hasn't hit many big cities."

I shake my head. "Only one. In the Flicker Court. This would be the second, and I can stop it."

She tilts her head. "Why?" She spins back to the scourge as if asking it.

It does feel alive, the writhing black magic bubbling and crawling. Is it sentient? I remember before the trials we were told it was controlled by a sorcerer, but we now know that to be untrue.

"Why would it avoid highly populated or important places?" she asks.

I shrug, considering all we've learned. "I suppose... the goal was never destruction. It was a threat."

If the Night Bringer started the scourge as a way to push the ruling fae into his plan, it makes sense.

"He needed me back in the fae realm," she says quietly. "He would enjoy destroying the most important areas in the world but instead he teased his power. He pushed his curse close to the areas that would utterly destroy the courts, but then pulled away... probably once they agreed to another part of his plan."

We don't know all the details of what led up to the trials, or who was involved in these negotiations, but someone was. Because now we know that the trials, and Caelynn's invitation, was all a farce to get Caelynn within their grasp, and eventually, into the Schorchedlands.

I tilt my head. "It was a complicated plot, just to get you back here."

She shrugs. "If I knew *he* was behind it, I would never have come. So he had to hide his involvement deeply. The threat had to feel legitimate. A plague was believable. And a terrible competition made enough sense. It was a temptation—I wanted to prove myself. I never even considered the Night Bringer could be involved."

I narrow my eyes, considering. "Would you not have come if they simply threatened me?" It's an honest question. She's incredibly selfless and did so much just to save me. It makes sense to think that plan would have work more easily.

Her lips part. "I don't know. Maybe. But maybe not. If I knew he was behind it, I'd assume there was no winning. And I'd been so far removed from the realm and you, I don't think that would have been enough to motivate me to face him again. You know, I really did consider allowing Drake to kill you during the trials."

I raise my eyebrows. Her eyes cast to the ground.

"I don't blame you."

She bites her lip. "Really?"

I shrug. "I was actively trying to kill you at the time."

"But *you* didn't know I was your mate. I did."

"I would have never believed you or trusted you until actively faced with my death. So, I don't see how you had another choice." I blink, thinking back to that day. That moment. I could taste it. My own death. Inches away. My betrayer turned savior.

My friends betrayed me. Truly betrayed me. And the female I hated with all of my being saved me.

I grew up in the court of light, where secrets were not

common. Or so I thought. I lived in so many shadows without ever realizing it.

"I can't believe we're discussing this like it was justified."

"Not justified. Just... understandable. It helps that you made the right choice in the end. You could have gotten yourself killed with that choice, even with the power we didn't know you held. We never would have guessed you had that much magic in your blood."

She shrugs. "Why would you? I was from the weakest court in the realm."

"You hid your strength well. And that helped to save my life."

She sighs and shakes her head. "So, we gonna do this thing or what?" she asks, staring back at the scourge, crawling toward us. It sputters, tar splattering inches from Caelynn's boots.

"Will you do me a favor and step the hell back?"

Her lips curl. "Worried?"

"Yes," I say emphatically. "I don't want to lose you."

She ignores that comment. "So, do you want to try to heal it, just to see?" she asks. "Supposedly, you never even needed the spell book to begin with."

My fingers tingle, magic rumbling beneath the surface, like it's eager to be used. Maybe I could do it. "I'm sure the spell book will help," I say. And I hand the backpack to her. "You should take it out. It likes you better."

She holds back an amused smile and then pulls the book out from the bag. A hiss resounds through the clearing. And like water being blown by a ferocious wind, the tar-like magic ripples away from Caelynn and the book.

"Not a fan, huh?" She smiles.

"Is there more to the spell book than we know?" I assume

the answer is an easy yes, but I still voice the question because there's so much we don't know.

"Most definitely. I forget that you can't hear it."

My eyebrows pull down. "What do you hear?"

"It talks to me. Like a fully sentient being. He told me... he's an ancient being that imbued his soul into its pages."

My eyebrows shoot up. "Ancient being?"

"He said there were many of them, ancient beings that apparently gifted our realm with the magic it now holds. He was once one of them before he put his soul inside this book to protect it."

My lips part. I trust Caelynn, and she's not exactly known to be a liar, but... it's hard to wrap my mind around.

"What does it say?" I ask. "When it speaks to you."

"It insulted Kari when she tried to touch it, saying she was unworthy. And that it belonged to me. I don't think it's had anything particularly nasty to say about you." She smirks like the book said something.

I frown. "That is really weird."

"Yeah." She shrugs. "It mostly answers my questions, though. It can even show me visions. Or, at least, it did once when we were in the cave."

"Cave?"

"Where I found it in the Schorchedlands."

Oh. I shake my head. That's a sharp reminder that I had nothing to do with retrieving this book. I shouldn't be taking credit for it.

"So, what does the book say about destroying the scourge."

Her brow furrows for a moment as she concentrates, looking at the leather binding of the book. I want to ask more questions—like does she not even need to open it to get answers?—but I withhold my curiosities to allow her to focus on our task.

"It says you may be able to destroy the spell without its help, but it would take a lot of your power." She flips open the book, and I blink back my shock that the pages are empty. Blank parchment with blotches of discolored brown. *It's empty.*

Then, ink appears on the open page. There are a few paragraphs of scribbled words and a symbol sketched across the page. Caelynn focuses on the page for a minute, and then she steps forward and holds the book out to me.

"Can I?" There's a slight jolt when my fingers first come into contact with the leather of the underside, and I wince.

"Don't be a jerk," Caelynn chides, and my brows shoot up. The weight of the book rests in my hands, and the burning fades, though there's a slight vibration. Almost like... grumbling.

"It doesn't like me, does it?'

"It likes you more than most other fae." She shrugs. "He's picky, though."

"Does he blame me for breaking the curse and freeing them?"

She shakes her head. "Not directly. I asked the same thing in the Schorchedlands—if he was angry that I'd come to get him. He said if he slumbered for all of time in that cave, he would have been content. But no, he wasn't angry. It was his purpose. To be used. Even if it maybe wasn't the best thing for the world."

All right then. I stare down at the diagram, lines and angles, and symbols. "Do we need to draw this?"

Caelynn shakes her head. "I just need to touch it, and it's activated."

"Would it work if I did it alone?"

She nods. "He said something about the soul stone? That allows you some ability to use it, but its power is somewhat muted."

The stone warms my pocket. I still barely understand what that stone is or means. Somehow, it holds the power of our mating bond? Our soul connection? Something like that. I've never known lumistones to be powerful. They're symbolic, but nothing more.

Power rumbles under my palm. The book vibrates against me, but I ignore the warmth that grows into a slight burn.

I hold out my hand, summoning my healing power. It's strange to heal something inanimate like stone.

The power rises, slowly building, but it's not enough. Not yet.

I close my eyes. The image of Caelynn drops into my soul. She's broken, in pain, and searching for me. My magic flares to life, flashing gloriously. I stumble back at the sudden intensity as a ray of bright light rises into the sky.

Caelynn reaches for me as I stumble, and the magic flares a second time at her touch. White blinding light streaks into the sky, soaring and roaring over the darkness that's taken over the land.

A groan leaves my lips as the magic grows, blasting over everything within miles. I can feel it stretch so much farther than I'd have ever thought possible.

Suddenly, the book is gone and the magic flashes back into my body, blinking out in an instant.

"Holy shit." My knees nearly buckle. Black flashes over my vision.

Icy cold pain locks my limbs. Caelynn is there, the book closed between her hands, looking at me like I've grown three heads. I straighten back up, but I wobble slightly.

"Holy shit is right."

"What happened?" I ask, which I know is a stupid question, but my tongue feels thick and my mind fuzzy.

"You healed..." she looks around, "I'd guess twenty square miles of the scourge in about ten seconds and almost burnt yourself out."

"I feel weird." Am I spinning?

Caelynn quickly stores the book in the bag and tosses it over her shoulder, and then her arms are around me. "Sit," she orders.

As if obeying her, my knees immediately buckle and I find my fingers digging into the ashen ground. My brow furrows. Is it safe to sit here? But I look down at the ground. It's black but dry. Scarred. "It's gone? Entirely?"

Caelynn nods against my shoulder.

My mind spins again, limbs heavy. "I feel drunk."

"You probably are." She chuckles. "It'll fade quickly, though. We'll have to be careful the next time we try that. That much power at once can kill you."

I swallow and nod, resting my cheek against her head. *Don't say anything stupid, Rev,* I tell myself. Because my body feels warm and unnaturally fuzzy. Like I'm a ten-year-old child instead of a fully grown, adult fae. *Yes, Caelynn is pretty, but you'll sound like an idiot if you say it.*

I guess I can't be that drunk if I'm able to remind myself of that. Or maybe it's just already fading like Cae said.

"Thank you," I whisper, words still slurring. "For helping me."

There's the echo of a laugh in her next breath. "You're welcome."

12

CAELYNN

I sit on the scarred ashen ground holding a slack-muscled Rev for a full ten minutes before his breathing evens out and he lifts his head.

He'd mumbled something about how he shouldn't say that I'm pretty then thanked me for helping him. I only barely held back the laughter.

"I think I can stand now," he says after several minutes in my arms, his voice back to its confident low tone. He doesn't sound like a lost child anymore, so I help him to his feet.

He wipes the soot off his pants.

"I feel... mostly normal," he declares.

"That's too bad," I tease, brushing off my own clothes. "I kind of liked drunk Rev."

"I'd be happy to allow you to meet drunk Rev again... in better circumstances."

I smile, but my stomach clenches. Will we have that chance? How long will I stay with him now that the scourge is well on its way to being defeated? Will I be kicked back to the human world soon? Even if I'm pardoned, it's not like I'm welcome in his court.

And then there's the Shadow Court to consider. *I need to go home.*

Will there be any more nights together?

I look up into the sky past the charcoaled branches and see the blue sky with puffy white clouds. I will certainly never miss the hazy red of the Schorchedlands.

Whatever comes, it will be good. For the both of us. Well, at least better than the alternative. At least we'll be alive, with hope for happiness.

If I'm banished, I'll go back and find Raven.

It's only been a few weeks since I left her in a boarding school, but it feels like years. She's been abandoned by so many in her life I'd hate if I became another name on the list of people who let her down. *She knows why I left*, I remind myself, *even if it hurt.*

"What are you thinking about?" Rev asks, and I blink, refocusing on my surroundings.

"Raven," I admit.

He frowns. "You miss her?"

"I haven't had much time to think about her. Saving your ass all the time."

Rev barks out a bitter laugh. "Oh, okay. Got it."

"She's probably better off without me, but I need to make sure she's okay. And well, I was thinking that I'd go find her if I'm sent back."

"I see." His jaw flexes. Does that bother him?

"I loved her," I admit. "But not in the way she loved me." I meet his stare. The quiet intensity sits between us for a long moment. I don't know why I needed him to know that.

"We should keep going," I say quickly, breaking the moment.

Rev brushes the hair from his forehead before nodding.

We continue walking forward quietly until we find healthy green vegetation.

Only a few minutes later, High Court Guards swarm around us, guiding us the rest of the way to Hynetaesi.

There are purple stones littering the ground here, moss with varying shades of green and white and pink scattered across the tree trunks.

"It's beautiful." I breathe.

"You've never been to the Crystal Court?"

"Only during our short carriage ride the day of the ball. And I spent about an hour in the Crystal Palace after I'd decided to follow you into the Schorchedlands. Kari demanded I'd need some supplies and new clothes." I shrug.

"Kari was right."

"She was, indeed."

Though beautiful, there's very little movement here. No birds or bugs or rustling creatures in the brush. Had they all fled from the nearing scourge?

These trees and flowers and gems would have been smothered by the curse in a matter of hours if we hadn't stopped it. A sense of accomplishment hits me. We saved this place.

Nearly a dozen guards march alongside us toward the city past the trees. The sound of rushing water fills my ears, growing louder as we walk. Then, there's whispering.

For the smallest of instants, I think it's the shadow sprites. But I know better. We're still five hundred miles from where the shadow sprites whisper through the trees of my homelands. "What is that?"

"A crowd has formed to see you," a guard tells us. "We've kept them back in case it was still unsafe. It appears that was an unfounded concern. The scourge is entirely gone."

I swallow.

"They'll be quite pleased by this news."

I suspect that will be an understatement.

"How do they even know?" Rev asks in a whisper.

"That spell of yours was fairly noticeable," another guard chirps.

"It lit up the sky for miles," the first explains.

"Oh," Rev mumbles.

"The magic was more intense than we anticipated," I say.

"The people will also be *surprised* to see you... my lady," the guard says awkwardly.

I almost laugh at the use of *my lady*, but instead, I purse my lips as his meaning sinks in. To be honest, I may not even be safe facing a crowd of Crystal Court fae. The High Court Guards will likely protect me out of sheer duty, but they'd like to kill me as much as anyone else. I consider for a moment the thought of disappearing into shadow so I don't have to deal with the backlash, but then Rev grabs my hand.

"Good," Rev practically growls. "They should begin to see you for what you really are, Caelynn."

"They're never going to trust me."

"If you always hide even the good, that will definitely remain true."

I narrow my eyes but follow his lead, unsure what his idea is. He wants people to see me with him?

The sound of rushing water rises until it's a crashing roar. The waterfall peaks through the trees, and the moment we reach the opening, the cheers begin before I even notice the fae. There is a line of guards in front of a crowd beside the stream. On top of the massive waterfall, there is another dozen fae, arms in the air as they cheer for Rev. There are hundreds of fae here of such varying sizes. A few pixies dart through the air. There are three stags and a hooved minotaur. Dark skin, light sparkling skin. Most of the fae here have bright purple eyes, but there are a few varying colors mixed in.

I can't help but smile at their joy, even though I know their cheers are not for me.

"Rev!" the crowd begins to chant.

"Savior!" another few scream.

The hair on my arms stands to attention. The magic of their joy swirling through the air is delicious.

"You're a hero," I say, voice light.

"You're the true hero, Cae," he says, not trying to keep his voice down—not that it matters, no one could hear him over the roaring crowd. "You deserve the praise so much more than I do."

I shake my head. "Just enjoy it, Rev."

He meets my eye for one long moment, and then he smiles and steps toward the crowd.

13

REV

I wave at the deafening crowd of fae surrounding a lovely waterfall over purple and pink iridescent crystal cliffs. They scream louder as I wave.

But I make sure not to leave Caelynn behind. I turn back and reach my hand out to her.

She frowns but finally takes my outstretched hand.

"This way, Prince Reveln," the lead guard instructs. We climb down a large boulder toward the rustling waters. We must wade into the icy water to cross the stream, and we're dripping wet when we make it to the other side, but I ignore the chill crawling through me.

I'm too distracted by the myriad of feelings flooding me.

Caelynn's hand in mine and the adoration of all of these fae. They think I've saved them. They don't know that it was really her.

I want to shout it to them. That she is the one they should be singing praises to. She is the one that saved them all. But I'm too wise to try it. They wouldn't believe me or accept it. Not yet. Just like Caelynn could have tried to warn me during the trials and I would have never believed her. Not until I saw it for myself.

Slowly. One step at a time, they'll begin to see what I see.

And that will begin by seeing her with me. Helping me.

Let them be surprised that I hold her hand, that she's the one fae I trust to help cure the lands. Eventually, that perception will correctly shift to not just help. But need.

I need her help.

I need *her*.

It may take years, but a plan forms so crystal clear in my mind. It will only work if I'm named the High Heir. Because the Luminescent Court won't accept her ever. But the realm? I think they could over time. Their hatred will melt away when they see her how I see her. When they see that I've forgiven her. When they see that she was the essential piece to their salvation.

My home court might hate her. But the rest of the courts will learn to accept her as mine. And one day, theirs.

There is a carriage waiting for us in the trees on the other side of the stream. The crowds continue screaming, pressing in toward us. The guards shout, and one of them pushes us with urgency.

"What are you doing here, shadow bitch?" someone screams.

I freeze. Anger so fiery it should scare me stirs in my gut. Caelynn pulls at my hand, prompting me to keep going. Get away from the crowds.

Then, a rock comes flying through the air right at her.

My mate.

My arm is out in a flash, blocking the projectile from its

target. A roar rips from my chest. It would have hit her in the back of the head. My palms are glowing in an instant, and I'm ready to destroy whoever would threaten her.

But the guards rush forward, crowding us, shifting us nearer to the carriage. The screams continue. Still so much joy. But deep inside of it, hidden beneath the surface, is toxic anger.

I will rip it out by the stem.

When I'm finally forced into the carriage, sitting beside Caelynn, my fingers are trembling and my heart pounds so hard it feels like it will escape my chest.

"It's okay," Caelynn says now that we're alone. She squeezes my hand tightly in hers.

"No, it's not."

"It is," she demands. "They have plenty of reason to hate me. You cannot change their mind just by holding my hand in front of them."

The pressure on my chest eases, the anger fading to a simmer. I shake my head. "You're right. It will take more time than that."

"Rev," Caelynn complains. "It would take centuries."

I shake my head. I refuse to believe that. They hate her the way I hated her. I can't blame them for something I felt too. "If I can change how I feel about you, they can too."

There has to be a way.

Because if there isn't, then there's no way for us to be together. And I won't give up that hope. Not yet. Not this easy.

14

REV

The carriage drives us the rest of the way through the forest, over rickety pathways, and into the city.

A city I've never been to but where everyone knows me. It's a strange feeling.

I take the half-hour ride to settle my mind. Caelynn's hand remains in mine, and I hold it tightly, but I lean my head against the closed curtain and breathe slowly.

It's incredible how intense the last few weeks have been. The anxiety and fear and pressure and confusion.

It feels good to know, so clearly, what I want. But it's frustrating to think it's possible I'll never be able to have it.

I want to be the High Heir. It's what I've been working toward. Now, it's right at my fingertips. The way people praise me. Fae from another court who adore me.

They knew my brother. They were eager to see him as the High Heir. The realm was broken-hearted when he died.

It's why they all hate her.

My lovely shadow fae still squeezes my hand like she's afraid to let it go. I'm afraid she'll let me go.

Because now, there is something else I want. And it's that dream I feel slipping through my fingers.

The carriage rattles to a stop.

Caelynn's fingers slip out of mine, and my heart sinks. I find her eyes, begging her not to leave. She gives me a sad smile.

"This is your moment, Rev. It's all right. I'll be waiting for you."

The carriage door opens, and the queen is standing there, her hand out for me. The light is blinding as I exit the carriage.

Nausea clenches over my stomach as the crowd roars for me. We're at the top of a hill, looking down at the massive fae city. Behind me are the largest buildings, stone towers rising into the sky, but below is a street of narrow townhomes. Short buildings with blue and pink and purple shingles and crooked windows. There are thousands of fae swarming the streets below.

"People of the Crystal Court," the queen shouts, her voice magically magnified through the streets, but even so, the sound of the crowd nearly drowns her out. She holds up my arm. "Meet your savior! The scourge has been defeated!"

The ground rumbles with their celebrating voices. My vision flashes black for one instant, terror rising up my throat.

The Night Terror, my mind seems to whisper.

The being I was no match for. That tortured me. Kept me in a cage.

She's here.

I don't know if that's true, but it feels like it. *That unnatural shaking.* I shiver. Panic overwhelms me, and my limbs begin to tremble.

Dark shapes shift through the crowd, in and out, waving like smoke.

Wraiths.

I blink, and they're gone, leaving me unsure if they were even real.

The crowd continues to cheer even as the ground trembles. These people love me. They think I saved them.

But it's this moment that I remember—I may have ended the plague, but I released something so much worse.

15

CAELYNN

Rev is pale when he reenters the carriage along with the queen. I lean in, hoping he'll meet my eye, but he doesn't.

"Are you okay?" I whisper, fingers reaching out to his knee. He nods slowly, but it's a lie. He's not okay.

I just have no idea why.

The queen eyes my hand on his knee, and I pull it back.

"Where is Kari?" I ask.

"She wanted to spend more time examining the damage. It's hard for her to believe it was that easy." He stares out the window. "Her court is saved thanks to you."

I nod. I could see that. She has to see it to be sure. To force her mind to believe it's going to be okay. It's good to have someone searching the lands to be sure there was nothing missed.

There are many other places we'll have to visit to heal the land and destroy the scourge but today was a big victory. Even after our healing, the lands were scarred. But I guess we can't undo the damage done. We can only save the realm from further pain. I wonder if, after it all, the grass and trees will regrow in those places.

"So," I say as the carriage begins to rattle forward. "What now?" I ask, thinking of Tyadin. Is he with Kari? Or will he head back on his own? I didn't travel to the scourge with Rev and the queen so I don't think the queen planned for me to remain with them on the trip home. Was I not supposed to enter the carriage? When people started throwing stones, it seemed I didn't have much of a choice.

I wonder if she realizes that we're mates, and if so, how does she feel about it?

Brielle is her granddaughter. Reahgan was Brielle's mate.

She probably hates me as much as anyone else. But she doesn't show it. Not even in the moments she stares at me with no one else looking.

"We are heading back to the High Court," the queen says.

I blink at that. "Should I get out?"

"No, dear. You don't think I'll let you out of my sight yet, do you?"

"Well, I didn't think you'd welcome me into your home either. Unless there is a dungeon there somewhere."

Rev's head whips up.

The queen chuckles. "You are a guest. For now." Her smile doesn't reach her eyes. "There are still several active spots of the scourge. So, until we discover exactly how much your magic is required to end it, you will remain as property of the High Court."

Rev coughs. "Property?"

The queen rolls her eyes. "Caelynn knows what I mean."

I fake a smile. "I understand." I do understand what she's saying—that she needs me. She hasn't decided if she will pardon me, and she likely won't until she feels confident she has me fully under control.

I'm a prisoner.

That's fine. I can deal with that.

I won't be going back to the Luminescent Court, which is good. I won't be going back to the human realm, which is also good. I'll remain with Rev.

There is only one downside to this arrangement.

The Shadow Court is still just out of reach.

~

We travel nearly a thousand miles in less than an hour. I spend the time zoning out, staring at the window frame but not focused on any of the scenery as we pass it.

The carriage rattles, and occasionally, there's a buzz of magic, which I assume means we've crossed through a portal. We were in a large city but not the capital of the court, and so there were no portals directly to the High Court island.

One more buzz of portal magic and the air warms suddenly. I blink and adjust my focus to the new world around me. Same world, I remind myself, though it doesn't feel it.

The High Court is an island on the Source Sea—the ocean that takes up most of our world. This ocean takes up most of the world, and it holds a great amount of magic. There is an entire tourist village on the coast of the Glistening Court where fae go just to bathe in its frigid waters. Supposedly, it increases your power for a full year. There is a tiny island in that area that has a vantage of the High Court palace in the distance. That is the closest most fae will ever get to the High Court—a far-off silhouette.

Somehow, this is the second time I've set eyes on this legendary castle.

Though I know better than to belittle myself and my legacy this much, I still have moments when I feel unworthy of such an honor. To meet with the High Queen. To enter the High Court palace. To stay here as a guest.

Prisoner, I remind myself.

Rev is determined to negotiate a pardon for me, but I know very well that the queen is far from offering that prize. She doesn't trust me. And we all know there would be significant backlash.

I pull in a breath. Salty cool air laced with power fills my lungs. I will admit there is something incredible about this place.

I exit the carriage and stare up at the magnificent structure. The island is fairly small, only a few square miles. Most of that space is taken up by the palace. Its spires wind up in pure glittering gold. There are diamonds lining the curved edges around the six major towers that glisten.

"Most fae never set foot on this island," the queen says with a smooth voice.

"I know," I answer without looking at her.

"It is a privilege."

"I know that too." I press my lips together. "It is simply a bittersweet one."

"Caelynn has yet to see her own court's palace," Rev explains for me.

"I see," the queen murmurs. "Is that an ambition of yours?"

I give her a sad smile and meet her amber eyes for the first time since our conversation in the carriage. Her eyes are blank. Emotionless.

"Yes." It's the only answer I'll give right now. I have many ambitions and visiting my home court's palace is only the beginning. But she is already slow to trust me. How will she feel if I tell her I want to rule that court? That I am its rightful heir. That I intend to rebuild its power and influence to one day retake its place among the High Courts.

Most fae would be very displeased by that idea.

"Come," she says and begins a slow walk toward the massive structure. My eyes dart beyond the building to the waves crashing against the banks in every direction. There are no beaches here, only high banks covered in dark glittering stone. There is a small forest with varied colors of trees, but otherwise, there is little to see.

There is the sea, that tiny forest, and the palace. That's it.

I know from my history books there is a courtyard with thousands of species of flowers within the palace, though. Fae from every ruling court have lived and ruled in this place at one point or another, and so there are marks of every element, even beyond the flags that line the walkway.

Thick golden doors crack and squeal as they swing open. The three of us walk slowly over the threshold and into the High Court palace. We stand in a large entryway with red glowing tiles on the floor and solid white marble walls. Straight ahead is the entryway to the ballroom, where every fae of importance is announced during events, but we enter a hall to the left.

Here, the walls are lined with portraits of every past High Ruler. The queen continues forward, even as I linger behind, eyes examining the portraits. They go back many thousands of years. My fingers graze the smooth stone wall under the right side of portraits. **Grimarian Thornweaver of the Twisted Court.** His eyes are green, but his skin dark as night.

The next has red hair and fair skin. **Helena Ignatius of the Flicker Court.** The next a woman with brown skin and long white hair. Her eyes are nearly white too. **Caroline Icenhour of the Frost Court.**

The rulers are so varied—in eye color, hair color, skin color, in stature and expressions.

Finally, I find him. I hold my breath, willing my lungs to remain calm. My hands stay steady as I look into those harsh golden eyes of the last Shadow Court High King.

Darren Shadowspell of the Shadow Court.

My lips tremble, so I press them tightly together. I blink rapidly to halt the tears threatening to overwhelm me. Is it wrong to terribly miss someone you only met after they died? Long, long after they died. There are five portraits of High Rulers after Darren.

Five hundred years. It actually feels like a short amount of time in the grand scheme of things. Five rulers, out of thousands. That's how long the Shadow Court has been out of favor.

And yet, it seems so impossible to regain that role.

"You okay?"

I jump at Rev's voice and blink back more tears. He stands over my shoulder. It's unlikely he knows the connection. He doesn't know who my wraith was. I nod and turn to find Kari, Tyadin, and the queen watching me from the end of the hall.

I force a smile and take a deep breath, bidding farewell to the fae who saved my life. In more ways than one.

16

REV

I pace in my room, the silence pulsing against my mind. I hate it.

When I close my eyes, I see the tangling roots, claws, and red eyes of the Night Terror. Her ancient power tearing me apart.

It's only been a full day since our lost battle against evil, so it makes sense for anxiety to continue to crawl through me. But the truth is, I'd almost forgotten.

I'd almost allowed myself to revel in the glory they showered on me, forgetting the truth of what I'd done.

But then, it hit me. As I looked out at the sea of faces, adoring me, praising me as their savior—I knew I'd condemned them.

I set that monster free. Who will she come for first? Who will she torture? Who will she destroy?

It's easy to fall into this wonderful life, where I am beloved and powerful, and forget what I've done. I tap my fingers against my leg as I examine my new bedroom.

It's huge and decorated much like my chambers at home

in the Luminescent Court. White marble walls, a four-poster bed with a shining silver bedspread. The biggest difference is the massive archway leading out to a terrace over the water.

There is a table and chairs in the corner closest to the door covered in trays and trays of foods and several types of drinks. There's a silver velvet couch, and two chairs surrounding a coffee table right next to a roaring fire.

Anxiety curls in my gut.

The queen took Caelynn off to another room down the hall and left me to my own. She told us to rest and that dinner would be served privately tonight. I appreciate that because we've had such little time to rest in all of this. And the magic I completed today definitely left me drained. In more ways than one.

I do want to be alone.

And I can't fucking stand it at the same damn time.

I munch on some of the fruits on the table and then lie down on the small couch by the fire. It's comfortable, and I find my muscles relaxing quickly.

There's a gentle knock on the door, and I jerk awake. I blink, eyes heavy. My mind is groggy as I pull myself to my feet and look around. I must have fallen asleep in seconds.

The knock sounds again. Could it be Caelynn? More likely it's a server bringing me my dinner. My stomach rumbles as a reminder that I could definitely use the sustenance.

Anyone else, I very well may slam the door back in their face. I cannot handle the bullshit politics anymore. Not today.

The door squeals as I pull it open, and the moment my eyes land on the fae in front of me, I realize I am entirely wrong.

How could I have forgotten about Ty?

My arms are around him before he can even blink, and a sob wells in my throat. God, I am messed up today. I pull back with an awkward laugh. "It's good to see you."

His eyes are big as he examines me. "Are you all right?"

I nod, though I know it's a bit of a lie. "It's good to see you."

His smile is small. "I was more excited to see Cae than you, I've got to admit."

I laugh. "I would be too." I shake my head and retreat back into my room, holding the door open for him. "Come on, we've got some catching up to do."

There are four jugs of liquid on my table. One is wine; I'll save that for another time. One is water. One is juice. I grab the last, a bottle of amber liquid I assume to be fire whiskey, and pour us each a glass.

"So, what happened to your grand adventure?" I ask. We take seats in opposite chairs by the window of the massive room.

He shakes his head. "There were more important things to worry about."

"Like Caelynn?"

He nods. "And you. And the scourge."

"I'm sorry. I know how excited you were to be a part of it."

He nods somberly, taking a long sip of the burning liquid. "How are you doing with everything?" he asks, shifting the questioning to me.

"Everything?" My eyebrows rise, and I smirk.

"You're the savior. You're curing the scourge. We're in a new era of prosperity." He holds out his arms dramatically.

I wince.

"Not feeling as good about it as you'd expected, huh?"

"It feels awful," I admit.

He blinks, his eyebrows high. "Imposter syndrome is a real thing. You know what you did is incredible, right?"

I nod. "The world oversimplifies everything. The scourge isn't the only evil we've got to contend with."

Ty smirks. "Oh, the world knows there is more evil around. That shadow fae of yours…"

I cough. "That's one of my problems, yes." I take a sip of the burning drink. It sizzles as I swirl it in the cup.

"What kind of problem exactly?" he prods.

"I need them to see her how I do."

"And how's that?" He leans in, examining me closely.

I smile, forgetting that the last time I saw Ty I hated Caelynn. I believed her when she told me she enjoyed killing my brother. "She's a hero. She's…" I close my eyes. "I couldn't even begin to describe the way I see her."

"Like a mate, perhaps?"

"No."

He frowns.

"Much, much more than that."

He pauses then grins. "It might be hard to make the world see her quite that passionately."

I chuckle. "Fair point."

"So, you've given up pretending you're not in love with her?"

I nod. "But I'm the only one of the two that's true for. She's… hesitant."

His eyes cast down at the sizzling liquid. "She's been hurt a lot."

I don't respond to that. Is that why she keeps me at arm's reach?

"You're not going to let her walk away, right?"

"Do you expect me to lock her up?" I laugh.

"No, but I damn well expect you to fight for her."

I slam back the rest of my drink, wincing as I swallow. "That I can promise."

"Good. I didn't want to have to hit you upside the head to see what's right in front of you." He finishes off his own drink.

"Another?"

"Getting drunk your first night back?"

I shrug, and the thought makes me think of Caelynn. "Do you know where her room is?" I ask suddenly.

Ty blinks and laughs. "Wow, that subject change gives me whiplash."

I roll my eyes. "After the spell today, I was a bit... loopy for a few minutes."

"It was that powerful, huh? I guess I should have expected that. It lit up the entire sky. Never took you for the flashy type." He winks.

I ignore that comment. "I felt drunk afterward, and I made a comment about really getting drunk with Caelynn. Hence the leap in subject."

"Yes, I do know where her room is. Would you like me to go fetch her? We can spend the night drinking and talking."

"Are you a servant now?" My eyebrows shoot up.

"No. Despite my sarcastic tone, it was an honest offer." He shrugs and rises to his feet.

"Or would you rather spend your time with the lovely shadow fae *alone?* Because I'm totally all right with that as well."

"A night of drinking with the two of you sounds wonderful."

"Very good, my liege." He curtsies. Literally curtsies.

"What the fuck, Ty?" I bust out laughing.

He moves toward the door, and my stomach is a bundle of

nerves. Anxiety crawls over my skin. But it's not the thought of Caelynn coming that has me nervous. It's the thought that she might *not* come.

That I'll spend the night here without seeing her. And I'm not sure my heart can take that right now.

17

CAELYNN

I shift awkwardly, in the chair across from the High Queen of the fae realm. Suddenly, in my mind, I'm back to being a teenage murderer. No one.

"What do you intend to do," the queen asks, her voice silky smooth, "if I pardon you?" Then she pulls her steaming cup of liquid to her lips.

Her movements are so docile, so domestic, but her eyes— her eyes cut through me. Her nails are red with sharp points that I'm certain are for more than show. She could carve my eyes out and set me on fire at the same time with just the blink of an eye.

I lick my lips and take a sip of my own beverage. It burns on the way down like whiskey but leaves a floral taste behind. "I don't intend to stay here... with Rev," I answer, hoping I got to the crux of her concern. I don't intend to go into more detail than is necessary about my personal ambitions.

Her eyebrows rise, expression slack as she examines me. "I must admit, that surprises me."

I pull in a long breath. How much does she know? I know she's noticed our closeness. Me touching his knee today in the carriage. Him constantly looking at me when we're in the same room. Does she suspect we're mates? Does she know? Has she always known?

"I will never be his bride in this court," I say, sincerely. "That is not something you have to be concerned about."

She bobs her head in a casual but incessant nod. "That is good news."

Somehow, the wince slips past my defenses, and I shake my head quickly, mentally reprimanding myself.

"I know you are smart, Caelynn of the Shadow Court. You know what would happen if he were to be foolhardy enough to choose you as his bride while under the High Court colors."

I bite my lip. I do. At best, it would instill distrust in the crown. At worst, full-out insurrection. This world believes me a true villain. They believe I am the symbol of a dark and dangerous court that has long since wanted to take over the entire realm.

"I believe Reveln intends to slowly reveal you as a hero to the world. The hero you truly are," she admits with a tone that suggests she means it. She sees me as a hero.

I'm not even sure what to think about that.

"He is a stubborn fae, but he too is smart. He knows the risks as well. But I worry his adoration for you will overcome his better senses."

Adoration.

"And he may even begin to succeed over time. The world's hate may slowly ease into simple discomfort. But there will never come a time, in your lifetime, that the world could trust a Shadow Fae on the High Court throne. No matter who stands beside her. Do you understand that?"

I nod. "There is only one way I would take my place on that throne, your Highness. And I am not stupid enough to think that is even a vague possibility."

She narrows her eyes and waits. She watches me, those amber eyes searching. But in the end, she chooses not to ask what I mean.

"I will not be his bride while he is the High King." I can feel the echo of claws digging at my soul. Shame suffocating, but I swallow it down. No matter how much I hate saying it, it's true. I will not be the queen beside Rev.

"Swear it?" she whispers.

I blink, and my stomach sinks to my feet. "You want me to... enter into a bargain with you?"

"A simple one. It would allow me to be confident my fears will not come to pass, and I can consider giving you both what you desire."

I swallow. She is implying she would pardon me, but her words are careful. She will not promise me a pardon. She will only consider it. Still, if this is what is required for Rev to achieve his goals...

"I am willing to promise, but..." I absently rub my wrist. The distant memory of my last true bargain still stings. Her eyes follow the movement. "I've never entered a bargain since that day." I don't specify what I mean, and she doesn't ask. Honestly, I assume the queen knows most if not all of my secrets.

She nods and then begins to stand. "I am ready and willing to name Reveln as my heir, and I will do so as soon as you agree to this bargain. It is your choice. I understand your hesitancy more than anyone, I assure you."

I pull in a long breath.

"But I will give you time to make your choice." Her golden tulle skirt shuffles as she twists. "One last piece of friendly advice before I take my leave." She looks at me over her shoulder. "Marriage is not the only way to be with someone. It would not have to be goodbye forever."

"Thank you," I tell her, unsure why I say it. Because she trusted me enough to have this conversation. Because she believes me a hero. Because she's willing to give me the honesty I desperately needed, even if it stings to hear.

Mostly, because she gives me time to decide.

The queen doesn't respond and instead slips from the room without a sound.

~

Only a moment after the queen departs there's a knock on the door and I open it to find a very wide-eyed Tyadin.

"Ty!"

"Was that seriously the High Queen leaving your room? What kind of alternate dimension are we in right now?"

I chuckle. "What's up?"

His expression grows serious. "I need your help with something. Are you free?"

"I'm starving. But otherwise, yeah. Of course, I'll help with whatever you need. We owe you a lot."

"I think we can solve that issue." He grins and pulls me from my room. I only have an instant to think about what I'm wearing. Form-fitting, black silk pajama pants, and a black tank.

"Wait!" I laugh as he practically drags me down the hall. "Where are we going? Do I need to change?"

"What you're wearing is perfectly fine, Cae."

"Hey!" a voice calls after us. "Where are you taking her?"

Ty pauses his trek to look back. "Kari," he says before I have the chance to take her in.

She's wearing a lovely, purple knee-length dress, her hair braided. Does she always look so made up?

"Oh good, we could use your help as well."

"What?" Her voice is high-pitched.

"Trust me," Ty says. "You'll want to be part of this plan."

"What plan?" I squeal, but Ty is already pulling me down the hall again.

With a groan, I consent and keep up with his fast pace down the hall, Kari taking up the rear. Other than the first moment he asked for my help, he hasn't seemed very serious. His energy is high, his smile huge. What the hell is he up to? What does he need help with that has him so excited?

We cross the palace to another wing entirely. This palace is so huge it boggles my mind. I know there are several wings, one for each of the ruling courts, with rooms fitting their element and tastes. There is even a Shadow Court wing, which is where my room is. Only feet from the parlor with the phantoms.

After twisting and turning several times, the walls fade into white marble with mirrored molding.

And just that quickly, I know exactly what he's doing. "Ty, I'm going to kill you."

"Oh, come on, we're just going to do a little drinking."

"You called it a plan," I say. "You're up to more than just hanging out with friends."

"No, that is exactly what I'm up to. I'm putting you both out of your misery and forcing you in the same room with alcohol, food, and friends. It's perfect."

Okay, that does sound good. But I'm still not sure I believe that's all he's about.

"You could have let me change," I complain again as he stops in front of a shiny silver door. I look around, not at all memorizing which door is Rev's...

"Why? You look fine, and we're just hanging out. No pressure."

Kari hooks her arms in mine. "If we're playing match-maker, we're supposed to dress her up first."

I groan, throwing my head back. "Why did I think having friends was a good idea?"

Kari laughs.

"Believe me, Rev will be impressed with you no matter what you're wearing."

Kari frowns. "Boys. They really don't get it."

The door swings open, and I have to force my lungs still, otherwise, I may have gasped or sighed or something else embarrassing. Rev's lips are curved, his posture casual. He wears silver silky pajama bottoms, much like mine, that hang low on his hips, and... well, let's just say I have to force my eyes up. His shirt is a simple, white short-sleeved tunic that's snug over his chest and arms. He looks fucking fantastic.

"I see we've got a full party now," Rev smirks. "I don't think this is what the queen had in mind when she told us to relax for the night."

"Well, it should have been," Ty says.

Kari sweeps me past Rev and into his room, her arm still linked with mine.

"You didn't have to lie, you know?" I tell Ty. "I would have come if you told me you just wanted to hang out."

Rev chuckles. "What did he tell you?"

"That he needed help with something." I eye Rev's room. It's a lot like his bedroom in the Luminescent Court, the biggest difference is that the far wall is entirely open to the ocean view beyond.

"Well, I suppose we do need help finishing off this bottle of fire whiskey?" Rev shrugs.

Kari groans, flopping down on the white lounger. "I hate fire whiskey. It's why Brielle and I were never friends."

"It's all we have at the moment. So, you'll have to deal," Tyadin says.

"Well, if we're doing this…" I say, holding out my hand for the bottle. Rev's eyes jerk up to meet mine, and I wonder where they had been previously. Was he… looking at my body? I shake the thought away because that is a rabbit hole I do not need to go down tonight.

He holds out the bottle, eyes full of interest. I chug for a few seconds then come up choking. "God, that's terrible."

"I told you!" Kari laughs.

Rev's smile does all kinds of things to me that I work very hard to ignore. He takes the bottle and pours a large glass for both of us. "No need to be such a barbarian. We have glasses." Rev side-eyes me and laughs when I glare at him.

He hands me a glass with a wink.

"Whimp," I mumble.

Rev freezes. "Excuse me?"

I smirk.

With an eye roll, Rev grabs the bottle and chugs from it for at least twice as long as I had. "You did say you wanted to see me drunk."

"That is not what I said."

Rev passes out the glasses of fire whiskey and takes a seat on the floor near the coffee table. It doesn't take long for the fire whiskey to warm me up, both literally and figuratively. Soon, I'm feeling fuzzy and comfortable, and the easy banter between Kari, Ty, Rev, and me is more than enjoyable.

For the first time since I was a child, I feel like… I feel like I'm home.

18
REV

Three shots, two glasses of wine, and three hours later, the laughter dies and joy makes way to sleepy eyes and quiet hushed tones. The four of us talked, mostly about nothing, but occasionally about the nightmares we faced in the Schorchedlands.

Caelynn brought up her concern over her human friend Raven. How it kills her that she's not even able to go back and check on her now that she's a prisoner here. We spent some time consoling her, understanding her fear and guilt, and Tyadin even offered to go to the human world for her.

Caelynn eventually changed the subject herself by starting a game of Never Have I Ever.

Food was delivered an hour ago, and while we all ate a little bit, no one got the full meal we needed. And a few minutes ago, Caelynn laid her head down on the coffee table and hasn't lifted it since.

"She's out," Ty confirms, leaning over Caelynn.

"Aww," Kari purrs. "We should draw something on her face."

"What?" My voice spikes. My mind is fuzzy, movements a bit slow.

She smiles, exposing two sharp canines. "Trust me. It's a human tradition. She'll appreciate it."

I shake my head. Kari chooses violence when she's drunk, that'll be something I remember. "I think that's a tradition we can skip tonight."

She grins and shrugs one shoulder. "Ty and I can get her back to her room."

"No." I stride toward Caelynn's slumped body and peer at her slack features. Her mouth is slightly open. Is she drooling? The corners of my lips tilt up. "She can stay here."

"You sure?" Ty asks.

"I want her to stay near me," I say, realizing my anxiety fell from my body the moment she entered the room today. "I'll let her have the bed."

"You need rest too, you know," Ty says.

Kari crosses her arms. "He's right. The queen is already planning events for the next few days."

I frown. My mind spins and nausea tickles at the edges.

"She's considering an announcement."

I shake my head quickly. Better to not dwell on that too long. "I'll be fine. And I swear on my life I'll take care of Caelynn."

"We'll help. And... hang out a bit longer." Kari says with a forced smile.

"Don't trust me?" I tease, but her expression tells me she's concerned for Caelynn and there's no reason I need to make that about me. Anyone helping Caelynn is helping me.

I slide my hands under Caelynn's knees and arms and gently lift her to my chest. She grumbles, but her eyes remain closed. Her arms and head fall limp as I carry her to the bed and carefully tuck her into the silk sheets.

My fingers touch her cheek gently. Kari and Ty watch from the other side of the room, but I don't care what they see.

She looks so peaceful like this. Angelic.

"You're both welcome to stay as long as you want. There's not much space to sleep, but…"

"We'll leave soon," Kari says. "I just don't like leaving her when she didn't choose to stay."

I swallow, knowing that she's only protecting her friend, and I understand it. I grab my bag and join them on the couch. My fingers burn as I grip the leather book and then place it on the table between us.

"Is that it?" Ty asks in awe. "The spell book?"

I nod. "It's not exactly what I expected."

"How so?"

I pick the book back up and pain streaks up to my elbow until I drop the book to my lap. Dammit. Stupid book. "He's a bit prickly."

Ty frowns and slowly reaches out fingers to the leather.

"I wouldn't do that," Kari warns, even as she stands. "It hurts. Badly."

"Really? Does it always hurt to use it?"

I shake my head. "It doesn't pain Caelynn at all. And me only slightly."

"Amazing."

Behind us, Caelynn twists in the bed and grumbles. Kari approaches and spends a minute sitting beside her. I try to ignore her soft murmurs.

With narrowed eyes and an expression of determination, Ty reaches out to the book a second time. This time, his fingertips land on the leather and it instantly zaps him.

"Ah!" he yells, whipping his hand back and shaking it.

I laugh, and Kari calls, "I told you so."

"So why only Caelynn then?" he asks.

"It belonged to her ancestors, I guess? It's... it's all really complicated."

Kari stands. "You ready?" she asks Ty.

"You're ready to go now?" Ty's eyebrows shoot up.

Kari nods. "Thanks Rev. For everything."

Ty hops up and gives me another forceful embrace and then exits the room with Kari. I turn back to Caelynn. Her eyes are still closed, but she frowns in her sleep. After a moment, she twists, turning her back to me.

The truth is, I'm desperate to be near her. I'm utterly petrified of a night without her within arm's reach.

And yet, I'm uncomfortable curling up next to her, considering she's not exactly... conscious. I sigh, knowing I'm not going to sleep no matter where I go.

I grab the book, pain radiating through my arms as I carry it to the other side of the bed where I settle in a few feet away from my snoozing angel.

I remember what Caelynn told me about the book being alive. That is has a soul and thinks like a sentient being. Somehow, Caelynn's magic unlocks the book. She's the key. Though the specifics to what that means, the why, are still beyond me.

I grab the stone from my pocket. Golden light flickers into the round jewel. Caelynn groans softly and squirms but ultimately settles back into her slumber. I gently touch the cover of the spell book with one hand, the stone in the other.

There's no burn.

I peel back the leather cover and find the same discolored pages Caelynn showed me, empty of any writing. Do I have to... talk to it? How the hell do I even begin to speak to a book?

Hello, excuse me, sir, could you please show me something?

I'm not even sure what I want to read about. When there are so many options at my fingertips—limitless knowledge, apparently—how could I possibly choose?

If I could know anything, what would I want to learn?

My eyes flicker to Caelynn, who snores softly. I want to know her... but not in a way a book can teach me. That, I've got to explore on my own.

I could learn about history. The origin of our world. The nature of the connection between the human world and ours.

My own history.

My mouth dries as I consider my father. Is that the kind of knowledge the book would hold? Is that something I even want to know?

Yes, I suppose I do. But not so deeply that it's where I should be digging when I have the chance to learn anything.

"Can you tell me about the origin of the Night Bringer and Terror?" I mumble. That would be helpful knowledge. The nature of their power, who they are, what they are. How to kill them.

A small sizzle sounds from beneath the pages, and I gasp as ink appears on the page. There are several blocks of text covering both visible pages. I turn the thick parchment and find another page filled with script. And another. The whole book is full.

Breath catches in my throat.

My mind spins, the fuzzy feelings in my limbs a sharp reminder that maybe now isn't the best time for me to dig this deeply into this information. But then again, what can it hurt?

I browse over the information about my enemy, only some of the words registering in my still cloudy brain. It's a story, about the Creator. The being that created all the worlds. There isn't any information about that being, but the book explains that the Creator gave a world to some of their highest-ranking creatures to reign over.

It was a full world with creatures of many kinds and magicless biomes.

These new rulers imbued their powers into the soil, imbedding it with magic and altering the world into what it is now.

There is a list of these ancient beings. Names I've never heard. And descriptions of their powers and where they resided. I don't see anything about the Night Bringer or Terror in these first few pages. I don't have the presence of mind to dig deep enough to figure out which of these names may be those creatures. They must have been known by another name, which to be honest makes all the sense in the world.

Next to each name is a vague physical description, power, and the land they claimed. Most of the descriptions are meaningless with no context I'm able to grasp but a few of them I can place.

Liliana- Passion and anger fueled her power which manifested itself in the form of heat so powerful it could melt the bones of lesser creatures. On the main continent, she claimed the barren lands over the northern mountain range.

That's the Flicker Court.

Ember- Claimed coastal land and fueled the soil with her soul fire, creating a forest so dense it became a prison for any who entered without permission.

I don't recognize the power, but the description of the forest must be the Twisted Court. I search through the others, trying to place them in the world I know now but not all of it makes sense.

"Can you show me a map or something?" I mutter to the book, not thinking much about the request.

The words on the page fade into nothing. "Wait," I cry just as more ink appears. A map.

"Thank you." I'm still unsure how to deal with this book. It doesn't talk to me the way Caelynn claims it talks to her, but if it's sentient I should at least be polite, right?

I spend a few minutes examining the map, but it still takes a bit of concentration to connect the dots between these ancient creatures and the courts I know. This must have been tens of thousands of years in the past. Much of the geography has shifted—there's no High Court Island, for example, and it's larger than the maps I'm used to. The courts I would rule if I'm chosen as the High Heir are all based on the main continent but that's not the only landmass in our world.

There is a very large mountainous island across the sea where the dwarves originated. The other is a massive span of tiny islands stretching nearly across the whole southern hemisphere. Water creatures and fae hybrids are the only creatures that tend to dwell in those places. On occasion, we banish fae to an island there instead of to other worlds. It depends on their danger level.

I'd never thought much about Caelynn's banishment to question the choice of Earth. If I had, I likely would have assumed Earth was chosen because of her age. She was still technically considered a child in the fae world, though right on the cusp. To banish her to a barren island would have likely been a death sentence.

Now, I suspect the real reason she was sent to Earth was to separate her from the Night Bringer. Another question occurs to me.

"Can the Night Bringer travel to Earth?"

The map fades out, and in its place, large block letters appear. **Yes.**

Then, a full paragraph appears below the word.

As of hours ago, both the Night Bringer and Night Terror have full mobility. So, yes, they could travel through portals to other worlds as any other being. Their power would be limited in that world, however, because they were not given dominion there.

"As of hours ago?" I whisper. More writing appears below the previous paragraph.

The curse that imprisoned the Night Terror was also meant for the Night Bringer, and there was a partial effect. He had his power, but he was bound to the underground. Before the curse was broken, he could not travel freely.

I blink rapidly, thinking that through. He was bound to the underground. He trapped Caelynn in the Cave of Mysteries. Though I know he'd also forced his way into bargains with other fae. I wonder how, but not enough to ask the question. Not with so many other things running through my mind.

"Caelynn was safe on Earth," I mumble.

Caelynn of the Shadow Court was safe from the Night Bringer's reach while banished to Earth, yes. She had other enemies, however.

That's why she was banished there. How much had the queen known at the time? Did she know why Caelynn killed Reahgan? Did she figure it out over time?

"Show me more about the ancients. Is there a name for them?" I ask, my voice growing in confidence now that I see how the ancient tome reacts to my requests.

So many questions.

My eyebrows shoot up at the new scrawled text. I can almost imagine the sarcastic tone. More words appear below.

There is no official name for the beings that once ruled your world. We have been referred to by many names. The kings. The ancients. The primals. Demigods. Beasts. And many other unsavory names.

I sniff as more text appears.

This time, I settle in and read the story of the king of all the ancients. His power sounds vaguely similar to my own. He brought light to the world and spread it even to the darkest of places. He was not always loved, though. Several beings opposed him, though indirectly, it seems. Those beings did not like being ruled. They claim they were given dominion over this world and can do as they see fit to the lands they claimed. Kasiel, the king of their kings, did not agree and instituted a set of rulers. Instructions, he called them.

I glaze over more about these creatures, flipping back to the list. There were twenty in total and each had a pairing. A mate. Kasiel, the king of light, had a mate who ruled over the shadowlands. "That's a strange pairing," I say, but my eyes dart to Caelynn snoozing beside me.

New words appear in the margins of the book. *Have you never heard the phrase opposites attract?*

I chuckle at the book's interjection and have to remind myself I am not going crazy.

Caelynn groans and rolls over. Her eyes meet mine, glossy and confused. "Rev?"

The corners of my lips tilt up. "Did you have a nice rest, angel?"

Her eyebrows furrow and she rubs her face then forces herself into a sitting position. "What happened?"

"You fell asleep."

She looks down at the cushioned mattress beneath her. "I crawled into your bed and went to sleep?"

"Not exactly."

Her eyes grow wider, and I hold back laughter.

"You fell asleep at the coffee table. I brought you here for a rest."

She looks down at my lap. "While you did some reading?"

"Something like that."

She rubs her face again then runs her fingers through her hair, attempting to tame the wild blond locks. "That's why Kari asked me if I wanted to go to my own room."

I blink but don't ask more. Kari just wanted to make sure Caelynn made the decision, that she felt safe enough to stay alone.

Caelynn scooches closer, eyeing the pages. "It's talking to you?"

"No, not with audible words. But it's been obliging in some of my curiosities."

She shakes her head, examining the scrawled script still on the page. "It's annoyed with you."

I smile. "It only seems to like you." I shrug, feeling only amusement.

"How did you get it to work for you? Didn't you say it burns?"

I nod and lift up the lumistone; it pulses with a yellowish light. "Tried an experiment. Seemed to work well enough."

"What is it, exactly?" She slowly reaches for the stone. We'd never had a chance to talk about the stone, or where it came from. I find myself vaguely relieved she doesn't already know the relevance of these stones in my culture. Most other fae would know exactly what it is.

Though none of that remotely explains why it holds magic the way it does.

I've had it in my pocket since we left the Luminescent Court for the Crumbling Court. It's been only a couple of weeks but it feels like a lifetime ago. We've each held it and used it at times in the last few days.

"It's a lumistone. They actually began as a fruit but when dried out they become gem-like. I have no idea how or why it would hold any power at all. It's not a magical stone. They're symbolic in my court, but that's it. They hold no power or worth outside of that." I wonder if I should tell her what it meant to me when I plucked it from that bush.

"I found it," she whispers, taking the stone between two fingers. "In the Schorchedlands. It was laying on the bank of the swamp just outside the flame wall where... we were separated."

I swallow and look down at my hands. I must have dropped it during my fight with the wraith.

"It was among the black pebbles Darren said were soul stones. All that was left of the souls that perished in that place. I picked this one up because it reminded me of you."

My eyes flit to her lips. *Not supposed to be thinking about things like that right now, Rev.* I close my eyes and breathe deeply. I run her words back over in my mind. "Who's Darren?"

"My wraith. That was his name."

"Oh. When did you learn his name?" Had she always known and just chose not to use it?

"He helped me across the swamps, and then we had a bit of a heart to heart. I learned his name, then when he promised to be on our side. Both of us."

"He was there after we crossed the fire wall." So much of that time was a blur, and we never talked about what happened while we were separated. "We both thought you were dead, and he... wasn't happy."

Caelynn swallows. "Then what happened? Darren told me you gave up on me and kept going to get the spell book."

I wince at that. "I didn't give up on you," I murmur. I don't know what I would have done if I had been given the choice. If I had been left on that bank without her and forced to choose—keep waiting, keep hoping, or continue on with the quest. I guess, at some point, I would have continued on. But the not knowing would have killed me. "Your wraith—Darren—fought me for a few minutes. He was in a rage. But then... Reahgan came. And the Manticore. They took me."

Caelynn's fingers find mine in the wrinkled sheets, and I cling to her like a lifeline. "Reahgan?"

I nod. "He made a deal with them somehow. But he was a fool. Thinking that working with them could save me. Could save any of us."

"Darren was a fool too. To think that me running away from the Schorchedlands could solve anything."

"But he chose you in the end." In those last moments, before Caelynn succumbed to the Night Bringer's internal attack, Darren tried to save her. Tried to save me too.

She nods, tears welling in her eyes. "That's why he was redeemed. He was given the chance to gain all the things he desired, and he chose the moral path."

I shake my head. "He chose you."

Caelynn blinks rapidly, then the tears are running down her cheeks. I shift closer, pulling her into my arms. She's still, quiet in my arms, but her fingers dig into my back. "No one ever chooses me."

"I do, Cae. I chose you, and I'll do it again and again."

19

CAELYNN

"I do, Cae. I chose you. And I'll do it again and again."

I shiver against his breath on my neck. I want to believe him. I want it to be true. That Rev would really choose me. Here, in this world.

But I don't.

He doesn't really know what that means. He thinks there is some way we can find to be together, and while even that is significant—that he would want to keep me as his—that is not what I'll ask of him.

Even harder than loving someone, is loving them enough to let them go.

And that's what I'm most afraid he won't do. If I give in to this, to him, I don't know if I'll have the strength to walk away.

And I have to. That's the one thing I know with absolute certainty. I have to go back to the Shadow Court. There are no other choices. No other possibilities for me. That is my place. My only real home.

I am warm in Rev's arms, though. And it feels so good it's

enough to make me question it all. I clear my throat and pull away. His arms let me go, but his eyes don't.

"How long did I sleep?"

"An hour, maybe. It's still fairly early. I can have dinner brought up for the both of us." We snacked on the dinner delivered earlier, but not enough to satisfy us.

I bite my lip. "All right," I whisper. "But then, I should go back to my own room."

Rev pauses, his muscles frozen. "You... don't have to."

I blink. "I think I do," I force out, even as my chest tightens.

Rev's gaze is trained on the floor, and he doesn't respond for a long while. Then, he takes in a long breath and stands. "I'll get us some food."

My heart aches as I watch him leave the room and wait for his return. *He wants me to stay.* I shake my head. That's such a terrible idea I can't even entertain the thought. We're both sobering up, and after some food, we'll likely be entirely in our right minds. But even then, can I trust myself?

"What were you showing Rev?" I murmur to the spell book still sitting on the ruffled bedsheets.

I slept in Rev's bed.

Again.

"He asked about the ancients. I showed him many things, stories from our time as rules of your lands, names and regions. He asked for a map of where the ancients claimed land."

"He was trying to connect each being with the modern courts."

"Yes."

I'm not sure what good that information will do, but you never know. It's a fascinating subject regardless.

I grab the book and set it onto the shelf by the massive window wall. Seems as good a place as any.

Rev is still somber when he comes back with a blue-haired fairy in all black wearing the High Court seal on a headband. The fairy pushes in a tray full of food.

"Wow, you were serious about dinner." It's got to be past bedtime for most fae. I expected a platter of snacks, pastries, and fruits, but instead, it appears they made full, fresh meals for us both.

"We're honored guests, the servants claim." He smiles, but there is still a spark of sadness that unnerves me. Is he sad because I won't stay? Because I don't want to take our relationship further?

I remember our intimate moments in the Schorchedlands. I told him I wanted him, but not there, not like that. Kissing him, touching him in that place, would have been awkward. We were exhausted, dirty, and uncomfortable in that cave.

The blue-haired fairy smiles and tinkles as she unveils the steaming plates of ridiculous smelling food. My stomach growls.

I sit at the table and claim one of the plates piled with herb-crusted fish and vegetables. He starts with cheese and fruits, weirdo.

The fairy dips into a bow, her wings fluttering behind her. "Thank you," I say, awkwardly, mouth full of food.

Rev holds back a laugh but the fairy doesn't react, she just politely backs out of the room.

We don't speak as we shove our faces with piles of food. I down a large cup of ice water quickly.

"They brought us some new beverages also." Rev smiles, pointing to a few bottles of fire whiskey and two bottles of fire-wine.

"I don't think either of us needs more."

"I don't suppose we do. Tonight." He winks.

"One drunken night wasn't enough?"

"With you? I will never have enough."

My heart skips and sinks at the same time. In only a short time, we finish eating, bellies full to the point of feeling ill. I take a seat on a velvety chair and stare absently toward the fireplace where a small blue fire ripples quietly.

Rev finds a place next to me, and he doesn't speak. Twenty minutes must pass like this, both of us afraid to say anything.

Though it's not exactly late, it's definitely bedtime for most non-nocturnal fae.

Finally, I force myself to my feet. "I should... go."

Rev flinches. His eyes find mine, desperation clear in them. "Wait."

I stand. "I like spending time with you, Rev, but this... can't go further."

"But that's not..." He fumbles for words, and it's so unlike him I pause. He approaches, chest heaving.

"What's wrong?" I ask. Is there something I'm not aware of? Has something happened?

When he doesn't respond, I frown and back away toward the door. I shouldn't stay, for so many reasons.

But as soon as my hand is on the handle, Rev slams his hand against the door. "Please," he croaks, and I swear my knees almost buckle. "Please don't leave."

I don't know how I continue standing. I stare at my own hand, still on the handle, breaths shallow. "Why?"

"Cae," he whispers. I look up, his face only inches from mine. His chest nearly touches my shoulder. That's not what strikes me. It's his eyes. They're darker than I've seen them since the Schorchedlands.

"I know this is hard for you. But I..." His fingers graze my cheeks, and I wince.

"I can't stay," I force the words out, heart-shattering.

"You don't want to be here with me?" His fingers fall away.

"Want and should are two different things."

He rubs his lips together, considering. Then, his shoulders slump, resignation in his eyes. He leans back, away from the door. My fingers still clench the handle.

"What about need?" he asks, his voice flat.

I bite my lip and slip my hand off of the door handle. Not that he's convinced me to stay the night, but obviously there is some kind of conversation we need to have. "That's different too."

"If you really need to leave," he says, his voice hoarse, "I won't stop you. I'm sorry for pressuring you." The sadness in his tone is like a damn dagger to the heart.

My stomach squeezes. "Rev—"

"I know our future is confusing and unclear." His voice rises slightly, forcing a casual tone. "I'm just afraid of being alone."

My heart cracks a little more.

"I'm afraid of being without *you,* specifically."

Breath rushes from my lungs.

His eyes find mine again, missing the same ferocity he had before. Now, I find only bone-deep sadness.

"We don't have to do anything you don't want. It's just... I won't be able to sleep if you're not near me. Not after everything."

I wait, letting his words settle in my mind. He's not suggesting anything; he just wants to be near me? But even that is terrifying. Even that means something I'm not sure I can allow. "I'm afraid."

"I know."

"Do you?"

His eyes are still dark, but there is a flicker of that silver I know and love. He shrugs. "I'm only afraid of losing you, but I realize you have other fears."

"I'm afraid of breaking." My voice is barely audible. So soft I'm not even sure if he heard me at first.

He closes his eyes. "I won't break you, Caelynn."

I shake my head. He can't promise that. "I have to go home, Rev." It's the first time I've admitted that to him—told him where my mind and heart really lie. "If I'm pardoned, I... can't stay here."

Rev stands straighter, his chest rises and falls in heavy breaths. "Okay."

"Okay?"

He nods. "We don't have to put any pressure on this, Caelynn. We can be whatever we decide. The both of us. All I know is that, right now, I have to be near you or I'll go insane."

"*Near me*," I repeat.

"Every moment you're not within my sight, I get anxious. I fear for your safety, even if that's irrational. After... after that night, I can't—" He shakes his head.

My God, my heart is in a damn puddle now. But there are still so many questions. So many fears. "What if that doesn't go away? The need to be near me?" The wounds are still fresh. So, theoretically, this feeling may dull over time.

Except, we're mates. So, maybe it won't. Maybe it'll only get worse.

"Then, I swear I'll let you go, even if it kills me."

I suck in a breath. This is such a dangerous place to be. Rev consumes everything when I'm with him. I close my eyes, and then I jump when I feel his fingers touching my arms. "Rev."

"Look at me."

I do, but I'm near tears again. I'm so confused.

He presses his lips into a thin line. "No pressure, I swear it. I won't touch you if you don't want it." He pulls his hands back, holding them up in surrender. "You can sleep in the bed, and I'll sleep on the couch."

I lean forward and press my forehead to his shoulder. I can't believe this is happening. Rev is begging, *begging* me to stay in his room tonight. My God, how did I get here?

"Okay," I breathe, and his muscles slacken, a breath rushing from him. We stand there—him afraid to move, afraid to touch me because I stupidly made him think that's what I want—for minutes that stretch into infinity.

"Can I hug you?" he finally whispers.

I let out a sad chuckle and nod against his arm. He pulls me into his arms. What the hell have I gotten myself into now?

20
CAELYNN

My feet thump over uneven ashy terrain, heart roaring in my chest. The pain and fear are suffocating. Darkness presses in on me. It bites at my soul, carving away pieces of it. My own shadows that once comforted me.

"Did you really think you could win this game? That you'd earned any freedom at all?" I shiver against the sinister voice inside my own mind, but I keep running.

Every breath sends more pain cascading through my chest, but I don't dare focus on that now. Now, he is in trouble. Now, I might lose him.

The Night Bringer laughs inside my mind. The magic inside curls around my soul, squeezing, crushing it. I stop running and claw at my chest, at the place the monster digs into me, slicing. Devouring.

But I can't reach him. My nails carve away at the skin beneath my collar bones, spilling my own blood.

He's inside of me, and I can't get him out. I can't reach the places he has dug into.

I can't reach him, because I am him.

~

I jerk awake. The room is pitch black and someone is screaming.

I'm out of bed, shadows covering me in an instant. My eyes adjust quickly to see a silver bedspread and couch ahead.

I'm in Rev's room in the High Court.

"Caelynn," his voice cries, and my stomach sinks. *Rev.* I rush across the room toward the couch. He insisted I sleep in his bed while he slept there.

My heart is pounding as I find Rev on his knees beside the couch. He groans, mumbling. "No. No. No no no."

"Rev," I beg, pulling at his hands that claw into his own neck. "Rev, what's wrong?"

His eyes flash up to mine, and he blinks, pain ricocheting off of them. "Caelynn," he cries. Then, his hands are on my face, "Caelynn," he says again, relief flooding his tone.

I fall to my knees beside him. "What happened?"

He presses his forehead to mine. "I told you I had those nightmares. Only now..."

I grip his chin and force his face up to mine.

"I almost killed you." He coughs on a near sob, and his palm lands over my chest. Gently pressing on the place his dagger left that tiny mark.

"It's okay," I say. "Truthfully, you probably should have."

"It would have killed me. Destroyed my very soul to do it. But God, I almost did."

"Is this why you wanted me to stay?" I ask. His breathing has evened out now, though the stress on his face is still evident.

He sits up, leans back against the couch, and runs his fingers through his hair. "I haven't had a night without you since the Schorchedlands. I didn't know for sure I'd have nightmares, but I'm not surprised." He pauses, his head falling back against the cushion. "I feel this panic, even during the waking hours, sometimes. When you're not nearby. When I can't make sure you're okay."

I shake my head to myself. What the hell are we going to do now? How do we navigate this?

We sit there, both breathing deeply for several minutes until finally, we both calm and our breathing evens out.

"Rev?" I whisper.

He meets my stare.

"Come to bed with me." My cheeks warm the moment the words leave my lips.

He pauses, heat flaring in his eyes, then his lips spread into an amused grin. "The shadow fae has finally made an attempt on my virtue?"

I smile. "I wouldn't mind having someone nearby while I'm sleeping either." I hope that's enough to clarify my intentions, though I suspect he already knew I hadn't meant what it sounded like.

Together, we slowly rise to our feet. I cling to his fingers and move toward the bed. He resists and tugs me back.

"Are you sure?" he murmurs against my hair.

My heart flutters. "Of course."

Our chests are just barely touching as his fingers rest against my cheek again. "You are so selfless, Caelynn. You'd do anything you thought would help me, even if it's not what you want."

I don't think that's as true as he thinks. I don't often choose myself, but I don't compromise myself either.

"But I can handle a nightmare or two. I shouldn't have even asked you to stay with me at all. I can handle it if you don't want to be here."

"Of course I want to be here, you fool." I shake my head. "I want to be near you every moment. Sleeping in your arms sounds like heaven." My cheeks warm a second time. "I'm just *used* to the pain of not getting the things I desire. It's what I expect. The fear of having a taste only to lose it again is new for me. I don't think... that I trust myself."

"Whatever happens from here on out, Caelynn, is you and me. We decide what we want. That includes how much or how little of me you desire."

I pull Rev toward the bed, and this time he obliges. I crawl under the covers first, and Rev gingerly shifts next to me. I curl into his side, and he tucks an arm under my head.

"Thank you," he whispers.

I smile, and my eyelids flutter, growing heavier. He's so warm and comforting. If I thought drinking and laughing with my friends was like home, it was nothing compared to this.

Rev's heart thumps beneath my ear, and I relish this sweet taste of heaven I've been given. No matter how fleeting it may be.

21
REV

I am so incredibly warm and comfortable when consciousness returns. Caelynn squirms in my arms, and I pull her in tighter.

"Rev," she complains.

My eyes fly open. My face is in Caelynn's hair, my arms around her waist. I chuckle as she squirms again, but this time, I release her.

"Sorry," I mumble. I wanted to fight harder to keep her at least for a few more minutes, but I remember our conversation from last night and I know she's still uncertain about us, about me and how close she's willing to be with me. Even if my skin stings where she was just touching me.

I don't want to put unneeded pressure on that, on her, on us. Guilt presses down on my chest. I'm doing too much of that as it is.

She crosses the room and peers out the huge window. "I'm pretty sure it's midday."

I blink the sleep from my eyes. "No one tried to wake us?" I sit up and stretch out my stiff muscles.

She shrugs.

"We needed the rest. If they didn't need us, then the extra sleep was well worth it." After a long sigh, I force my heavy body out of bed.

I walk to the door and find a folded slip of paper by the door. Eyebrows high, I bend down to retrieve the note.

When you wake, we will convene in the dining hall. Bring Caelynn.

I wave the paper. "We've been summoned."

Caelynn frowns. "What?"

"The queen left a note for both of us to meet her in the dining hall once we wake."

She stomps forward. "What else does she say?" She reaches for the note, and I pull it back from her, holding it behind my back.

"Nothing."

She sneers. "Then, let me see it."

I smirk and hand her the paper. She frowns again as she reads the simple message. She turns the paper over to the other side. "There's nothing more to it. Why did you keep it from me?"

I shrug. "Seemed like fun."

She rolls her eyes. "I'll have to go back to my room to change. But I'll meet you down there."

She slips from the room without another word, and the moment she's gone, the ache in my gut begins anew. I remember her words from yesterday.

What if it never goes away.

Then, I will have a very uncomfortable future. She told me last night that she wants to go home.

As High King, I could help the Shadow Court more than she could by residing there. If I succeed in my plan to reveal the true Caelynn to the world, maybe she'll start to see what a Shadow Fae beside the High King could mean for her court.

I shake my head. I'm getting ahead of myself. I'm not even High Heir yet. And even once I'm named, I'll have years to wait before I become High King. We have years to figure this all out.

One step at a time, Rev.

Right now, Caelynn is here. For how long, I don't know. But I decide quickly that I will not beg her to stay the way I did last night.

Because Caelynn deserves to be given anything and everything she wants. I can't give her everything, but I can give her the freedom to choose.

22

CAELYNN

I shut the door to my room behind me and then press my forehead against the cool obsidian stone, panting.

What. The. Hell.

I spent the night with Rev. I mean, I've spent nights with him before. In fact, most of the last several nights, I've slept in his arms. But this was different.

Every time before was simply about survival. We were trapped together. We were trapped together because of choices I made, not him. We worked together because it made the most sense. And eventually, because we didn't want to see harm come to the other.

I know that was part of why Rev wanted me there—because though we're safe, we don't *feel* safe. Not yet. One doesn't just run from suffering and forget it ever happened. I get that. But also—

I bite my lip hard.

Maybe it's not all I'm making it out to be. Maybe I'm freaking out over nothing. Maybe it's really just friendship.

I don't want it to be just friendship.

But it has to be. Right?

I tap my fingers against my knee anxiously and then force myself to march to the closet and look through the clothes the queen has provided for me.

I have to convince the queen to pardon me so I can go home.

I have to find a way to get back to the human world and check on Raven.

I have to destroy the Night Bringer.

There is much more to add to that list, but those are the most important.

The queen has provided me an entire wardrobe fitting for a Shadow Court Queen. Has she guessed that's what I intend to do, or does she simply want others not to forget the dangerous court I hail from?

No matter her motives, I suppose it does make sense for her to give me shadow clothing. She can't give me High Court gold or colors of any other court. She could put me in servant's clothing, or a prisoner's tunic—those would be exceptionally fitting—but she must keep up some appearances.

Instead, she'll make it clear I belong elsewhere. I'm just a means to an end. I pull on black leather pants, a black tank, and a sheer cover that billows behind me as I walk.

I've never dressed like this before. I didn't have access to high-quality materials growing up. I was a countess, technically related to the crown, but a far enough relation no one actually cared. And our whole court was poor enough that even royalty didn't have many luxuries. A tailor was never something I'd ever even thought to have. We couldn't keep up with trends.

On Earth, I went shopping on occasion but was given very little to buy clothing, so I ended up with hand-me-down jeans and band t-shirts.

There's jewelry in a box in the corner of the room. Black jewels. I run my fingers over the cool sleek stones, admiring them for a moment, but I don't want to wear them. I'm outside of my comfort zone enough as it is.

I march from my room, channeling all of those old masks and shadows to cover my newly exposed and vulnerable heart, and head toward the High Queen's meeting.

～

Heat radiates from the dining hall the moment I pull the double doors open. The room is massive—like the queen could hold a decent-sized ball in this room alone. Scarlet banners cover golden walls. A massive chandelier engulfed in fire sways slightly above the massive table.

I'd like to spend time examining the unique chandelier, how the flames flicker gently over every prong, or the patterned tile on the ground, or count the chairs lining the long table—I estimate fifty on each side—but there are scrutinizing stares waiting for me at the end of the table, so I hold my head high and gaze steady.

Most of these fae are my allies—but not all of them.

It doesn't matter that Ty, Kari, and Rev sit beside the queen. I still have a lot to lose even with my allies to support me. And that's not including the strange fae that line the other side of the table.

Three fae males, each with their own crown. One wears High Court gold—the queen's mate. By marrying the High Queen, he established a firm legacy but gave up any actual power. His own children will have his wife's name, court, and element.

His narrowed eyes are blue. He's from the Glistening Court, which would make the king sitting to his right—

126

wearing a crown of silver with blue gemstones scattered across it—his brother.

There is a small resemblance between the two crowned males.

The other male wears a simple yellow crown that sparks. Crackling Court, certainly.

"Caelynn," the queen draws. "We've been waiting for you." She side-eyes her husband, whose expression is more tense.

He doesn't like me.

Unsurprising. Nearly every ruling court could easily rally entire armies in order to trample me personally. I killed the last High Heir—Rev's brother. That alone is reason to hate me. But my court has always been feared, regardless of how low their magical strength has become.

My court has been neglected and hated for hundreds of years, their power diminishing quickly. And eventually, that led to anger and dissension against the High Court. Whispers of rebellion have been spreading for many years. Long before me, though my assassination of the High Court heir certainly fans the flames.

They all think I'll continue that uprising.

I suppose they're not entirely wrong. I certainly intend to raise the Shadow Court out of the ditch it's been pushed into, but I won't do it by war and insurrection.

I know how and why my court fell, and while it frustrates me, I understand it. I accept it. I do not hate anyone for what happened.

I simply will not allow it to continue.

"Apologies, your Highness," I say smoothly, eyes hooded.

At the head of the table, the queen nods and motions for me to take the seat farthest from her, beside Tyadin and across from the three powerful males. On Ty's other side is Kari, followed by Rev.

I quietly take my seat but continue a casual perusal of the crowned males. The queen is the most powerful fae in the realm, but I've come to an uneasy understanding with her. These males are new to me.

"This is Caelynn of the Shadow Court," the queens says to the males. "This is my husband, Thompson, and his brother, King Briar of the Glistening Court. And King Raijin of the Crackling Court."

I nod. "It's nice to meet you."

"I wish I could say the same," the Crackling Court king sneers in my direction. I can't help but smirk.

The queen quirks a brow. "I've called this meeting because we have important business to attend to regarding the scourge."

I keep my eyes trained on the queen and refuse to give any more attention to the king who clearly hates me.

"There were three active outbreaks of the scourge in the realm. Yesterday, Prince Reveln successfully destroyed the largest. The two remaining are closest to these two courts. The Glistening and the Crackling. Once we are able to neutralize these outbreaks, the scourge will be nothing more than an old scar."

"It was my understanding, *Zanterleisha*," the Crackling court king says in an icy tone— apparently, I'm not the only one he's unhappy with, "that the savior was supposed to travel to my court to neutralize our threat *today*. Instead, you drag me into this façade of meeting with a betrayer."

The queen's face remains passive, but there is fire in her eyes. Almost literally, they glow with heat that tells me she's fully contemplating melting him where he stands. "We had spoken of tentative plans to end the scourge in only three days' time. That turned out to be overly ambitious. Our saviors require time to recuperate after executing such an elaborate spell."

My lips part, but I avoid outright gawking. She said, saviors.

Plural.

She included me. Was that a slip-up? Or did she do it on purpose?

"We can go now," I say. My anger has been washed away by waves of guilt. I saw what the scourge did to that town in the Crystal Court, and I will not rest if it means stopping that from happening again.

"Caelynn." The queen's stern voice breaks my panicked thoughts.

I blink and meet her gaze. Her fire has cooled, and I breathe out slowly.

"We are meeting here to discuss a new *realistic* plan to end the scourge. All plans are fluid as we do not know how and when the scourge will move. Our priorities may shift, and I have no doubt that Prince Reveln and his allies will kill themselves in order to complete this mission if the risk calls for it."

The Crackling Court King eyes me, his shoulders slightly relaxed.

"But I will not allow them to destroy themselves for your pride. The scourge is not actively moving. It is twenty-five miles from the nearest settlement and seventy-five from the closest city. The situation in the Crystal Court was dire. It is not dire in your court. Not yet. If that changes, so will our plans."

The yellow-crowned king wrinkles his nose and crosses his arms.

"What is really going on here, Zanterliesha?" he asks, his

tone is calmer, but his eyes are dark as he studies me. "What is she doing here?"

I freeze, unsure what our story is here. These are ruling court kings; they may be allowed more information than the average fae, but I still suspect the extent of my involvement is to be kept as close as possible.

"As with all things, Rai, this is more complicated than the public will realize. More complex than even you will understand. Reveln is our savior, but he cannot do it alone. He has allies. And if you'd like to complain to Reveln about his choice of allies," she waves in Rev's direction, "he is right here."

The king curls his lip, but his expression slackens as he faces Rev. "Your brother's murderer." His voice is nearly a whisper.

I blink, registering the emotion in his voice. This king knew Reahgan.

"I loved my brother, Rai. That has not changed."

"You vowed to kill her."

Rev inclines his head once. "That is one vow I will never complete."

"Why?" The Crackling Court King stands, his chair screeching against the stone floor.

Rev's expression remains calm, his eyes a gentle silver. He pauses, like he's unsure of his next words. Then, he lets out a bitter laugh and shakes his head. "It's a long fucking story."

The Crackling Court king does not like this answer. He bares his teeth. "Tell me! Make me understand why you would take this *bitch* as an ally? Why you would sit beside her? Honor her? Pardon her?"

Rev stands now, slowly, leaning over his hands that are planted on the table. "Call her that one more time, Rai,"

"Oh, I see now. You're fucking her."

A flash of light blasts the Crackling Court King across the

room. I'm too shocked to move as the room erupts into chaos. There are roars of anger and screams, and then a wall of flames rises all the way to the ceiling, blocking the warring males from each other.

"Calm yourself now, Reveln," the queen commands. "Or I will be forced to reconsider the choice I have already made."

Rev is shaking, still standing over the table. I rise slowly, moving back from the heat of the flames over the table. I approach him and press cool fingers against his forearm.

He winces and turns to face me. His eyes are dark, his expression pained. "How do you do this all the time? How do you handle their hatred?"

I shrug. "You get used to it."

"I can't do that. I can't just accept it."

I swallow. "It helps when you believe it's deserved. I always have."

He runs his fingers through his hair. On the other side of the fire, the three males stand, watching us. One of them, the Crackling King, I assume, screams in a rage.

"Can't you put yourself in their position, Rev?" Kari asks softly, standing on Rev's other side. "If you hadn't had the chance to get to know Caelynn, if you only knew her as an assassin who killed someone you cared for, then someone else you cared for befriended her... you would react significantly worse than even Rai."

Rev drops his head into his hands. "This is harder than I'd thought."

"You love her," Kari whispers. "It's understandable."

I suck in a breath.

"But *they* will never understand it," Rev says.

I stumble backward, did he just admit he loves me? He didn't exactly say it, but he didn't deny it either.

Ty's hands steady me, and we pull farther away from Kari

and Rev, still chatting. They understand this world better than Ty and me. We've always been outsiders. I tell myself that's why Kari and Rev are whispering together, and that it has nothing to do with his emotions for me. Because... shit. I can't deal with that right now.

You love her.

23

REV

My teeth are still chattering as I stand there, telling the queen that I'd like a private assembly with King Raijin. He was once a friend of mine, and I need the chance to talk with him in a casual setting. To help him understand a few things.

Kari convinced me that the High Court Rulers shouldn't know the extent of my feelings for Caelynn. And I know she's right, but it's hard. So much harder than I'd anticipated.

One step at a time, I remind myself.

Step one, Caelynn is a necessary ally. They might not like it, but we need her. Just like I did in the trials.

Step two, she's a welcomed ally. Someone we trust, even though it seems to make little sense. Just like I trusted her to help me get into the Schorchedlands.

Step three, believe in her.

Step four, fight for her.

I don't know if any of that will be relevant in my quest to convince the realm to accept Caelynn as a hero rather than a villain, but it does help to have quantifiable goals. *Don't get too far ahead of yourself, Rev. Don't force it.*

"If you raise a hand to him again, Reveln."

"I won't," I promise the queen.

She nods, and the fire, blocking me from the other side of the room drops. Rai's eyes are glowing in rage, flickering like lightning, but his body is still.

I hold my hands up in surrender as I approach.

"I'm sorry," I tell him. "I'd like to swear an armistice for the next hour and have a private talk. If, after that, you'd like to remain an enemy, that is your choice."

He breathes slowly through his nose, his muscles still tense. "You swear, that no matter what I say about your *whore*, you will not attack me?"

Rage simmers in my belly, but I push it down. One step, Rev. One step. "I swear." My voice is hoarse as I force the words.

He narrows his eyes. "I'll only allow it if there is scotch. Lots of scotch."

I bark out a laugh. "I assume we can arrange that." Scotch isn't my favorite drink, but I'm not at all opposed to a stiff beverage.

"Before you go and get drunk, we have two important things to settle," the queen barks at us. We turn our attention back to the front of the room. "But I'll make it quick. First, this weekend, there will be an event held in the palace. Everyone in this room will be expected to attend and be in good spirits, regardless of how your heart-to-heart ends up. And tomorrow, Reveln and his allies will travel to the Glistening Court and complete the spell to end the active scourge. We will allow him two days of rest, and then the Crackling Court will get its needed treatment. Again, this plan is fluid, and any movement of the scourge could alter the plan. Caelynn of the Shadow Court will be a *guest* under the High Court colors and therefore protected, until all active scourge is destroyed. Understood?"

Guest.

I'm fairly certain every soul in the room, including the guards, understands that to mean prisoner. She is treated well, but she has no freedom. Not yet.

I nod, as does Rai and Briar.

Caelynn... I don't even see anymore. Ty is also gone. I bite my lip but shake my worry off. I'll find her soon and make sure everything is all right. First, I have politics to attend to.

It only takes minutes for the queen to have a meeting room set up for the two of us in the Crackling Court hall. Even so, I spend extra time pacing in the main hall, surrounded by portraits of past rulers here in this incredibly powerful court.

Zanterleisha Ignatus of the Flicker Court. She has been the High Queen of the Realm my entire life. Will my portrait hang beside hers? She's implied she made her decision.

I shift down to find the last Shadow Court king, four portraits down, and try to see what Caelynn saw. She loves her court. She hates how it's treated. I've never set foot in a Shadow Court village, so my experience is small. But if she were their queen? I'd easily say they are deserving of respect.

But, then again, I'm obviously a bit biased.

I stare into the harsh eyes of the final Shadow Court High King. His cheekbones are sharp, his expression severe. The look in his eyes makes me think he's the type that would enjoy pain.

Darren Shadowspell of the Shadow Court.

I frown. That name is familiar.

"He is ready for you."

I jump at the voice and turn to find an antlered fae smiling at me. "Thank you," I mutter and shake my head from those thoughts. Caelynn's heritage is something I can dig into another time.

I march across the palace until I find the Crackling Court wing, where Rai is waiting for me in a meeting room built to make fae from his court feel comfortable.

I take in a long breath before entering.

Here, the walls are dark blue with streaks of glowing, splintering golden stone. The furniture is all bright white and the torches flicker and pop with yellow light.

I've never been a huge fan of Crackling Court aesthetics.

In the center of the room is a stone table with two large bottles of scotch and two glasses. Rai is seated when I enter, the glass in his hand already half empty.

"You waste no time," I comment.

He smiles. "I needed to relax." And the few sips of scotch seem to have done the trick. He reclines in the chair, one leg hitched over the other casually. "Come on, boy." He nods at the chair across from him.

Raijin is over fifty years older than I am. He's been king of his court for only five years though. He was closer in age to my brother, which is why they'd been friends. I was the annoying little brother, but after Reahgan's death, Rai and I grew closer.

His younger brother died in the trials. Luckily, his death had nothing to do with Caelynn nor I. He was a tentative ally of mine, but we were never close. We simply were not enemies.

"So," Rai begins as he pours a generous glass of scotch and hands it to me. "What is it you'd like to say?"

I accept the glass with a quick thanks and take a larger gulp than I probably should. Rai only smiles.

"Too much, likely," I say. And truthfully, I don't know how much I should say. How much should I tell him about

Caelynn? About my brother? "It feels overwhelming, all of it."

Rai nods. "It was overwhelming when I took my father's crown, and that was small compared to what you've endured."

I nod and take another gulp of the bitter liquid.

"I appreciate your apology, Rev. And I am still admittedly angry about that..." He shakes his head. "That *shadow fae* being involved in anything to do with the High Court. But I'd like to hear you out."

"Kari advised me to put myself in your position. And she's right to say that I would have reacted significantly worse than you did, if I were on the outside, and someone who I know cared for Reahgan befriended his murderer without me understanding the *why*."

"So, tell me. What is the *why*? Somehow, she holds the key to the cure?"

I raise my eyebrows, he'd put that much together, had he? I assume the queen's comment about Caelynn being a "guest" in the High Court until the scourge being destroyed was a strong clue. "In a way," I answer.

He bobs his head in a casual nod. "Strange how this world works, isn't it?"

I laugh at that. "Caelynn isn't what you think. She isn't what I'd expected in the slightest."

"So, what is she then?"

A hero, is what I want to say. My savior. My friend. My mate. "Complicated," I decide to go with. "She... It's hard to hate someone who hates herself just as fully. Hard to punish someone who has punished herself more deeply than you could ever imagine. Hard not to forgive someone who has sacrificed deeply just to help you."

He watches me closely. "She's manipulated you."

"No."

"How do you know that?"

"Because if it were up to her, she'd be dead. If it were up to her, I'd still hate her. Because she has honestly risked her life —given her life—to save me more than a few times. It's a miracle she's still living after all she's done."

He frowns, finishing his drink in one go.

"I've spoken with Reahgan," I admit.

Rai chokes on his last gulp, coughing. "What?"

"He was in the Schorchedlands."

"He... is a wraith?"

I nod and finish my own drink. He leans forward to pour us both another.

"And your brother's wraith," he says smoothly, his voice controlled, as he pours two more glasses of scotch nearly up to the rim, "advised you to forgive the shadow fae?"

I bark out a laugh. "No, no. Most definitely not."

He frowns but nods. "Good. I don't think I could have believed your story if you'd said yes."

My smile is sad. "Reahgan was Reahgan even as a wraith. He wanted her dead. He wanted me to succeed, though he was a bit torn about even that."

"He helped you?"

I open my mouth to speak but pause, words failing me. "He tried, in his own way. And instead, made it harder for me."

Rai chuckles. "That sounds like Reahgan."

We sit in silence, sipping our drinks for several more minutes.

"You trust her, truly?"

"I won't claim that Caelynn is perfect. She has made mistakes. But she is not the villain we've made her out to be either. And to say that I trust her would be an understatement. If you were to put my well-being at risk and asked me to choose anyone in our world—any world—to help me, I would not even consider another."

He stares down at his drink, brow pinched for such a long while I wonder if I should just leave him be. If our conversation has run its course.

"There is only one I'd trust so deeply," he murmurs. Then pauses again, for a long while. I don't know for sure who he means, but my first thought would be his queen. His mate, Bethany.

"I suppose it was also an understatement," he meets my gaze, "when I said the world works in strange ways."

"Yes," I whisper. "It was definitely an understatement."

24

CAELYNN

My mind continues to spin for the rest of the day, long after I fled from the meeting with the queen. Apparently, they had ended it quickly and Rev held a meeting with the Cracking Court King to try to salvage the situation.

Lord knows we don't need another enemy.

But it wasn't the king's reaction that had me freaking out. It was Rev's.

You love her.

Somehow, in my panicked rush to get those thoughts out of my mind, I had found my way to Rev's room and stolen the damn spell book. I am so tired of playing politics and waiting for my enemy to come to me. Tired of wondering when the night ancients will strike. Because they will. I know it.

It has only been two days, but I feel it in my damn bones. They're going to rip it all away from me. The moment I grip this incredible life, that's when they'll strike.

And so, in my panic, I rush to take hold of what little power I have.

Right now, all I have is information. So, I'm going to take it.

I take the spell book across the High Court grounds to the edge of the island. There is power here, palpable and pulsing with the salty waters. Maybe it's usable. Maybe the key is here, where the fae chose to build their strongest fortress thousands and thousands of years ago.

I kneel next to the bank. Water crashes violently against the sharp black stones, sending scattering drops here and there. Three drops land on the open pages of the spell book.

It rumbles, but I can't tell if it's a pleased expression or an annoyed one.

"Does the Source Sea hold exceptional magic?" I ask the book. It's the first question I come up with to test my grasping theory. I have so little to go on.

"A great battle was waged on this island millennia ago between several of my kind. Blood was poured into the waters here. Their souls' essence remains. Their power was imbued into the waters here."

So, that's a yes? "Does it really build power in those who bathe in these waters? We're talking a massive ocean spanning thousands of miles; are all of the waters magical or only here?"

"The Source Sea does hold power, but not unlike that of the soil in your courts. It can be used to build magic, but the effect would be slight. The closer to the source, the stronger."

"Is that what fuels the magic of the High Court? The sacrifice of past ancients poured into the waters?"

"There was once a king of all kings. A ruler of our kind. His power was not elemental but all-encompassing. Limitless. He could destroy the very planet, were he so inclined. And he nearly was once. He was betrayed by his mate, who attempted to steal his power. He believes, out of jealousy. To become more powerful. His rage split the land, creating two large continents instead and shattering the southern end into islands."

His rage created the geography of our world as we know it? "Like, in minutes?" I ask stupidly.

"He split the land in minutes, yes, but they remained close together, shifting into the continents and islands as you know them over time."

I shake my head. "Right. Go on."

"It is his power that fuels the High Court island. It is his legacy that your kind unwittingly continue. His power, they siphon into their High Rulers. It is here he ruled, taking the smallest batch of land as his own. And it is here that he slumbers."

~

"He slumbers," I repeat slowly. "Here." Sleeping, not dead.

The spell book rumbles against my open palm. I hadn't even realized I was leaning against it. We need an ancient being to aid us in the fight against the Night Bringer and his mate. We've discussed this.

"How many ancient beings remain in our world?" I whisper. "That could potentially aid us against the night ancients?"

Three.

The words are written, scrawled on the otherwise blank page.

"Who are they?" I demand.

The High King of our kind, Nexus. Slumbering beneath the High Court island.

The beastly ancient, Aurelius, who remains as a nomad inside the Twisted Forest. He is the weakest of our kind.

And, Carolina, who slumbers in the Black Lake.

"Why did you stop speaking and start writing?" I ask quietly, eyeing the words. Is it just paranoia, or is it somehow significant?

"*I do not like this subject,*" the book whispers.

"Why?"

"*You intend to raise one of my kind to aid you, but you do not understand the risks.*"

"Well," I drawl, "that is why I have an all-knowing book —to tell me those risks."

The book vibrates softly.

I sigh. "You understand my predicament, right? You know that the night ancients will come for me and I do not have the power to win that fight, not even with you."

"*I do.*"

"I need as much information as you can give me in order to make the right choice. Tell me how I may be able to destroy the Night Bringer and his mate. Tell me the risks. So that I can choose."

"*If you raise the King of all Kings, and if you could manage to convince him to battle the night ancients, he would win.*"

I pull in a long breath, my mind already wheeling. He is here, beneath my feet now. The secret to winning this game after all...

"*But,*" the books hisses, "*his rising would destroy the High Court, and that is only the beginning. He will not listen to you, child. He would not fight for you.*"

I narrow my eyes. "You cannot see the future," I remind the book.

"There are some things I can know without knowing."

I shake my head. "How?" I whisper, mind still reeling. I want to have patience and listen to the wisdom of the book but I also know he is biased in this subject. I just need as much information as possible. "How do I raise an ancient?"

A spell appears on the page. "*It will kill you if you do this.*"

My heart throbs, pounding. An eagerness overwhelms

me. A desire to destroy. Maim those creatures that hurt me, that ripped my life apart.

"*Enter the waters*," a voice instructs me. I blink and rise to my feet. Overwhelming desire rushes over my body, prickling my skin.

"*Stop*," another voice demands.

I chuckle, a sinister sound that sends a shiver over my body, as I walk slowly toward the water's edge. I watch the dark and powerful waves crest and then crash against the stones. Water splatters against me.

I lick my lips and taste the salt. I taste the power.

"*He would kill you if you were to wake him.*"

"*But he would kill your enemies first*," the other voice answers.

"*Lies*," the book hisses against my palm.

I stand precariously on the edge of the sharp stone jutting out over the violent waters just feet away, holding the book against my chest.

The king requires a sacrifice.

"I do not fear death," I tell the book.

"*I know.*" Its voice is soft. Achingly sad. "*But you will not get what you desire this way.*"

"Hey!" a voice roars behind me. "Get away from there!"

I blink and shake my head, recognition dawning. I gasp as I realize how near the edge of the waters I stand. My foot slips, and I scream as I topple over, sliding down the stone toward the fierce waves.

Pulling the book tight against me with one hand, the other grasps for the edge of the ragged bank, fingers clawing at the slippery smooth stone, but there is an unnatural pull that tugs at me.

My fingers slip.

The guard grabs me by the upper arm, heaving me up. He tosses me to the ground and I choke on desperate breaths.

Three guards stand around my fallen body. I wince as spears jerk toward me and stop at my throat. The sharp points sting, pressing tightly against the exposed skin under my chin.

My teeth chatter. My mind spins.

I suck in heaving breaths, chest rising and falling.

"What are you doing?" one of the guards barks at me.

I close my eyes.

"*Don't tell them you know.*" The book rumbles against my chest. "*Lie. Say you were only curious about the waters.*"

"I was just curious," I whisper. "The waters are beautiful, and I heard they hold power."

Two of the spears ease their pressure and pull back. One remains, just as tightly as before.

"Go take a swim," the guard with the spear against my neck says then spits at the ground beside my face. "You won't survive more than a minute."

"Will it be the waters that kill me—or your spears?"

One of the guards chuckles. The one holding the spear sneers. "The rocks will tear your body apart," he tells me, and I shiver, realizing how close I'd come to that fate. I could have shadow walked back to the solid bank, but in my panic, I hadn't even thought to do so.

A fourth guard approaches casually. "Wound her, and the High Prince will have your necks," the new-comer drawls easily.

High Prince? Was there an announcement I hadn't heard about?

Two of the guards scramble away from me, believing the threat. But the spear remains at my neck. The guard above curls his lip in disgust. He leans in so I can see his yellow eyes. "We still see you for what you are, shadow bitch," he tells me.

"Continue bewitching the prince, and I'll find a reason to kill you myself."

I swallow, but then the pressure of the spear disappears... My teeth still chatter as I sit up, eyeing the three guards marching back toward the front gate.

"You should have let her fall," one guard says to another. The others chuckle in agreement.

The final guard holds out a hand to me. I grip it, and they pull me to my feet.

"All right?" they say, pulling back the veil to reveal a lovely face with plump lips. A female with purple eyes.

"I am. Thank you."

She nods. "Don't get so close to the waters. They weren't kidding that you wouldn't survive the swim."

I nod. I pick the spell book up and rush away from the only friendly guard and retreat back to my room. I suppose I came out here for a distraction. And I sure as hell achieved that.

25
REV

The carriage rattles to a stop. Caelynn remains frozen, her eyes still distant. She's been quiet since the meeting yesterday.

My fingers brush over her clenched hands, and she jerks back.

"Would you like to stay here?" I offer.

"No," she says, her expression blank.

"What's wrong?" I ask, not for the first time. "You've been so tense since the meeting with the queen." Since Rai called her my whore two days ago. She came to my room last night but didn't seem in the mood to talk.

We slept in each other's arms without anything more happening between us.

Her eyebrows rise. "It's not that," she whispers, but I'm not sure I believe her. "It's everything. The Night Bringer and his mate. Have you had any more dreams?"

"No, have you?"

She purses her lips and peers out the window.

"Tell me."

She shrugs. "It's nothing. I just hate waiting around for them to come for us."

"They can't." I lean in and pull her chin so that she's facing me. "We—you and I—are safe from them."

Her smile is forced.

"Are you ready?" I ask, nodding out the door of the carriage. Today, we are completing another healing spell—this time on the Glistening Court.

Caelynn exits the carriage without another word.

Before us are the remnants of another village and a forest beyond. This village has been destroyed for more than a year. The ground is still scorched with streaks of black and covered in ash.

There are three high fae from the Glistening Court waiting for us. The first two are the king and his heir, Illiana.

Illiana wears a flowing silk dress with a blue ombre pattern and a tiara of simple silver. Neither likes me now that I've aligned with Caelynn.

And the third is the king's nephew, who wears the apparel of a guard.

"Is this near where we traveled for the trials?" Caelynn asks as we approach the waiting party.

"Yes. We were maybe ten miles west of here."

She looks back at the mountain range just visible over the horizon. The mountain range of the Shadow Court. We're very close to her homelands.

We greet the Glistening Court royals stiffly.

"Where is the active scourge?" I ask the king. His expression is carefully controlled, betraying no emotion.

"In the forest beyond." He points past the ruins and to the sagging trees. "My nephew, Caleb, will escort you to the location that requires healing."

My eyebrows rise. "Do we require an escort?"

The king forces a smile. "The active infection is quite small, though it travels regularly. It is closely tracked by members of the guard in case of growth or unexpected movement, but it is sluggish and fairly predictable compared to past infections in these lands. Because of its size, it would take you some time to find it. We conclude that an escort will save us all time."

"I see," I say with a nod. "In that case, I greatly appreciate the help." And that's the truth. I'd like to get this over as quickly as possible.

Caleb smiles sincerely, but it fades quickly, and his gaze jerks up to his uncle. Is he afraid to show any sincere appreciation? Also quite telling.

After more awkward pleasantries, Caelynn and I follow the young fae through the rubble of the old town and into the trees beyond. We move swiftly, but even so, the hike takes nearly twenty minutes. We finally stop in a damaged clearing, not unlike the last several miles we traveled through.

"Is it here?" I ask, looking around. The trees are covered in black ash, leaves brown and decayed, and there is a nasty smell in the air, but there is still green grass in patches here and there.

Caleb points to a set of three trees, entirely blackened. In the center of the tree is a rippling black void.

I shiver. Well, now I can see why it would have been a challenge for us to find this bit of active infection. The black void shifts, twisting down lower on the tree.

This is also why this portion of the scourge is considered less of a threat. Unless it grows significantly, its damage would be rather limited.

I turn to find Caelynn kneeling on the ground, the spell book open. Caleb follows my gaze, and his eyes widen.

"This might be a good opportunity for me to try it on my own," I say, watching the small infection as it wriggles.

Caelynn nods. I also need to practice using my magic without her help. Still, I picture her in my arms, the Night Bringer's voice on her lips. I feel that anger, that pain. And my magic flares to life in my palm.

The same being that did that to her, did this to our world. And I will destroy it.

The rage burns through my very being, and I practically growl as I blast my healing light into the tree with the black void.

It hisses and writhes, and in only moments, the black sludge slides to the ground in a puddle. Puffs of black smoke rise into the sky.

I shake my burning hand and bend down to examine the puddle.

It doesn't move, not even the slightest of ripples. After a full minute of watching, I stand, content.

"That was it?" Caleb whispers. "That's all it took?"

I shrug.

"That won't heal the rest of the lands," she says.

I give her a nod and approach the spell book. I achieved my goal of practicing my magic, now I don't mind using the spell book to jump-start the rest of the healing process. Scouts informed the High Queen that the twenty square miles that my magic reached the last time around have already begun growing fresh vegetation and more than that—the healing is spreading. Places I hadn't reached have begun spouting bits of green grass.

If I do the same here, with the spell book's help, we can erase the scars left on our land entirely.

I place my palm on the book and close my eyes. Caelynn

places her hand on top of mine and the moment her skin contacts mine the roaring white light explodes from us.

I clench my jaw against the intense heat and Caelynn's fingers cling to mine.

We pull our hands back in unison and blink as our eyes meet. Her cheeks are flushed, and I find I like the way it looks on her.

"Wow," Caleb says, blinking rapidly.

Caelynn quickly deposits the book back in the bag and slings it over her shoulder.

"We have somewhere to be," I tell the young fae. "Would you take a message back to the queen?"

The boy blinks back his shock and then nods rapidly. I pull a note from my pocket, pre-written, and hand it to him. She already knows my intentions and only agreed to it if we complete the healing in a short time. Which we certainly did. Less than an hour, including travel time.

"What was that?" Caelynn asks with a frown.

"We'll meet the queen back at the High Court for dinner."

"And until then?"

I smirk. "I have a surprise for you."

Her eyes flare golden, even as an adorable frown appears. "What do you mean?"

"I mean, I talked with the queen, and she gave me permission to take you somewhere."

Caelynn swallows then turns her attention to the southwest, toward her homelands.

"We only have a few hours," I murmur, holding my hand out.

26

CAELYNN

I have a pretty good idea where Rev is taking me, but even so, my mind spins through so many thoughts it's hard to keep them straight. I take his hand, and he pulls me through the trees. We follow a pathway that feels familiar, though there is nothing particularly striking. The forest here is lovely and untouched. Bright green foliage and thick tree covering. Birds chirp, and there's a light tinkle of water from a stream somewhere nearby.

A few stones are scattered here and there, and I get the sense that I've been here before. I just don't remember when.

Then, atop a hill to the right of the pathway, there's a stone arch. I stop, frozen in place because it all clicks. "The trials."

Rev turns back with a small smile, his eyes soft and glistening with that lovely molten silver. He nods behind me. "That's where Kari would have died. If you hadn't saved her."

I purse my lips. "It sounds a lot less heroic when you add in the fact that I dealt her the blow that nearly killed her. Two sides to every story and all."

"And yet, Kari herself would still call you a hero for the act."

I don't dwell on that thought for long. What I did was basic decency, not a hero's act, but it's not an argument worth having, not now at least. When I know what lies just beyond that portal.

It's where I'd thought Rev would take me; I just hadn't expected this route.

The thought of going back to that place is both exhilarating and terrifying. It's everything to me. Those lands hold nearly all of my hopes and dreams. But they also hold all of my fears.

We walk the rest of the way to the stone arch, the magic only barely rippling. "I wouldn't have thought this would still stand." It was only created for the trials.

"I asked to be sure."

Of course, he did. He'd really planned this, hadn't he?

"Ready?"

I pull in a breath. Yes. No. I hold out my hand because he's here and I'd like to experience this with him. His smile is heart-shattering. His fingers curl around mine, and I allow joy to overtake all of the anxiety I've felt since the dream. Since that day I nearly leapt to my death in the Source Sea.

I still don't know what that was. It had to have been the Night Bringer—but how? I never even told Rev what happened because I didn't want to worry him. But I won't worry about that now. Now, I get to go home.

Together, Rev and I step through the portal into my homelands of shadow and enigma.

My eyes are closed as we take that first step, but I can feel it. The rushing power of *home*.

Darkness surrounds me. Shivers cascade down my back.

Finally, I open my eyes and take in my favorite place in any world.

Shadows shift and wind howls past my ears, tossing my hair around in a whirl of power, welcoming me to the world of secrets.

Murmurs and whispers flutter through the blowing leaves of the shadow maples, growing louder. Incoherent voices drift over the wind, filling our ears, allowing us to hear little else.

Welcome home, the voices whisper for me alone.

27

REV

I hold my breath as I watch her.

I've never seen a more beautiful sight than Caelynn as she first steps back into her homelands. Her eyes glow golden, her hair billows in the wind. But it's her expression that takes my breath away.

I couldn't even describe it. Awe. Bliss. Wonder. Adoration.

Caelynn stares at the canopy above, the sky beyond a dark blue, even though it's still midday. She sucks in a long, deep breath, eyes closed, expression serene.

This forest has a distinct scent—damp wood and fresh foliage. Of wild power and danger.

It's the smell of her. I breathe it in deeply, savoring the luscious scent of the Shadow Court.

"Thank you," she whispers, and for one wild moment, I consider throwing her against one of these dark trees and seeing just how far that appreciation would take me. The rush of desire passes quickly though. This is about her, not me.

"You're welcome."

Shadows shift through the trees, and my heart picks up its

pace. They seem too big to be shadow sprites. But then, several wispy creatures dart from the tree cover and streak toward us. The little shadows cling to her limbs, dancing over her.

Her smile lights up, and my breath catches, not for the first time.

Then, something tickles the back of my neck. Little fluffs of inky blackness swirl around me and then leap onto me. I wince but remain still as the shadow sprites examine me.

Friend. Ally, they whisper into my ear. I gasp. I hadn't ever heard the sprites speak the last time. They talked to Caelynn, but not to me or Tyadin.

Yes, trust. Friend, the voices whisper, hurried and excited. The sounds bounce around, one ear to the next, to my feet and back up.

"They're speaking to me," I say.

Caelynn stops to watch. Her eyes are full of intensity that sends my mind spiraling into those very naughty places once again.

Will you stay? Stay here?

"What are they saying?"

"They're calling me 'friend'."

Belong.

Family.

Family. Family.

I suck in a breath.

"Now?" Caelynn asks with a smirk.

"Family," I breathe.

Her smile slips, but her eyes remain electric. "They're claiming you as belonging with them. With us."

My heart shudders. "Yes."

Caelynn takes in a long, slow breath and then turns toward the forest. So many emotions well inside of me. Good and bad. Fear and longing at the forefront. I have an aching need to make her happy. To ensure she has everything she could ever want.

And yet, I know that's impossible.

I can give her this, though. I can and I will find a way to free her from her punishment so she can take it back. So she can belong here once again.

I follow behind Caelynn as she walks down a well-worn path, deeper into the shadows. We walk for a few minutes like this. The path slopes up, up until the hill crests, giving us a scant view of the rest of the shadow lands through the trees.

"You can just make out the palace," she says, bending down a bit, tilting her head. "Just barely." She points through the trees, and I follow her guidance.

On the horizon, I can just barely see the points of three towers. "It's so far."

"I've seen it closer, but not by much," she admits.

I shake my head, still unable to believe that. She's a countess, a loose relation to the queen of her court. Well, officially, that is.

"You're part of the lost line, aren't you?"

Caelynn's head whips toward me. "What?" she breathes.

My lips part. "Darren," I say. "That was the name of the last Shadow Court High King. The one who's portrait you stared at in the High Court hall."

She bites her lip but nods.

"And that was also the name of your wraith. Your... ancestor."

She doesn't respond to that.

"It doesn't make much of a difference," she says, her voice lifeless, distant. "I was going to be given the crown either way."

"It might not change the ending," I say, "but it definitely changes some things. Like the meaning behind it all."

She doesn't respond to that; she just stares out at the palace so very far away. A distant hope she's never had the chance to seize.

"Of course, that's only if the queen ever frees me," Caelynn whispers.

"If she doesn't, I will."

Caelynn's eyes meet mine, her expression serious.

I shrug. "It would be a long wait, but I swear I will pardon you if the queen continues to refuse or delay. You will be freed one way or another."

Caelynn presses her lips together. "Thank you."

My smile is sad, but I give it all the same. "You may not agree with me, but it's what you deserve."

"Maybe. But what I don't deserve," she says, turning back to the tiny palace in the distance, "is your forgiveness. Your appreciation. Your friendship."

Love, I almost say. But I don't. I hold it back because I don't know if it would help our relationship or hurt it. If it would make her feel the way I want it to, or if it would only break her heart.

I take another step forward so that I'm right beside her, then my fingers find hers. The contact is like lightning that first moment. Then, it settles into the warm buzz of contentment. "You're wrong," I tell her. "You've more than earned all of those things. And it's high time you start forgiving yourself."

She squeezes my hand tighter. "It's scary," she admits.

"Trusting and caring for someone is always scary. But it's worth it."

Three sprites hop to our joined hands, murmuring over us.

"I think they're pleased." I smile.

"Just don't break it to them that they can't keep you."

My heart sinks. I pull off my backpack and drop it on the ground at our feet then pull out a bottle of wine.

Her eyes go wide. "What is that?" Her lips curl, and my gaze pins there.

"We have some time. We don't have to leave yet."

Her eyebrows rise. "Is that so?"

I pop open the bottle of wine. "I didn't bring glasses, though. Hope you don't mind sharing."

"Don't you know I'm a princess?" She gives me an exaggerated curtsey, and I laugh.

"Apologies, my lady."

She laughs, and the sound sends a shiver of indescribable pleasure through me.

We find a place to sit together, and she takes the bottle from my hands and chugs. She licks her lips when she pulls it away, and I don't try to hide how much I like it.

We sit in silence for a while, watching the shadow sprites and the other shadows dance through the trees. I learn quickly that the larger shadows in the tree coverage are phantoms, like the ones in the High Court parlor room we visited weeks ago. They make a short-lived appearance, dancing for us and then slipping back into the trees.

Caelynn leans her head onto my shoulder, and I have to hold back a sigh. Will it ever be like this again? Will these few days with her be all I ever get?

Suddenly, Caelynn is on her feet, and I flinch.

"What?"

The ground rumbles beneath our feet. "Something is happening."

The shadow sprites are in a tizzy all of the sudden, swarming around us. "What? What is it?"

Caelynn swallows. "The Night Bringer."

My heart hammers in my chest, and I have a sword in my hands before I even realize what I'm doing.

"He's not coming for us," she says, eyeing the sword. "But he's doing something."

Run, a sprite whispers in my ear, and I shiver. *Leave, flee.* More join the chant, pushing us to leave.

"They can't hurt us," I tell the sprites, but those words do nothing to calm the shadowy creatures.

He's coming.

He's rising.

He's RISING.

Caelynn gasps, eyes wide, panic clear in her expression. I pull her into my arms, wrapping her up in my warmth and protection.

"They cannot touch us," I say through clenched teeth, even as my own fear rises. Do I still believe that?

The sprites push us back toward the portal. Caelynn grips my hand and pulls me along. I hate that this is how our trip to her homelands is ending—with more fear. More pain.

But one day, that pain will end. One day, she'll be free.

28

REV

I watch Caelynn staring at the same page of the spell book for near hours.

She's been digging into the depths of the knowledge this book holds, and I've only gathered a few bits and pieces. Because the book belongs to her. I know I can use it, but it will never work for me as it does for her.

I let her concentrate because I trust her judgment and it's easier to get information without a middleman.

Tomorrow, the queen is holding a ball in my honor. She's implied she'll be making an announcement. I shake my head against the anxiety that churns my stomach. It's a good thing. My dreams are coming true.

And yet, there is still much uncertainty.

Caelynn frowns as she reads. It's adorable, at first. Then, I notice more lines of stress appearing on her face. She covers her mouth with her hand.

"What is it?" I ask, no longer able to hold it in.

"I... I don't know what to make of it."

I frown and shift closer. "What?"

"Drake has a younger brother. Do you know him?"

My eyebrows rise. "Blane? I've seen him. I don't know much, though. Why? What's his part in this?"

She bites her lip. "I don't know."

"You have a book that knows everything. How do you not know?" I poke her in the arm, trying to lighten the mood. Something has her visibly shaken.

"The book only knows things that have happened. He can't read minds or know someone's intention."

"So, what about him then?"

"He has Raven."

My brain freezes. Drake's brother has Raven? The sweet human girl I saved during the trials. The girl Caelynn may love.

"Why?"

Caelynn schools her emotions—one of her greatest talents—as she tells me what she knows. She'd decided it would be a good idea to see if she can check on Raven via her all-knowing book. His information is limited because he cannot reach other worlds.

He doesn't know exactly what transpired at Raven's school. He only knows that Drake's brother and two other fae traveled to the human world for a few weeks and came back with Raven. She was in the fae realm for two days. Then, she went back through a portal to the human world.

I sit, mind spinning through all of that information. "Why? What would they want with her?"

"To use her against us?" she muses.

I blink. I suppose it would work for Caelynn. She'd give up many things to help her friend.

"The enemy of my enemy is my friend," Caelynn mutters.

Does she think this somehow has to do with the Night Bringer?

"How much does Drake hate us?"

I bite my lip. "He desires power. I don't think he holds many personal grudges. Besides, we don't know for sure she's in trouble."

"I could know if I were allowed to leave this damned place."

I hold up my hands. "I'm sorry, Cae. Do you want me to go? The queen might allow me."

She shakes her head. "Not until we finish the healing, she won't. And besides, it has to be me. You going would only make me even more nervous."

"Ty offered." I shrug.

She sighs. "Maybe I'll take him up on it. If she's back at that school and okay, I'll drop it."

I narrow my eyes, unsure I believe her. After what the book told her, Raven has had run-ins with fae. Fae that aren't our friends. Even if she's back at school, I doubt she'll let it drop just like that. But I nod anyway because it's worth a try.

"I'm not going to be able to sleep tonight," she admits, shutting the book quietly and then wringing her hands.

"Then, stay and we don't have to sleep." My voice comes out huskier than I'd intended.

Her eyes widen, and her breaths come out in pants. For a moment, just an instant, I think she's not going to turn me down. I believe in that instant that she wants me. Wants *this*. And that moment of hope, as foolish as it is, has me molten.

"I don't know if that's is a good idea."

"Why not?" I tease, forcing a smile.

She runs her fingers through her hair.

"I'll take every second I can get. I'll gulp it down and savor it. I'll memorize every moment of this so that if you're gone, I'll have something to remember. Something to cling to."

Caelynn flinches. She steps back. "Rev." Her voice is desperate. Fearful.

I hold my hands up. "I'm not trying to pressure you into anything. You tell me where your line is. I'll take every inch you're willing to give. We don't have to touch. We don't even have to really talk if you don't want."

"Okay," she whispers.

"We can do something else. Something fun, maybe? Honestly, I could use a drink, and you could use a distraction."

Her eyebrows rise, interest stirring in her golden eyes.

I turn to the coffee table, mind whirling through the different options. I do recall a few different sets of cards and even dice in the drawer. My heart lifts at the thought of us playing a game. As silly as that may be, it would be the most normal thing we've ever done together.

I can't do all the things my mind has conjured with my incredibly beautiful mate. I could dwell on disappointment, or I could take the good that may come from something else.

"Let's play a game!" I say, excitement taking over.

I chuckle at Caelynn's incredulous expression, and I memorize it. Her. Every moment, big and small, they matter. And I'll savor each and every one.

29

CAELYNN

Rev's smile loosens something wild in my heart, and I quickly grip the couch in front of me in case my knees buckle. Why am I so damn pathetic? "Play what?"

"Cards," he says with a flick of his eyebrow.

"Cards?" I repeat.

"Have you ever played? I know a few human games. Poker, Big Two, Pisti. Oh, I also have dice, and I know Pirate's Dice." His grin is wide and boyish.

"I... only know poker. Texas Hold'em."

"Poker it is then!"

"I've never seen you so excited." I fold my legs beneath me at the coffee table. "Are you always like this about card games?"

"And dice," he adds with a wink. "No, I just think it's a good idea. For us to have a little tensionless fun for a change."

My stomach twists at the way his eyes turn intense, even as his fingers begin flipping through his deck of cards. "There are likely better ways to ease tension than cards," I mumble.

His fingers halt their movement. "I can certainly think of a few." His voice is husky suddenly, and my muscles clench. Dammit. Why do I have to say things like that? I'm trying not to fall in even deeper with the sexy as hell male I can never have.

At least, the male I can't keep.

"But any activities I could come up with have their own added levels of tension built-in," he says, voice smooth, calm. "And when they're done... well, I'm afraid you'll run from me again. I don't want that." He looks down at the cards in his hands. "So!" he says quickly. "I suggest cards as a way for us to just be us. With no expectations or fears or all the other things we constantly seem to be grappling with. And when it's over, there won't be new questions to mull over. We'll have a good time, and that's it. Nothing more to it."

I allow a small smile. "That does sound nice."

"Good," he says, continuing his shuffling.

"And how about a drink to aid with our relaxation?" I ask.

I swear his eyes glow with deep joy. I force air through my stupid, stupid lungs.

I stand and cross the room to grab the bottle of votive liquor the High Court has stored here. "Don't stack the deck while I'm not watching," I call over my shoulder.

"No promises," he teases.

I turn back with the bottle in hand and a grin spread over my face. He pauses as his eyes meet mine. I nearly trip when I see his expression. One of sincere awe.

"What?" I whisper.

He gives himself a tiny shake and then refocuses on his quick deal of the cards. "I just never see you smile, not like that."

My lips part. *Oh.*

I don't respond to that and instead sit back in my spot

and uncork the bottle. "What is this stuff?" I ask, sniffing the bubbling liquid within.

He eyes the bottle. "Something new. The queen has discovered my lack of appreciation for her chosen drink."

I examine the elaborate golden label. "Stars of the Sky. Made in the Luminescent Court."

"Hmm, if it's what I think it is, I've never drank it from a bottle. It's saved for only special occasions, in which a server will always pour it first."

I pour the liquid into two glasses, and it sizzles and pops like Pop Rocks. It even sparkles, little silver sizzling balls. "Wow," I breathe. I realize I've also had this drink before.

He gives me a knowing look and a small smile. This is the drink we had before our first dance. A decade ago.

The moment between us had been perfect. But, as with everything in my life, short-lived. It was only days before I killed his brother.

I don't know how he feels about it, so I say nothing and shift my focus to my cards. Jack-Ten. Not bad for a starting hand. "What do we bet with?"

"Drinks?" His eyebrows rise.

"This will be a short-lived game." I grip the bottle and pull down a long swig.

"Ah!" he says, jumping up. He grabs a tray from the corner of the room full of pastries and cookies and chocolates. He quickly disperses the tray of goodies and then takes his seat again.

I swallow down the feelings that stir in my gut just at the sight of his smile and his bright silver eyes. "I wasn't sure I'd ever see it again," I whisper, unsure why I even said anything at all.

"What?"

My lips part, but I pause, fingernails rubbing against the

hardwood of the white oak coffee table. "Nothing," I say because admitting I'd meant the silver in his eyes seems… embarrassing. Would it be? I'm not sure. But somehow, saying the words feels impossible.

"There are a lot of things I didn't think I'd ever see or do again."

"You really missed poker, huh?"

One side of my mouth tips up, and Rev's face falls into that awed expression again. "What?"

He shakes his head.

"We're such good communicators, you know?" I say.

At this, he laughs. It's not loud or hysterical, but it's real. A real laugh. And warmth spreads over my chest.

"One day, we'll figure it out."

"Maybe," I shrug. "I bet three brownies." I gently place three chocolate blocks in the middle of the table.

"Pre-flop?" he exclaims. "You must have a monster over there." He stares down at his hand. "Brownies?" he says like he can't believe I'd risk such a prize on the first hand.

I can't help but let a small laugh escape my lips.

"I fold." He drops his cards.

I roll my eyes. "Scared-y cat."

"They're *brownies!*"

I laugh again and then deal another hand. Two-Seven this time. If I remember correctly, that's literally the worst hand possible. "Bet," I say and drop one wafer into the pot. "Trying not to scare you off this time."

He twists his lips. "Raise." He drops a brownie into the pot with full-on eye contact.

"What? Are you kidding?" I grumble as I toss a brownie into the middle. "Unlike some people, I'm not afraid of a challenge."

"Hey!" he exclaims. At least we get to see a flop. I drop three cards face up in the middle. Queen, Ten, Seven.

I have a pair. I almost smile but remember—poker face. Right. I look down at my pile of treats and notice a marshmallow rice treat. I toss it straight into my mouth.

"Hey! You can't eat your stack."

"Try and stop me," I say, mouth full of gooey goodness. "Bet," I say and drop two wafers this time.

He rolls his eyes and drops two wafers into the pot. The next card is a King. Dammit. Not looking good for me. Rev takes another swig of sizzling wine and hands it to me. I throw back another swig.

"Check."

One eyebrow hitches up. "Bet," he says, and he places another brownie into the pot with the most serious stare. I almost laugh. He really means business with these brownies. That should probably be my cue to fold. He's got me beat. I'm certain of it. And yet... I don't want to.

I call his brownie bet, and his deadpan stare doesn't change. Last card. Eight.

I purse my lips.

"Didn't like that card, huh?" he asks.

I smirk. "Never underestimate a shadow fae."

His nose wrinkles.

"Bet," I say, meeting his serious stare with one of my own. *Call my bluff.* I drop three brownies into the pot. He's given me his weakness, and I'm gonna exploit it.

"You're kidding! No way you have a better hand than me."

I school my features into the mask of indifference.

"Dammit," he grumbles as he stacks his brownies, measuring their worth to him. He'd only have two left. He stares at me for another full minute, and my serious expression almost breaks. Almost. I blame the wine. Or the fact that he's taking this way more seriously than I am.

He groans, holding up his cards like he's going to fold. Pauses. "Dammit!" He tosses in his brownies and turns over two pair. Queens and Kings.

I laugh out loud and show him my losing Two-Seven.

He stares at my turned-over cards while I take another drink. "I seriously almost folded to you."

I laugh again, pushing the pile of treats toward him.

After another ten hands, I've only won three of them. Between my losses and several I've snacked on, I'm almost out of treats. Not to mention, my toes are quite toasty and my lips tingly.

"Are you a light drunk?" Rev leans in, a smile on his lips.

"I'm used to shitty Earth drinks. And the low-shelf ones at that. I don't know. Maybe I am." I lean back, head resting on the seat cushion of the velvet lounge chair "This was a good idea," I mumble.

Rev deals another hand. "You're not done with me yet, are you?"

"With you?" I murmur. "No. Not yet."

The room is quiet for a moment. "When will you be?"

I lift my head, feeling heavier than usual. "Whenever I become strong enough to leave you behind."

I look down at my cards, barely caring what they are but looking because that's what I'm supposed to do.

"What do you want, Caelynn? What will you be leaving me behind for?"

"The Shadow Realm," I say wistfully. "I've never really had a choice. I cannot leave it to crumble. I won't. No matter what I have to sacrifice to reclaim it."

He looks down at his cards.

"It's not like we really have a future here, right? I mean,

you do." I realize I'm rambling now but, well, liquid courage and all. Despite what Rev might think, I'm not drunk. I'm just... looser than usual. "But I don't. Not in this court. I don't belong here."

"We could find a place for you, Cae. If you wanted to stay."

"It's a fantasy. The thought that I could belong here."

"I don't see it as fantasy. It's just... hope."

"Hopeless hope." I smile.

"It would take time. But it's possible."

I shake my head. I look at my cards again. Ace-Ace. Wait, is that what I had before? I shake my head. That's a damn good hand. I eye my dwindling stack of treats. "All in."

Rev blinks. Looks at his cards and then back at me. "You sure about that?"

I smile.

"You sure, you're sure?"

I push all of my treats into the center. There are three cookies, four wafers, and a chocolate.

"Fine," he declares after a long swig of wine. "I raise you."

I hold my hand out. "You can't raise an all-in."

"Sure you can. You add in a stake. Take it or leave it."

"No. That's not how it works."

"You scared?" He raises his eyebrows.

I roll my eyes. "You're cheating, but I'll hear you out. What's your bet?"

"A kiss."

I suck in a breath.

"If I win, you kiss me."

My eyebrows shoot up. Not what I'd expected, but... maybe it should have been. "And if I win?"

"You don't kiss me."

I purse my lips. Is that really a win? I'm confident I could convince him to take the wager back, but… I've got the best hand I can possibly have right now, and why not? Liquid courage, am I right?

"Call."

Rev's eyes flare for a moment before he smiles. "Flip 'em."

I turn over my pair of Aces, and he blinks.

"Dammit." He flips over Ace-Ten. I smile. My chances of winning are sky-high.

The board cards are all meaningless low cards of varying suits. I win, but my stomach sinks.

Rev doesn't move. He stares at the cards like he lost something immense there. My heart aches. I should be happy I won, right?

I bite my bottom lip. Do I have enough liquid courage? He doesn't look up at me, and I think that's what does it. What gives me a chance to move without second-guessing. Without freaking out.

I crawl forward quickly, and just as his eyes flit up to mine, my lips are on his.

30
REV

The kiss is brief, just a quick press of her lips against mine. A tsunami of emotions slams through me. Confusion and pain and desire and relief. I'm not sure how I can feel all of those things at once, but somehow, I do.

She pulls back but remains close, her nose nearly touching mine.

I allow one side of my mouth to curl up, even though smiling is about the last thing I want to do. "You know you won, right?" I ask it playfully, but in truth I'm afraid.

Was she confused and thought she lost the wager? Did she only kiss me out of guilt? Out of obligation? Because the truth is, I hadn't expected her to kiss me. I only threw it out there as a playful tease. To push her and see how she'd react. I didn't think she'd take the bet. And once she did, I had planned to wave the kiss off if she seemed even the slightest bit hesitant. I don't want her to kiss me if it isn't what she wants.

"Yes."

My stomach flips. She knew she won and didn't need to kiss me. She chose to. I let that truth hit me one more time—

that sweet, sweet torture—and then my hand curls around the back of her neck, pulling her into me.

This time, when she kisses me, it's rough and desperate. She doesn't pull away, and I can barely breathe for all the want that washes over me. I grab her waist and pull her into my lap.

Caelynn.

Her lips part to allow me deeper access, and I take it, running my tongue along hers, tasting her, feeling her in all the ways I've been denied. Her hips press against mine, and I groan.

I twist, pulling her down to the ground, and lean over her, shifting my lips to her neck. She's sucking in breaths, soft moans on her lips. My mind finally catches up to the situation, and I slow my exploration of her body.

Shit.

I want this so badly, I forgot that... she may not.

"Rev?" she questions through desperate breaths.

I swallow, terrified of what she may say next. I pull back and study her expression. "Do you want me to stop?" I force those words out all the while silently begging her to say no. *Please, God, say no.*

She doesn't respond for such a long time that my heart begins aching.

"Caelynn?" I whisper. Her eyes are pinned to mine, her chest still heaving. I pull back a bit farther, but her fingers dig into my shoulders, halting my movements.

"Don't move," she commands.

The side of my mouth twitches, and I obey, frozen over her, chest just an inch from hers. She shifts back, sitting up straighter, watching me for another moment, and then her hands begin to move.

Her eyes stay steady on mine as her fingers glide over my

tunic, gentle touches on my stomach, drifting down. She finds the bottom hem of my shirt and slowly tugs it up.

My heart hammers in my chest as she pulls it up. I keep everything tense, frozen in place. My arms block my shirt from rising any higher. She raises an eyebrow.

"You said not to move."

She gives me an annoyed look, and I lift my arms up with a crooked smirk. She rips the shirt over my head, and I settle back to where I was.

"Good boy," she says with a twitch of her lip.

"I aim to please." The color in her cheeks deepens, but she otherwise doesn't react.

Her eyes roam over my body hovering over hers, chest heaving. Her fingertips continue her slow exploration of my body, over my shoulders, down to my chest and abs. And, okay, yeah, I clench just for the chance it's more impressive to her.

She takes her time, studying me with intent eyes, and I do my best to remain still despite the sweet agony she's causing me.

She traces my body, dipping along every edge like she's memorizing me. My God, I'd love to do the same to her. Except, I think I'd use something other than my fingers.

"You're beautiful," she breaths.

I laugh. "You think *I'm* beautiful?" Has she seen herself? Even when I hated her, when I thought she was nothing more than my brother's murderer, I'd wanted her. Now?

The only reason I'm not buried deep inside of her at this moment is because it's not what she wants. She deserves to have everything she wants, everything she needs, and sometimes, that means time. Or space. And sometimes, it means it means nothing.

She knows what I want. I've been pretty open about that.

I'll let her take her sweet time. I'll let her walk away from me if it's what she needs.

"It's not a contest," she teases as she reaches around to my back, digging her nails into the skin. I groan. She puffs out a breath, her eyes blazing golden.

"Tell me what you want, Cae," I say, not for the first time. "If you want... more, I..." I close my eyes, trying not to push her too hard. I'd love to press into her and show her how much I want her. I'd be more than happy to beg. But she deserves not to be pressured, no matter how hard it is to refrain.

"I want..." She breathes hard.

Eyes closed, I press my forehead to hers, waiting.

"I just want this. Just... being here with you. I'm not..."

I nod against her, understanding. I've been clear with her, and she's been clear with me. Taking this too far, too fast, terrifies her because there doesn't seem to be any future in it. Even though I disagree. I can't convince her of that until I find I real way to make it work. As it is... it's just desperate hope. I pull back into a sitting position. She rises with me.

"Is that okay with you?"

I smile, though I know it doesn't reach my eyes. "I've been pretty clear with what I want, Cae. But you're in control here. I've told you once, I'd take every inch I can get. Every second with you is heaven." I pause. "I never expected there to be so much torture in heaven," I laugh, "but it's worth every second." I meet her stare.

Her eyes flicker to my lips then back up.

"And you are welcome to kiss me, or touch me, any time you want. No expectations. Just because you turn me on—" Her lips part at that, and I relish it. "Doesn't mean you owe me anything. Until you say otherwise, I'll let you have full control of what we do or don't do."

She takes her bottom lip between her teeth, and I watch closely, trying to ignore the ache in my gut. She takes in a long breath and then smiles sadly. "So, if I... were to say I want to go to sleep?"

My lips quirk. "Just being here with you is enough for me. Well... I mean, I'll always crave more of you. There is never truly such thing as *enough*. But just being near you, that's all I need to stave off the desperation. The panic. This bone-shattering need for *you*."

Her lips press together, holding back a soft whimper. I stand, holding out my hand to her. She flicks an eyebrow like she's annoyed I'd offer a hand.

She takes it, rising slowly. The heat between us like a solid thing. I force my feet to move toward the bed, shirt left discarded on the floor between the table and lounge chair. I slip beneath the silk sheets first and hold the cover up. Caelynn crawls in and curls up beside me, head on my shoulder.

"Just in case I haven't been clear enough about this," I whisper against her hair. "There is no part of me that blames you for the things I used to. My brother's death or anything else. If our circumstances were different, I'd make you my bride in an instant. I'd take you and flaunt you. And I mean now. Not if the past was different. I mean if... you'd let me."

Caelynn stills in my arms, her breathing heavy. There's so much more I want to say. Things I'm desperate for her to understand, but just like I can't force the world to trust her, I can't force her to believe in herself. I can only show her what she means to me.

One step at a time.

31

CAELYNN

I lie with Rev for hours, mind unable to rest.

He stays tense but still for near an hour before his breathing finally evens out. I stay with him, in his warm and caring arms. We took a step forward today, and while every part of me enjoyed it, it terrifies me.

Because I want more.

I almost took it. Almost threw caution out the door and gave in to the desire that's been clawing at me.

And that's the problem. I want Rev. He wants me. But it's not that simple.

Rev says he'll take every inch I allow him. The problem is, I don't think there's ever an end. When I give an inch, I want another. And another. And another.

There is no end to the want.

And if I let this take me, if I'm swept up into the whirlwind that is Rev, I'll never find my feet again.

I don't want to be the "shadow bitch" standing behind the High King. I certainly don't want to be the reason the people he rules distrust him. I'm ready to swear not to marry him, and he doesn't know that yet. But even if he did, part of me wonders if he'd ask me to stay anyway. That he'd like to keep me as a lover out of the spotlight.

I don't want to be his dirty little secret hiding in the shadows for the rest of my life. I don't want to rely on his choices, on his accomplishments, and neglect my own.

Not that my pride is too large for that. Remaining in shadow isn't hard for me. Being someone else's secret isn't out of my realm of experience either. I could do it, I'm sure.

If it weren't for the Shadow Court.

There's another promise on my mind. One I made without magic that I fully intend to fulfill. The vow to reclaim my kingdom. I don't know if it makes me a bad mate, not being willing to sacrifice that for him. But I'm not.

I slip out of Rev's warm embrace and find a place on the window's edge looking out at the front of the palace. Its dark, shadows shifting over the stone-covered ground. The waters rush and ripple in the distance. The ocean that hides a power that could destroy the Night Bringer.

My mind runs through so many things slowly, methodically, like the rushing waves below, crashing against the stones and swirling away. I think about Raven. The hopelessness I feel when it comes to her. She's so far out of my reach right now.

I think about Darren. I think about my father. My mother. My mate sleeping peacefully behind me.

Mate.

I think about all what-ifs. What it might have been like with Rev if it weren't for those monsters. They did this to us, and yet they're out there, free.

Freer than we are.

Freer than I've ever been any single moment in my life.

A desire sweeps through me, tasting bitter and sour. I want to crush them with my bare hands.

I'm possibly the most magically powerful fae alive, and I'm nowhere close to being strong enough to achieve that. I'm weak compared to the only beings that truly matter.

The plague is receding, curling back into itself. A plague that killed thousands of fae. Hundreds of fae children. Sucked the magic from entire cities.

And it was only the beginning.

The Night Bringer did this. All of it. And now, he's even stronger.

There are three things that I want, and I know I can't have them all.

One, to destroy the Night Bringer and his mate. No matter the cost.

Two, the Shadow Court. I plan to reclaim my court because I am the only being alive capable of bringing it back to its former strength.

Three, Rev. I wish I didn't have to list him last, but to me, Rev is a selfish desire. The first two are what I *must* do. What I won't forgive myself for if I fail. But Rev... Rev is what I *want*.

And I am the Shadow Court bitch. I don't get to have happiness.

32

CAELYNN

I slip out of Rev's room early in the morning. My mind meanders through all of the same things I've pondered for the last two days. Thinking about the spell book, the Night Bringer, and what the sprites had said. The spell book didn't have anything of note to tell us about the Night Bringer's plans. I asked what he was doing while we were in the Whisperwood, but the spell book didn't have an answer. That cave system right near there was one of the Night Bringer's most frequented spots for the last few centuries, so it may not have had any meaning at all.

And though he's no longer bound to the underground, the books says he still uses his former means of travel out of convenience.

He has been moving around a lot, but those beings know we have the book and are apparently taking that into consideration as they make their plans. And as ancient mates, the Night Bringer and Terror are able to communicate without words, making it even harder for the book to uncover their plans.

We do know they've spent more of their time in the

mountains between the Glistening Court and the Whirling Court.

My mind is so wrapped up in these wonderings I don't even realize I'm not hiding any longer as I pass through the halls, and I freeze when a familiar face stops on the stairs to stare at me.

Kari's lips spread into a wry grin. "Where are you coming from?"

I'm still wearing my pajamas and heading toward my room, away from Rev's. It's pretty obvious where I've been.

Her hands fall to her hips, and she quirks an eyebrow. I can't think of a response, to be honest, so I decide not to respond at all. I continue walking and just pass right by without a word.

"Aww come on," she says, following after me. "I was just teasing. I think it's great."

"What's great?" I stop, my heart giving an uncomfortable squeeze.

She frowns. "You and Rev."

I shake my head. "There is no me and Rev." Again with that damn heart squeeze. Why does it have to hurt all the damn time? Kari approaches slowly like I'm a spooked animal.

"I mean... we're a team," I say. "We care about each other, but there is no *us*."

She doesn't respond; her sad eyes just watch me.

"So, I don't want people to know I spend most nights with him. We both have nightmares. It helps." I shrug. "But soon we'll be apart, and it will be like it never happened."

"I doubt that," she mutters to the ground.

"What?"

She jerks her head up. "I'm sure it's complicated, Cae, and

hard. But everything that's happened—it doesn't just go away when you go your separate ways."

"I know that," I say.

"Do you?"

"Yes," I say it adamantly, even as my heart continues its stupid, stupid ache. "I've been preparing for it for a long time."

Her lips purse. She blinks like a thought just occurred to her. "Hey, we should hang out more. Girl talk is one hundred percent necessary. Today, maybe? If you want. After lunch, we can go to the pools in the dungeons. Then, prepare for the ball together. I'll do your hair and everything."

My eyebrows shoot up. "Dungeons?"

She shrugs. "It's just an underground area where there's a salt hot spring—that also happens to be near the dungeons. It's fabulous, though, trust me. We can spend some time relaxing and talking. Might be a good break from," she waves vaguely, "everything."

"That sounds amazing," I admit. "After lunch?"

She nods, her smile growing wider.

A few hours later, Kari knocks on my door with a smile even bigger than before. "Ready?" she asks and then wraps her arm in mine without waiting for a response.

"Are you nervous for tonight?" she asks as we wind through the halls.

"Yes," I admit.

"Balls are always nerve-wracking. But also exciting. It'll be fun."

We march quickly through the massive High Court palace, down a winding set of stairs toward the west wing, down, down, down until the air turns cool and the silky-smooth stone shifts to gray cobblestone.

There are no windows here, and it's hard to tell how far down we've actually gone. Until we finally reach a dark and dingy level. We walk through the hall, and my mind spins with recognition.

"I've been here before." I stop, and Kari spins to face me.

"What do you mean?"

I suck in a breath, looking at the barred room down the hall to the left. I hadn't even remembered. I don't think I even realized it was the High Court they'd taken me to back then but now that I see it... "It's hazy, the memories. But I was kept here after—"

"Oh, right," she mutters. "I'd forgotten I befriended a convicted murderer." Her chuckle is awkward. "Sorry, was this in bad taste? I didn't think—"

I wave her off. "I wouldn't have thought of it either. Honestly, I barely remember any of it."

"None of it? Like, the... act?"

"No, I remember that well. The after... it's all pretty hazy. I... disassociated, I think is the right term. I gave up. Knew my soul was shattered and my life was over. None of it really mattered after that. I didn't care that I was convicted or banished. It was simply my new reality."

Kari doesn't know all of the details about that part of my life. She watches me for several moments before apparently coming to a decision because she grabs my arm and pulls me farther down the hall. "If you want to talk more about it, we can in the hot spring. Or we can never speak on it again. Your choice."

I appreciate the option and find this lovely hot spring isn't far from the actual dungeons. We walk into a cavernous room, past a set of guards who simply nod. The ceilings are domed with glittering multicolored jewels. The pink and blue and purple stones reflect colored beams of light all around the room. "It's beautiful."

Kari smiles. "It's part of my court's heritage here. Though, the location leaves a bit to be desired."

I look over my shoulder toward the hall that leads back to the dungeons.

"They don't keep anyone there often. Most of the time, it's individual courts that deal with criminals. Your case was… unique." No one has ever successfully killed a High ruler, not even an heir. Not until me.

I nod absently and strip my clothing off quickly. I shiver the moment my toe first touches the steaming water. It's hot!

"There are steps here." Kari points to an area where pink tiles lead to the pool. I follow her into the scalding water, the heat clawing at me for only a moment before the sear settles and it becomes an incredibly pleasant feeling.

I groan as I settle into the water.

"Nice, right?" Kari grins.

"It's incredible."

We're quiet for a few minutes, just soaking. I don't mind talking about anything really, even my time in the dungeons behind us or the events leading to it, but I've never been good at starting conversations. I'd rather hide away.

"So," Kari murmurs. "Do you really intend to leave Rev behind entirely when the scourge is gone?"

I bite my lip. Yes. No. I don't know. "I don't have a place with him here. That's all I know."

She nods, her hand gliding over the dark waters, watching the gentle ripples as she does. "I can see how a public relationship would seem… improbable."

"Impossible." I shake my head. "I've literally sworn to the queen I wouldn't marry Rev while he's king."

Kari gasps. "You swore? Like…"

I hold out my arm, showing her the soft white lines of the fire tattoo inside my wrist.

"Why?"

"She made it a condition on naming Rev heir… and the possibility of a pardon."

"Wow. Okay." She blinks slowly, still taking it in. "That's crazy. But it doesn't actually change much, I suppose. You can still be in a relationship with someone without marriage."

"Even if I'm pardoned, I'll be five hundred miles away. In a court that is not involved in the ruling court's politics. It's… it's all impossible. It doesn't make sense to even try. It will only end in heartbreak for the both of us."

"Won't it already?" Kari whispers.

I don't respond to that. Whether or not we resist what's between us, it will still break our hearts, the both of us, when the time comes, but… "Maybe, but not as badly as it would if we gave in completely."

Her eyes narrow. "What do you mean give in completely? You spend every night with him."

"I wasn't lying when I said we simply sleep near each other to stave off the nightmares."

She leans in, eyes still narrowed. "You're telling me you haven't… acted on your mateship?"

I flinch.

"I honestly don't think I even believe you. Your connection is obviously really strong. Like him using your power to unlock the spell book."

My jaw drops. I didn't know she even knew about that.

"And what you told me about his healing magic flaring to life just by your touch. Not normal stuff. That's like epic soul-mate love shit. The kind of connection that only comes when the bond has been sealed…"

"You sound like medieval folk talking about consummation." I roll my eyes.

She shrugs. "It's how I always understood it to work."

"Well, we haven't. We've kissed but nothing more."

"Is there a particular reason?" Her words are slow, careful. "Like does he not want—"

I cough. "He wants to. I don't. I mean—" I shake my head. "I *want* to but don't for all the reasons we already talked about. I know how hard it will be to walk away, and it'll be even harder if we give in to... whatever is between us."

"You're soulmates, Caelynn."

My eyes widen. "I realize we're mates, yeah," I spit as anger simmers in my chest. "I've known that since I was seventeen years old and I murdered his brother. I spent ten years mourning the love I'll never have. The thought of having just a taste and losing him again—" My jaw clenches, and I turn away, hiding the tears in my eyes.

"Yeah," she whispers. "I can see how that would be... hard. I didn't even realize you knew back then. Did he?"

"No," I whisper. "He didn't know until the trials."

She whistles, and we're quiet again for a long while. My face burns red, pain I'd been trying to avoid rises to the surface.

"I don't know all the details about your relationship, Caelynn," Kari begins slowly. "I don't know all the details on what happened to you back then. But I see who you are now. I see how Rev looks at you. And if Rev, of all people, can forgive you for your actions, then I highly suspect you deserve that forgiveness."

I breathe in through my nose and out through my mouth. My head throbs with heat and pain.

"And I just have to say, if he wants you and you've

successfully avoided all physical intimacy, then you have some serious self-control. Holy shit. Have you seen him?"

I spin to face her, my cheeks red and eyes wide. I almost take her bait, I almost let jealousy rise to the surface, but then I see the amused expression on her face and I force out a breath. I rub my face with my hand. "You're ridiculous."

She shrugs. "How do you do it, though, really? Not give in to the desire?"

"I just think about what it'll feel like to leave. It's just around the corner. One way or another, we won't be together very, very soon. He's not mine."

"You use your pain to your advantage," she mutters. "You've always been good at that."

I nod and slip under the water, heat pulsing over my skin.

When I rise, water dripping down my face, Kari speaks again. "You ever think you'll regret it? Not taking it while you've got the chance? You'll live the rest of your life without him. You've got him now. Later, you may wish you'd taken what you could while you could."

I bite my lip. "Maybe. But I don't trust myself. I know what I need to do, and if I give in, I'll only get lost in him..."

Kari hums and lies back, floating absently. Her coarse, curly hair floats in the water behind her.

"It gets harder and harder to stay away, though. And... yeah, maybe you're right that I'll regret it later. It's just really scary."

Kari sits back up, sinking low so that her lips are below the dark waters. Then, slowly, she rises, her purple eyes piercing. "You could simply set boundaries."

"What do you mean?"

"I mean, make it clear, what you want and how. Set rules. Like, only oral. Or no kissing. Or a damn blindfold. I don't know. Or keep it simple and say that anything goes, but it's only for one night. When the sun rises, you pretend like it never happened."

My mouth goes dry at all of the pictures this conversation conjures in my mind. *Anything goes.* It sounds temptingly amazing. I'd get the chance to see all of the things Rev really wants. What he pictures in his mind when his eyes glaze over and I know he's thinking about me that way.

I shake my head. "If only my life weren't so eternally complicated."

Kari chuckles. "I will admit, I've had my moments of being jealous of you and Rev, even knowing all the complications you've faced. It's still so obvious how much he adores you. And how right you are together. But this conversation put some of those feelings to rest. I pity you now."

I laugh. "I pity me too."

But the truth is, I already feel like I've gotten so much more than I deserve. So much more than I'd ever thought possible. The intimacy between me and Rev is incredibly thick, even without anything physical. He's forgiven me, as much as that still boggles my mind.

But maybe I'm thinking about it the wrong way. Maybe it's not so much about what I deserve but what he does. Maybe, if I treat it like that—like I'm giving him something, it won't feel so wrong.

The pressure on my chest eases slightly. And that's what makes me realize that that's the core of my hesitation.

I still believe I don't deserve him.

33
REV

I pace in my room for a full thirty minutes in the evening. Already, carriages are arriving at the High Court palace.

My jacket is white with golden buttons and a golden tunic beneath—a gift from the queen. There is meaning to the color that is too obvious to ignore.

I'd usually wear silver only. The color of my court. But today, I will be wearing gold. The color of the High Court.

I swallow. She's going to name me High Heir tonight. Soon. In hours. Minutes, maybe. This is everything I've wanted since my brother was killed. Well, not everything. But it's my most consistent desire.

It's what I've been working toward all these years.

But all I can think about is Caelynn. I haven't seen her since last night.

There's a light knock on my door, and I jump. I swing the door open to find a shocked dwarf staring at me.

"Eager much?" Ty chuckles.

"I was hoping it would be Caelynn."

"Sorry to disappoint," he mumbles as he enters the room. "You'll see her soon."

"Will I?"

Ty nods. "She'll be there."

"Have you been with her today?"

He nods. "She's fine, Rev. Calm down. She spent some time with Kari earlier, I know that much." He looks down at my tailored jacket. He blinks back more surprise but then smiles. "Nice jacket."

I nod. "See why I'm freaking out now?"

He chuckles. "It's what you've been working toward for years. You deserve it. It'll be fine."

I bite my lip. So, why do I feel so terrible? Why does it feel like the moment those words escape the queen's lips, it'll tear me away from Caelynn forever? "What about Caelynn? What happens..."

Ty steps forward and grabs my upper arm. "You'll figure it out. The both of you. You've got time. Remember, she's trapped in this palace with you for at least another few days."

I take in a long breath, unable to find any humor in his joke. "I'm honestly terrified of losing her."

"I know."

God, this feeling is awful.

"Caelynn and I went for a walk around the palace grounds a bit the other day," Ty begins casually, walking toward the drink station in the corner. He pours us each a glass of some clear liquid. "We saw the harbor, walked through that pathetic little forest." He chuckles.

My stomach turns sour, jealousy simmering there. Not because I'm threatened by their relationship, but because I would have liked that time with her. He hands me a glass.

"We found something interesting on the south side of the palace."

I gulp down the drink much too quickly. "What?"

"The ruins of the Shadow Court portal."

I blink.

The eight ruling courts in our realm have a place on the High Court's council and have direct access with the High Court. On the island there are eight portals. One for each of these ruling courts. But there were once more of them.

The Shadow Court was once one of the ruling courts. They once had a portal on these lands.

Could it be rebuilt? Could I be the High Heir, living in this palace for one hundred years, while Caelynn is in her own land, and we still be mere feet from each other?

I take in a deep breath. "Thank you."

He smiles.

"I don't know how easy it would be to convince..."

Ty shakes his head. "Easy doesn't matter. Possible is what matters."

I pull Ty's stocky body into my arms. He hugs back, squeezing me tightly.

"It might be selfish, but I'm glad we didn't lose you to the dwarves. Yet," I add, knowing he likely still desires to be part of the dwarfish community across the sea if they're able to reclaim their land.

"Come on," Ty says. "It's time to make your grand entrance."

34

CAELYNN

Shadows have always been my home. The one and only place I belong. And so, it's to the shadows that I retreat again as fae from around the realm gather to celebrate Reveln.

The savior.

The almost-High Heir.

Everyone here knows what will be announced tonight. They know what he'll be. And they are all excited. All of them happy.

Because Rev is indisputably the best choice. I could list all the reasons the people of the realm love him. He's the previous heir's brother. He belongs to a powerful court. He won the trials. He cured the land of the plague.

The people don't know the rest of the story, and that's okay. For now.

I am not foolish enough to think the Night Bringer will just slink off into the darkness with his mate and forget the people who challenged him.

But for now, Rev is the hero of the land. And I sincerely believe he deserves it.

I'd like to walk down those massive stairs with him. I'd love to be beside him in the glory. But that has never been in the cards for me.

No, my place is in the shadows.

His place is in the light.

The room is full of gathering fae, the lights dimmed, making it very easy for me to slip to and fro without a glance in my direction. It was easy to sneak my way into the grand hall without being "introduced."

The walls here are decorated with living vines, flickering in blue flames and flowers with sparkling centers. There is a massive chandelier over the steps that drips with incredible, eternal ice crystals.

Every court that has ruled here has left its mark.

The queen enters before Rev, and she eyes my hiding spot in the corner of the room, but she doesn't react.

I rub my wrist where the new bargain mark stretches over my skin. It's not the same mark as the Night Bringer's. This one is a tiny flame, nearly the color of my skin. No one would notice this mark. But I feel it.

I swore to the queen yesterday that I would not marry Rev so long as he is High Heir, or King. I hate that I needed to make that vow. But I understand it.

I know that being Rev's wife would be a disaster to his reign. And he deserves the chance to have the position he's worked so hard for. The position his father tried so hard to take from him.

"Prince Reveln of the Luminescent Court."

All attention turns to the top of the stairway, where Rev begins his descent into the room, hand gliding over the banister made of intricate golden vines with flowers. They look like metalwork, but they're real living plants. A gift from the previous Twisted Court High King a few centuries back.

Rev's eyes are luminescent, and I smile, watching him. He's beautiful. Powerful. Gracious.

He's perfect.

Rev reaches the main floor, and he looks around, searching the crowd. For what?

Me? I wonder.

I bite my lip.

His first step echoes through the hall, but the step after is lost in the encouraging murmurs. The floor is translucent glass, thick and glistening but clearly showcasing the tossing waves that crash a hundred feet beneath the hall.

The Source Sea surrounds the High Court. It's where legend claims all of our power comes from. I know a different story, but that doesn't mean there isn't some truth there.

Tyadin enters next. A large minotaur booms his name over the crowd, and a round of applause rings out for him.

Tyadin has quickly become the most renowned dwarfish fae in the realm for his role in helping Rev defeat the scourge. He too is now considered a hero.

But me? They still find excuses to blame me for everything wrong with the realm.

More appreciative words rise from the crowd as Kari enters.

"If it weren't for Prince Reveln," someone whispers from the crowd near me, "I'd have loved to see her as the High Heir."

Murmurs of agreement scatter through a group of lovely fae women with flaming red hair. Flicker Court, I'd guess.

"Yeah, but Rev totally deserves it."

Kari wears a lavender gown with sparkling jewels. Her dark skin is strewn with silver glitter, just subtle enough to make her shine. She is beyond beautiful.

"Maybe they could marry?" one of the girls whispers. I

don't really consider their words until Kari reaches the main floor and a handsome dark-haired fae bends down and presses his lips to her hand.

My stomach sinks. Rev.

"Oh, she would make such a lovely High Queen, even if it meant being the wife of the High King."

The action is meaningless. I know that neither Rev nor Kari would pursue any kind of relationship. Not now. Not like this. But it is a reminder that... one day.

I intend to leave. Rev will be High King.

And it stands to reason that, if we aren't together, someone else will take my place. One day. Maybe a decade from now. Maybe fifty years.

But one day, Rev will be pushed to marry.

"Well, I still keep hearing that he's mesmerized by the shadow bitch. Could you imagine?"

"No, that has to be false. I know Rev. I know how much he hated her."

"Well, it's common knowledge that they've been working together. She's here." The short fae with twisted braids looks over her shoulder, as if looking for me. The spy. If only she knew I was right here. Within reach. "Somewhere."

"Probably spying like a creep. Shadow Court fae are so creepy."

"I couldn't possibly believe he's befriended the female that killed his brother. There's got to be more to the story. Maybe she was innocent?"

The group giggles, like that's the biggest joke of all.

"No, she's guilty. But you never know what a shadow fae can do. She probably hypnotized him."

I bite my lip. It's not the first time I've heard that reasoning.

"Fae can't glamour other fae."

The tall one shrugs. "You never know."

The dark-skinned fae crosses her arms. "I don't know, but she's definitely up to something."

I shift away from the gossiping females, my heart aching. It's not a surprise what they think of me. I've always known that's how I'm seen. Even before my conviction.

Shadow fae are not to be trusted.

Those fae think I've seduced Rev or *hypnotized* him, apparently. Others think I'm blackmailing him. Others don't know but don't care. They won't trust me, no matter what.

It's incredible the secrets one uncovers when invisible in a crowded room. I shift through the gathering, barely managing not to run into people who can't see me. The whispers and rumors are everywhere.

Most of the chatter is positive. Word about the Crystal Court miracle has spread, and the relief is palpable.

Fae from the Crackling Court murmur here and there about their own troubles. The Scourge is still active in the Crackling Court, but they're hopeful that it will be eradicated completely in the next week.

Every other court acts as if the scourge no longer exists.

I turn my attention to the ceiling. The only remaining mark the Shadow Court has left in this part of the palace. In the hall, there is a line of portraits where I know there are at least three of my ancestors pictured. And high above us, there is an entire wing devoted to my court. It's neglected and small, but it remains, and that's what matters.

I stare up at the ceiling. It's a deep black void, unending, covered in gobs and gobs of glittering stars. Like its own expanding galaxy.

Without the dark, there would be no light. My mother used

to say that. It's a bittersweet thought. Because I know I own all of the darkness.

I belong to the shadows. And so, in the shadows I will remain.

35

REV

I step into the sea of faces, heart pounding.

The applause is deafening. They cheer for me. Pat me on the back.

The tattoo on my wrist pulses—or is that just my imagination?

Anxiety continues to claw up my spine, but I do my best to force it down. To remain calm and not show what I'm feeling, just like Caelynn would. I harden my expression, just like she would.

I search through the sea of faces, the bodies pressing closer and closer, but I can't find her. She is what I need to settle this feeling, I'm sure of it.

But she's not here. Not in the crowd. I can't even find her hidden in the shadowy corners.

But Kari is here, her lovely purple eyes shining as she bows before me. I smile and do the proper thing. I grip her hand in mine and bend to press my lips to the back of her hand.

The crowd gasps and whispers, even though it's not a

significant action. Any female I highly respect would get the same response.

But then again, though I may not be the High Heir yet, the likelihood is high enough to make me the most eligible bachelor of our realm. Any females aspiring to be queen will now be interested in me.

That reminder sends another wave of anxiety through me.

If only Caelynn were here, I wouldn't have to endure the constant barrage of, well, anyone, but I know from experience how savage the females can be. In the past, I'd enjoyed it. Being desired by some of the most beautiful fae in the land.

Now? I have no desire to lay eyes on another for as long as I live.

"You all right?" Kari asks, wrapping an arm through mine. I give her a small smile in thanks. She's come to the same conclusion as I have.

Without someone to take their place beside me, I'll have others lining up.

I place my hand on hers. To others, it looks like an intimate gesture, only perpetuating the suggestion that we could be a couple. To us, it's a signal that I appreciate the help and want to keep it up. For now.

The realm would love it. Kari and I.

And if it weren't for Caelynn, maybe I'd have even considered exploring the option. After all, I'd be lucky to have a fae as powerful, intelligent, and caring as Kari standing beside me.

Instead, I have a lovely shadow fae that is ten times what Kari could be. Except, the world will never know it.

No, not never. I refuse to believe that.

Even if Caelynn doesn't want to be with me, even if it's not a fight she's willing to take, I'll still fight for her. I will convince the realm that she is a hero. That is my life's mission, no matter what my future holds.

I will protect the realm. I will protect her. I will change their minds.

I am ready to take on this impossible mission.

"Have you seen her?" Kari asks, through a dazzling smile.

"No," I whisper, the ache in my gut growing larger.

"Will it bother her? Me with you?"

I swallow. "I hope not."

Kari's smile fades slowly, subtly. "Then, let's keep it light. Perhaps a dance later in the night?" She turns and inclines her head then spins, her dress swishing as she slips into the crowd.

Immediately, there are three fae vying to take her place, standing shoulder to shoulder. Two young females and one male. "Excuse me ladies, but I have business to discuss with our little hero, here."

I narrow my eyes at Drake. His golden eyes glow. His hair is swept back into a long ponytail that hangs down his back.

One of the females frowns, but the other flicks an eyebrow suggestively at Drake. He's also a powerful male in our realm.

"Little hero, huh?"

He hands me a glass of sparkling liquid; his fingers graze mine, and he pulls his hand back quickly, shaking it like I'd shocked him. I ignore his reaction and return his smile. We are not friends. I've never liked him, to be honest. But we don't have to be enemies at all times. Politics and all.

"What business did you wish to discuss, here of all places?"

"Well, considering you're likely to be announced High Heir in say, the next ten minutes or so…"

"You want to apologize for trying to kill me since I'll be High King?" My lips twist into a snide grin.

"Not exactly."

I sip the drink. "Did you know this was my favorite?" I ask as the sparkling wine buzzes over my tongue. It's a Luminescent Court drink, so I suppose it wouldn't be a tough guess.

"Incidentally, I did. I know a lot of things you wouldn't expect."

I narrow my eyes. "Like?"

"Like where a sudden gaggle of mindless wraiths have been wandering through the Whirlingwood. Or where some powerful being destroyed a cave system in the Glistening mountains, leaving a trail of oozing tar in its wake."

I purse my lips but work to keep my expression as passive as possible.

"Does the queen know what you've done?" Drake asks with a forced smile. "That's what I keep wondering. Is it all a façade or part of the plan?"

I turn my attention to the queen standing on the short balcony at the front of the room. Watching me. "I have hidden nothing from the queen."

I haven't told her all the details, but there is very little she hasn't uncovered all on her own. Or knew even before I did.

He nods. "Good to know."

"Is that it? Some strange events you wanted to bring to my attention?" I do note that these events were rather close to his court. Is that a coincidence? Or is he the only fae brave enough to bring them up in front of me? He's not afraid to accuse or challenge me.

He chuckles, his eyes glowing even brighter. Is it just me or are his eyes brighter than before?

"Indeed. Thank you for your gracious audience, *High Prince*."

I narrow my eyes as he twists, pressing into the crowd behind him. I only have a moment to ponder the strange conversation before there are three more fae vying for my attention.

I force a smile at the young females standing before me but stare over their heads, desperate to get even a glimpse at my mate among the shadows.

A petite fae with skin as dark as night curls her fingers through mine and smiles. She's lovely, with intricately braided hair and a golden dress. Whirling Court? Her eyes are hazel. She's not powerful.

The girl next to her has darker skin too but not as dark as the female gripping my fingers. The third has smaller eyes and a round face.

"Dance with me," the first fae whispers, her voice tinkling like a bell. Once upon a time, I'd have loved to take her up on the offer. But not today. Today, there is only one fae on my mind. Only one I want my fingers touching.

"You're quite lovely, but I'm sorry I have to decline tonight."

She sucks in a breath, shocked to be rejected.

"What about me?" the round-faced fae asks, her hand resting on my chest. I grip her wrist quickly.

"No," I say sharply. And stomp past her. The fae gasp and complain the moment I march away. My sharp rejection may look badly upon them for the night. I may have even acted too harshly, but being touched grated my nerves. I don't want them.

I want her.

And then, I see her, a shadow shifting in between moving bodies. But then, she's gone.

I eye the luxurious fabrics swishing and flowing as fae

pass. I follow what feels like a path of wisping shadows. Aching to find her.

The light from the frost-covered chandelier above casts little shadows scattering around the room. Is she here? Or is it only my imagination? I stop when I reach the open area where fae dance. Mostly male-female pairings, but a few female-female and male-male pairings as well.

I always wonder how female pairings manage not to trip over each other's dresses, like the silky gowns of the two closest to me. They twirl together in harmony, the fabrics following almost as if the wearers have control of them as much as their own limbs. I suppose that could be true for those from the Whirling Court.

"They're beautiful, aren't they?"

I jump and look down at the gorgeous blond fae who appeared beside me. *Caelynn.*

She's wearing all-black, shimmery material that dips low down her chest exposing the swell of her breasts. Across her waist is a black stone ornament with a raven on it.

She looks up at me, her golden eyes glistening. She smirks, and then just like that is gone. The soft black smoke of her magic dissipates in a moment. I blink, almost wondering if I'd only imagined her.

Then, I find her watching me from across the dance floor.

I shake my head. My little phantom, haunting me.

An amused smile plays at my lips. I need to get her in my arms. For even a moment. My one-track focus takes over everything. I begin to march around the dance floor. People call my name. A few hands grab at my arms and even the hem of my jacket. I ignore all of them.

I may never have another chance to dance with my angel. I won't let the chance go.

Caelynn disappears again. This time, the shadows

sprinkle and pop between people around me. She's teasing me.

With a chuckle, I curl around and stand at the edge of the dance floor. A pretty blond fae with a blue dress and hazel eyes stands beside me. "Looking for a dance partner?" she says smoothly.

I smile. "I am. But I am seeking someone in particular."

She purses her lips. "I see." I glance down at the girl and notice the blue and gold tattoo over her pointer finger.

"You're married," I remark. Wondering why she's approached me if she's taken. I don't know her.

"She's there," the girl remarks, nodding to a shadow shifting to the music. I suck in a breath. How did she know?

"She's not trying to hide from you. Just from everyone else."

My eyebrows pull low. Who is this female that knows so much about Caelynn?

"Watch the ground. The shadow shift begins from the place the light touches first. The ground is almost always last."

"How—"

"Now's your chance." The girl nudges my arm. I look to the ground, right by the dance floor. When I glance back the blue-dressed girl is gone. I shake my head from the strange experience and move toward Caelynn like a predator seeking its prey.

36
CAELYN

I watch Rev from the shadows as he speaks casually to a blond fae in a blue dress. She smiles knowingly, and his eyes grow wide as he looks down at her.

With him distracted from our cat and mouse game, I allow myself a moment to enjoy the show.

The fae on the dancefloor spin and twist. Easily the best dancers in the group are the two ladies with red and blue dresses, respectively. Their fierce eyes are only for each other.

Some say fated mates cannot be the same gender. Since so many believe the fated connection has to do with the couple's future child together, it makes sense. But then, I see a couple like them and have to wonder if those rumors are full of shit.

Or perhaps, it's simply true that the greatest loves are those we choose, not those chosen for us.

Either way, I could watch the adoration in those ladies' eyes for hours.

I'm so distracted by the dancers' passionate stare that I'm shocked when another set of eyes flash in front of me with his own passion displayed in the silver glow.

Before I can even gasp, his fingers wrap around my wrist

and pull me into the light. My shadow magic flickers out, and I know that I am visible to everyone around me because the crowd gives a gasp of its own.

Prince Reveln stepped into the dance floor alone and pulled a partner seemingly out of nowhere. And not just any partner. Caelynn of the Shadow Court.

"What are you doing?" I say breathlessly as he spins me. My muscles nearly clench in panic, in confusion, but then his arms are around me, moving with me, and I can't help but relax against him.

"Just go with it, angel."

And I do. Because his arms are around my waist, his breath on my neck, and the music pulses to a rhythm that even I can't resist. And in only a moment, I'm dancing in fluid motions with Prince Reveln.

What even is my life?

"This is such a bad idea," I say, still breathless. Still unable to break through the magic swirling over me, over us. Pulling us together in ways I could never define. The logic is there, knocking on my mind. But my body ignores it.

"I remember the mistake I made at the last ball we attended, and I refuse to make it again."

"What mistake?"

"Leaving you alone to face the scrutiny. We're a team. I won't leave you alone like that again."

My heart twists at those words. I remember that moment too. When Rev refused to walk into the High Court with me. I didn't blame him, but it still hurt.

"You didn't have to dance with me to achieve that."

"I didn't. But, well, I wanted to. And maybe I wouldn't have needed to if you didn't run from me like a scared kitten."

"Scared?"

He ignores that. "I would have walked in with you on my arm if you hadn't hidden. Or avoided me all day."

"Also a bad idea."

"Why?" he asks in a tone that suggests he knows exactly why but simply doesn't care.

"Because you're the most beloved fae in all the land right now. And I'm the most hated."

He pulls me tighter against him, and I let out a desperate breath, just one step away from a moan. Damn, I have to get a grip. But my body feels no such inclination. I melt into his warmth, his magic clinging to my limbs. Can others see it? The mix of shadow and light, twisting together in their own beautiful dance.

His breath tickles my neck, and I shiver. "Sounds like more of an excuse than a reason, angel."

I lean away, but he pulls me back in with the swell of the music. I let go and move with him.

"Why do you call me that?" I breathe between another spin.

"You don't remember?" he chuckles.

"Remember what?"

Rev leans in close, his lips brushing my ear as we spin. "We're already here," he whispers, hands squeezing me tighter as if to prove his point. This is real. My heart hammers in my chest. "Can you give me one dance? Where we forget who we are. Where we forget all the reasons we can never be together, and just enjoy it? One dance to relive in our minds for the rest of our lives. One moment no one can ever take from us."

"A memory not even we can soil." That didn't work out the last time. Or maybe it did. I don't know. It was that moment, a beautiful kiss beneath the shadow phantoms, that Rev's father ripped away from us—and I allowed it. Because it was what Rev needed at the time. So, it's bitter, that memory.

The moments between, those small fragments, will remain unscarred in my mind forever.

The music dips down, settling between songs. I could walk now. Move away and forget this ever happened. Or I could give him his one request and allow us to have one full song, one dance, where we forget the prying eyes and outraged whispers around us.

Where I stop worrying and fearing the future and enjoy this beautiful moment.

"Just one," I whisper.

Rev's eyes flare an incredible silver, swirling with desperate desire, and for the first time, I let my own shine back. A rumble grows in his chest. So low and pained that I wonder if anyone else could have heard it, or if it was only for me

Then, as the music swells into a new song, he pulls me in, spinning. A smile plays at my lips, and I squeeze his fingers still curled around mine. This time, when he spins me to the tones I release all of my tensions and live in the music.

The melody pulls at my soul, and my body moves with it.

So much of my life has been fighting the current threatening to drown me. This is the exact opposite. This is how it should be.

Our small moments of destiny complete.

My body spins away from Rev, but his hand remains clenched on mine. My hair flies back as I arch my back to the crescendo of music. He yanks me toward him. I curl in until my back is pressed to his chest.

His lips are at my ear. "You better not make me sleep alone tonight, angel."

His tone is husky but playful.

My lips curl in a smile that's full of pure joy.

And even though I know it's a mistake. Even though the crowd around us is certainly sparked with anger at our display of intimacy here, in the middle of the High Court ballroom, I don't care.

Because right now, I am Rev's. And he is mine.

Too soon, the song fades. Tears prick my eyes as he allows my fingers to slide from his. Then, I shadow leap, and all that's left of the moment is the dissipating splotch of black smoke where I'd just stood.

And back into the shadows I slink.

37
REV

And just like that, Caelynn is gone.

I watch the black smokey magic fade into nothing, and then I am entirely alone. The music begins anew.

Couples around me spin and twirl together, and still I remain.

Then, a new set of hands are on mine. Kari's smile is sad as she pulls me into a simple dance. Awkward and dull compared to my dance with Cae.

"Bold move," she says with a knowing smile.

"Worth it."

"You mean it was worth the heartbreak after?"

"Worth anything."

We dance, swaying and twirling to the music. Is it just me, or is this song sadder than the last? Beautiful but bittersweet. *This is the future I'm destined for*, I realize, staring blankly at the place she is supposed to stand.

The ghost of what was supposed to be.

All because those creatures took it from us. They are the reason Caelynn is hated. The reason she's considered a villain by fae across our world—because of what they forced her into.

"I'm sorry," Kari whispers. "I wish there was a conceivable way for—"

"I know. It's okay." We continue to move to the music, and I realize the wisdom in what she's done. The whispers are now roving through the crowd of Kari and I dancing. And though many will remember the shadow fae's intimate moment with the High Prince, it'll be overshadowed by this. By the real-life implications of a possible powerful union between the Crystal Court and the Luminescent Court.

"I won't marry another," I tell her, looking out over the crowd. I don't believe she's done any of this tonight because she's hoping to be my future bride. I know she cares for Caelynn and she's aware we're mates.

But even though I trust her intentions, I say those words just in case.

"Good," she mutters.

I give her a small smile.

"The world might not accept you two together, but fate has other plans. And I, for one, would never get in the way of fate."

My broken heart swells. Those words, stupidly, give me hope. Fate. We're fated mates. Which means some powers beyond the ones we see want us together.

I know that doesn't mean everything will work out. I know there are mates that don't remain together. My brother had a mate he barely got to know before his death.

Others, I'm certain, never meet their mates. They live entirely separate lives until the day they die.

But even knowing all of that, it does ease the pressure in my chest to remember that while it feels impossible or stupid, it's right. Even though the world is often so wrong.

The song comes to an end, and I give Kari a quick bow. "Thank you," I whisper.

She nods back, and I slip off the dance floor and into the crowd.

"Rev," someone says. I keep moving. Multicolored eyes from every corner of the room follow me. Hands reach for me.

"Rev," another voice joins in.

I twist and shove my way through the layer of pressing bodies toward the front of the room where I know I can get a reprieve by joining the queen in her overhanging seat.

"Rev! Rev, Prince Reveln." They begin as soft calls by varying voices but quickly make way to shouts as I reach the stairs. There are a dozen guards blocking the entrance to the queen's booth. The two in the center shift to allow me entrance without so much as a glance in my direction.

I let out a relieved breath as I reach the top of the short staircase.

The queen's amber eyes meet mine, a question buried deep. Does she disprove of my actions on the dance floor?

"This is only the beginning," Zanterliesha murmurs, taking another sip of her drink. "It is a burden and a blessing."

I nod and slump in the chair beside her, looking out over the crowded room.

There are many fae I recognize. Many I've met but don't actually remember. Others who I've never seen before.

My fingers tap on my leg anxiously.

"She is still here, hiding in shadow as she does," the queen tells me. "There." Her finger points to a spot near the middle of the room.

I have to squint to make out her form, but I swear the moment I do, my muscles relax. She shifts through the crowd, and I watch as close to the ground as I can, as the strange female suggested. It is easier for me to catch her shadow magic with that tip in mind, though the crowd increases the challenge.

Across the room, another fae of significance enters the hall. "Brielle of the Flicker Court," The minotaur hollers from the top of the massive staircase.

I sit up straighter, staring out at the bright red-headed fae as she descends the large stairway. This is the first I've heard of Brielle entering society after the trials. Making a late entrance for dramatic effect, I'd guess.

"Can she see?" I whisper, noting the way she clings to the banister with clenched muscles. Her steps are smooth, though. She hides whatever discomfort she feels well. Only those who know her well would notice the added tension.

"Her sight is not what it once was, but she is able to get by."

I bite my lip, remembering that it was Caelynn who blinded her during the trials. I don't know if she'd intended for it to be a permanent ailment. It's been months, and Brielle's only now able to see well enough to leave her home court.

"Will it go away entirely, over time?"

"I don't know. To be honest, I don't believe so."

"I could try to heal her," I say but shiver. Healing is a very intimate action, and I am certain I would not enjoy what I'd feel if I were to reach into Brielle's essence.

"That is not necessary."

"I thought you'd hate her."

"My niece?"

"Caelynn," I correct. Brielle is the queen's niece, and she would have been the queen beside my brother had he survived.

"Ahh. Well, I do adore my niece, but that does not mean

I'd blame anyone else for her own actions. I was relieved to see Brielle survive that final trial, if I am honest. If I was in Caelynn's shoes, I'd have destroyed her."

I raise my eyebrows. Brielle killed a human girl during that final trial, all to get to Caelynn. All in the name of revenge. And after Raven's death, Caelynn went ballistic.

"I understand her better than most," the queen murmurs, and part of me wonders if I was meant to hear those words. "I understand why you care for her," she says louder, firmer. "But I am pragmatic. I must advise that you will never, not in your lifetime, squash the resentment the realm feels for her, not entirely. Not enough."

I bite my lip. The conversation took a sharper turn than I'd expected.

"I know what you are attempting, and while it's admirable, and I won't stop you from trying, you must know that if you accept the position of High King, Caelynn cannot be your queen. You will risk the wellbeing of the realm if you marry her. I cannot allow that."

I frown. Is she not moments away from announcing me as the heir? And she brings this up now? And expects me to agree to it?

"Cannot *allow* it?"

"I know that you love her. I can see it. And if I can see it, others will too. Even that concerns me. But, so long as she remains outside of the High Court officially, we can manage the damage."

"You're telling me that I cannot choose who to marry."

She shakes her head. "I am telling you that with a convicted murderer as your bride, your reign as High King will be disastrous."

My lips part.

"As High King, you will be married to the courts. You must always do what is best for the realm, and not yourself."

My stomach sinks, but that I can understand. And Caelynn herself has said she doesn't want to stay. She doesn't want to be my queen.

Queen Zanterleisha's amber eyes dim as she examines me. Then, she nods, as if deciding something right then, and she stands, her eyes glowing so bright it's like a living flame.

The music quiets the moment her fingers grasp the banister and she looks over the crowd. The torches lining the massive room flare—their light and heat rages and then fades again.

The crowd hushes quickly.

"We have come to celebrate a great victory," the queen announces, her voice booming over the room. A rainbow of brightly colored eyes of nearly every shade stare up at her. "To celebrate a great fae."

There's a roar of applause. The queen motions for me to stand and approach the banister with her. I obey, barely able to force air through my tense lungs.

"We are getting ready to enter into a new age." The queen pauses for another round of intense cheers. "We have all the hope in the world that this new age will be a prosperous one. Of peace. And power. Of hope and of glory. But remember that with every age comes a new obstacle. Some new evil that must be prevailed over."

Whispers scatter over the crowd.

"We must never stop fighting. Not even when the light is so bright and beautiful that we can't imagine any evil remaining. But as we fight, we must also remember to never stop hoping." She smiles gently at me. "Our next age will certainly be one of luminescence."

A few chuckles scatter over the room.

"I am certain it will be beautiful and glorious. I will advise your new High Prince, and also the people of the realm, to be prepared for the battle that must constantly be waged. Against ourselves. Against our foes. Against those who choose themselves over others again and again. I am confident in the hands I will leave you in. Because he has personally fought these battles and won. He faced evil greater than any of us will ever fully comprehend. He has loved and lost and given himself again and again. For the better of you all. I believe in Prince Reveln, more than any fae I could have ever chosen. Because Reveln has been tested. He has been hardened, and yet remains caring. He is sympathetic but knows when to take up his sword. He has been sharpened but knows how to hold back. He will be a fierce and gentle leader for his one-hundred-year reign.

"To this great realm, I give you, your new High Heir: Prince Reveln of the Luminescent Court."

38

CAELYNN

The cheers are deafening. The floor beneath us trembles with the rush of adoration for Rev. My Rev.

No, not mine.

Now, he is the realm's. Their heir. Their future king.

My heart swells and stings. I am proud of him. So happy for him. And yet, I mourn for what we will never have. Which is a silly thought because High Prince or heir of the Luminescent Court, it makes no difference. I could never stand in either of those places with him. For more than one reason.

There is only one place in this realm that I belong. Only one that I can make my permanent home.

And he has his.

And yet, it still feels significant for him to be named High Heir. It still stings, somehow. Maybe simply because I am still here in shadow while he basks in his glory. He got his victory. Mine is still so far away.

Seven hundred and fifty-six miles, to be exact. I had stared at a map and measured the distance from the High Court palace to the Shadow Court palace yesterday. If that isn't a clue of how wrapped up I am in all of this, I don't know what is.

Because even if we both get everything we want, we'll be seven hundred and fifty-six miles apart.

"Tonight, we celebrate our new High Prince and the process of destroying the scourge. In the places Reveln has touched, magic and life are returning. By the end of the week, the scourge will be completely eradicated from our lands. The scars may remain forever in some places, but let it be a reminder of what we have lost. And a reminder that nothing is promised. We must continue to fight for our lives and our freedom. For the world our children will be raised in."

She pauses to allow the applause to rise again.

"And," she continues, "we celebrate the brave fae who have given selflessly to assist our new High Prince in his dangerous mission. Kari of the Crystal Court. Tyadin of the Crumbling Court. And even Caelynn of the Shadow Court." An uneasy rumbling of voices simmers. "Not every hero is what we expect or even wanted. Alliances are not always easy. But the strongest heroes do what must be done to achieve their goal. Including aligning with once-enemies."

I suck in a breath just as the boos begin. The queen speaks louder, over the barrage of rapid whispering. Some are shocked. Some angry.

"Banish her," someone calls, but the queen simply glares in their direction. No one else picks up the call, but his words linger in the air, a reminder of the hatred that continues to swell in the hearts of the fae in this realm. The hatred that I will live with forever.

～

I find a nook in the corner of the hall where I can stand on a small set of stairs by the servants' entrance.

"Let us celebrate what we have all prayed for—the end of the scourge. And honor our hero and soon-to-be leader—Reveln, the High Prince."

I swallow, but the discontent shifts easily back to applause and murmurs of approval.

Music begins again, and the crowd falls back into its expected rhythm. Dancers dance. Others mingle, their conversations more hushed than before.

There's a shift in the crowd. People part for a golden-haired male wearing a mustard yellow jacket and golden earrings. I watch Drake as he strides toward the back of the banquet hall. After two steps, he stops.

With a smug smirk he turns to my place in the corner and winks.

Drake was my ally in the trials for grand total of two days before I betrayed him to save Rev. But I interacted with him enough to know he's power-hungry and arrogant as hell.

And his brother has Raven.

Maybe. He had something to do with her, and that's enough to push me forward.

His expression shifts, though, as he stares out over the crowd. His eyes turn intent with sick joy. I follow his gaze to the shadows streaking around the edges, so fast it's hard to make them out.

My heart stops.

The smokey magic sends waves of recognition through me. The moans are hard to make out over the music and content voices of the fae. No one else notices them. But I know them well. The sounds of their moans dwell in the background of every one of my nightmares.

I spin back to the stairway entrance to find Drake halfway up now, his arms crossed. At first, I think his wary expression means he too is surprised by the wraiths, but then he reaches for his wrist. The fabric pulls back for only a moment, enough for me to see black streaks of a thorn tattoo. A bargain tattoo.

39

REV

My mind is still reeling over the announcements. I knew it was coming, but that didn't stop the flood of emotion that came along with it being official or hearing the words aloud.

I am the High Prince, replacing my brother before me.

I don't emulate him any longer. I know what he was, deep in his soul. What he did.

And yet, I can't help but feel like he would be proud of me now. That I'd finally lived up to his legacy. But do I even really care about that anymore?

It does feel good to finally prove myself. To be chosen.

It's a slap in the Luminescent Court King's face, and that's also a wonderful thought.

But I still search for Caelynn in the shadows of this beautiful ballroom in the most powerful court in our world, knowing she remains bound. I have my victory, but hers still eludes her. She deserves to be free to enter the Shadow Court, to return to her beloved homelands.

My heart aches as I descend from the queen's booth, and into the crowd. I force a smile as I accept pats on the back and bows and handshakes from those I meet in the crowd. I push through, meeting more of the fae that are ecstatic to see me named heir. Eager to see me crowned.

Some adored Reahgan and are torn about my alliance with Caelynn. Others are simply thrilled. My chest is tight as I continue on.

A shadow shifts a few feet in front of me, and some of the crowd gasps.

My heart drops because I know immediately that the acidic smell of decay does not belong here. This smoky magic is not Caelynn's.

The moaning of the dead simmers just behind the crescendo of music. But I recognize them immediately.

Wraiths. In the High Court.

My heart pounds as adrenaline rushes through my limbs. My magic pulses in my palm, ready to attack. But the wraiths are hard to make out in the crowd.

My light flares from my palm and I shoot a blast of light into the starry sky above, lighting the whole room. The wraiths hiss, streaking away from the blinding light. Fae scream, ducking away from the shadowy cloaks of the dark spirits.

Three wraiths turn to face me, hovering and hissing. The one in the middle opens its too-wide mouth, exposing rotted black teeth. Wraiths are pure magic, their forms only imitating the physical. But their imitations are certainly unnerving, and their bites can still kill.

The three wraiths converge on me as others leap into the crowd. I waste no time blasting my magic into the coming wraiths. Two disintegrate in an instant. Ash floats through the air, and darkness flashes over my mind.

The memory of the same fate reaching my brother's spirit.

I blink and shake it off, searching for more wraiths to destroy. More fae to save. Anger roars through my veins, and my power continues to build. The room, once filled with a symphony of incredible music, is now a cacophony of screams of terror and cries of agony. The moans of the dead, eager to extinguish life where it stands. Many of the powerful fae fight back, their magic flashing here and there.

Guards charge into the crowd, attacking the wraiths as more fae flee from the hall.

A wraith grips a young fae prince by the throat only feet from me. Their teeth tear into his chest, and the boy roars in agony. Black blood splatters. I whip light at the wraith, and it disintegrates in a flash.

The boy falls and is instantly surrounded by bystanders seeking to save him from his injuries. I want to help him, want to heal him, but I don't have a spare moment.

I turn my gaze up to the queen's platform, and my stomach drops.

There are three wraiths surrounding the High Queen. Her eyes flare red, flames dance in her hand. *She's powerful,* I tell myself. She'll be fine.

"Stop this, now!" Caelynn's voice rings out over the room. I spin, along with everyone else in the room, to see her at the top of the stairway with another fae male.

I have no idea what's happening. What has she figured out?

Everything freezes, though. The crowd stills and so do the wraiths, gazes turning to the spectacle above.

"*It's her,*" someone whispers near me.

"*The shadow fae did this.*"

"*I knew it.*"

My heart throbs, fingers shaking, feeling helpless.

Because my mate, the fae I trust above all others, is in the spotlight finally. With her blade pressed against Drake's neck.

And I know that though Caelynn is saving everyone from this attack, that's not what *they* see. They see her attacking a powerful fae. They see her as part of this.

"She sent the wraiths. See how they obey her command?"

40

CAELYNN

The moment the attack began, I knew who was at fault, and so, I acted.

I could have leaped into the crowd to save a fae or two from attack. I could have killed a handful of wraiths and appeared as the hero in their eyes. Instead, I leapt to what I knew was the source.

The commander. And I stopped the attack after only minutes.

Drake chuckles, even as his throat bobs beneath my blade. Blood trickles down his throat as the skin begins to split.

"Do you see your mistake now, Caelynn?" he whispers.

Anger squirms inside of me, mingling with the fear. Yes, I see my mistake.

I did what was right. And yet, it makes me the villain once again.

"They hate you. They will always hate you."

"I know," I whisper.

"Did you think you'd won? That the game was over?" he chides sweetly, like I'm a foolish child.

"No." I swallow, staring out at the accusing eyes. The pity

and fear. They fear *me*, not the fae in my grasp that I know is really responsible.

I am such an easy scapegoat.

"Pardon her!" Drake cries out.

I press the dagger deeper, but my muscles tense as his words register. *Shit.*

"Pardon Caelynn! It's what she demands!" His voice trembles in fake fear. His act is disgustingly genius.

My fingers tremble, even as I clench the dagger tighter.

He is beneath my blade, but it is me that is at his mercy. Because I see it, the recognition flaring in their eyes.

"What did you do, Drake?" I whisper.

A low murmur of approval rumbles in his body, but he hides his pleasure from everyone else.

"They'll destroy you too," I warn him. Knowing he won this chess match. I lost tonight, in only moments.

"All you had to do was work with them," he murmurs, like talking to a child. "They rule us, always have, even when we didn't realize it. Every move our kind has made was with their permission if not outright demand. Give in to it, Caelynn. They'd still take you back. They'd forgive your misdeeds against them if you'd only give in. Accept their reign."

Everything within me screams against his words. I long to shove the blade into his throat and let his blood flood the High Court ballroom. But I know that would only solidify my fate.

I wouldn't earn banishment this time. I would be hung. Publicly. Because no one but my few allies would believe Drake is the bad guy.

"I will never submit."

The queen steps forward, the crowd parting for her. Her face is calm, but anger simmers in her eyes. Eyes pinned to me.

She believes Drake's act too. My teeth chatter, muscles growing weak.

"Then, that is why you will lose," Drake says.

Queen Zanterleisha stares up at me. "Release him, Caelynn."

Quiet stretches over the room filled with fae and wraiths. Blank eyes of the dead stare at us. Me. A chill washes over me as a whisper floats through my mind.

This is only the beginning.

My knees almost buckle. Was that the Night Bringer? Or only my imagination?

You can't touch me now, I whisper to myself, even knowing I don't quite believe it.

A rumble of sinister laughter sends a wave of absolute panic through me until I realize it's Drake. He's laughing at my panic. He can feel it.

"We will not bow to your demands," the queen roars. "Release him or face death."

Archers appear on the rafters. Five of them. Bows stretched and ready, their aim better than any human snipers, I know. And yet, I'm certain I could shadow leap and escape their shot if I desired.

But I hadn't intended to kill Drake. I only intended to threaten him into calling off his wraiths. Wraiths he somehow has the power to control. Due to a bargain, I suspect. What else did he earn in exchange for helping those monsters?

"Where is Raven?" I ask, my voice pathetically quiet.

Drake laughs again. "I suspect you'll find out soon enough."

"Caelynn," Rev says, his voice softer than the queen's but still firm. "You need to let him go. We'll figure this out." He holds his hands up in surrender. His eyes fearful but not in the way of the others.

Sadness drops over me like a cold blanket, overtaking every ounce of my anger. I knew I would lose him soon but it came even faster than I'd thought. Or maybe I really had started to believe in that hopeless hope.

I release Drake and the dagger at once. He falls onto the steps on his hands and knees, panting pathetically. Then, he scrambles down to the main floor and is wrapped up in the comforting arms of those from his court, while I stand here with arrows still trained on my chest.

He is the victim in their eyes.

And I will forever be the villain.

41

REV

"She's betrayed us," the queen murmurs to me as the crowd begins its chaotic whispering again. "She brought them here." There is unmistakable misery in her tone. Guilt that even she had begun to trust the true villain.

"No," I growl. "She had the culprit in her hands."

"Drake?" The queen shakes her head in disbelief as the wraiths waft up, moaning mindlessly. They hover a few feet above the crowd and turn their empty eyes to Caelynn. My stomach clenches again.

Drake is held in caring arms. His mother, the queen of his court, his sister, and several others I couldn't name. They pamper him, sweetly chattering comforting words in his ear. Were they in on his act too, or are they as fooled as everyone else?

Red rims my vision in a way I haven't felt since the day Caelynn entered the trials. The urge to kill is the same, only now I have a new target. The wraiths fly higher into the starry sky ceiling until their forms disappear into nothing.

All of this, I realize, it's all a setup to frame Caelynn for this attack. And it's working.

The wraiths do not reappear, and their groans fade into nothing.

There are still cries and groans in the crowd below, but the wraiths are gone. How many did the wraiths injure? Did they kill anyone? Concern for my people fills me, but there is only one fae I *must* hold to know she's all right.

I march across the hall and up the stairs.

The crowd watches me intently as I approach her. Everyone seeking to understand what is happening. With me, with Caelynn, with the wraiths.

The easy answer is that Caelynn, the villain of our realm, orchestrated a wraith attack. But they adore me, and I adore her.

Will they trust me enough to believe in her because I do?

I don't even try to hide the adoration and desperation I know is pouring off of me as I rush toward my mate.

Her black dress is seamless, the Shadow Court raven just below her breasts still glistens against the starlight above. But blood drips down the fingers of her right hand, all the way to her wrist. Again, she's the hero, but the world will only see her as the villain.

My fingers are on her cheek before I realize what I'm doing. "Are you okay?" I whisper.

She presses her lips into a thin line, lashes fluttering. "They think I did it." Her voice is low, hard. She presents anger, but I know better. Her eyes are so dim they appear black. This is how she shows her pain.

"I know," I breathe.

There are three hundred or more fae in the room with us, but it is dead still. So silent that for a moment, I believe it's only us.

Her dim eyes meet mine, and I know she's not okay. My palm flashes, magic reaching out for her. My fingers slip down to her neck, and without any effort at all, I search her body for injuries.

There's a tiny flare of pain behind her ribs and a pressure behind her eyes. I ease both, and she shakes her head, but her lips curl into a tiny smile. "Only fools use their magic for such pointless endeavors."

"I'm not sure it requires anything from me anymore. My magic seeks to heal you now. It would take more energy to stop it."

Her eyebrows shoot up.

"If only it could ease the pain that's not physical."

Her smile slips, revealing her agony for only an instant.

"She's a witch," someone whispers from the crowd, followed by a few murmurs of agreement and dismay. *"She's hypnotized our prince."*

I clench my jaw.

"See?" Caelynn's lips stretch into a bitter smirk. Her shield solidly back in place.

The crowd begins shifting, whispering. They're still interested and curious about Caelynn and I, but some have begun asking for help. There are certainly injured fae among the crowd.

"You and Drake have matching tattoos now," she whispers.

I blink at that and follow her stare to my wrist. I pull back the fabric to reveal just the tip of the thorn bargain tattoo. My bargain was with the Night Terror—in exchange for their freedom, they would never cause harm, directly or indirectly, to Caelynn or I, or our courts, or our future children.

If Drake attacked the courts, it couldn't have been from a forced bargain with the Night Bringer. They are magically bound to leave us be. Especially after I was named High Heir.

They can't touch the High Court—and by extension, I would think, every court under our rule.

So... "How?"

"They must have found a loophole." Caelynn shrugs.

Stomping feet grab my attention. I take in a deep breath through my nose. "We'll have to discuss this later," I say just as several guards approach.

I suck in a breath as I notice their drawn weapons.

I tense, magic flickering in my hand, ready to defend her. Desperate to keep her safe.

"Step away from her, Reveln."

I spin to find the queen only a few feet away.

"No," I say, my voice steady, even though it's a roar in my own mind.

Caelynn's gentle fingers find my forearm. "It's okay," she whispers.

"No, it's not." My voice is hoarse now. Desperate.

"If you fight them, it will hurt more than it helps."

A flood of pain radiates through me. Helplessness crumples my resolve. I take the step away and watch the guards place magical manacles over Caelynn's wrists and march her from the hall.

42

CAELYNN

The bite of cold metal stings my wrists. I wince, only once but that's already too much. I let them see too much.

"This is ridiculous," Rev barks.

But the guards are already guiding me away. I march peacefully, following their lead. Even so, I'm shoved and prodded.

"She didn't do anything."

"Shadow witch," one of the guards spits at me.

"It's all right, Caelynn," Rev calls, his voice filled with pain. "I'll fix this."

And I know he'll do what he can. I know he'll fight for me. But the damage is done. He can't change what every fae in that room was convinced they saw—me commanding the wraiths. It fits so nicely into what they already believe.

Rev's voice fades away quickly, and we're plunged into darkness. The guards grow even more rough as they force me down the dark spiral staircase. A hand presses into my back and shoves me forward. I trip and slam face-first into the cold stone wall. Uneven gritty material scrapes into my chin.

I don't give them the satisfaction of a groan.

I can see better than the guards, but even so, it's easy to lose my footing when shoved periodically and without warning. A shoulder flies into mine, and I'm knocked sideways into the wall again.

"Does that make you feel better about yourself?" I seethe but continue marching.

A few of the fae chuckle under their breath.

The truth is, I could best these guards without much work. The manacles are magical, meant to suppress any outright attack, but they put me right into my element in this shadowy walkway.

I could use that to my benefit. Opening all of my senses, I focus on every shift and move the guards make. It's almost a full minute before another guard attempts another "accident". This time, I feel him tense. And I freeze, halting my movement just as he tries to ram into me.

He stumbles, missing me entirely and instead crashes into the next guard who roars, slamming a fist into the first's face. They holler and grumble at each other, but we've already made it to flat ground, to the open walkway surrounded by cells.

My cozy new home.

"Quit your antics now or you'll risk demotions, the lot of you." A woman guard approaches from the bottom. Her eyes are bright purple, her short silver horns curl against lavender braids. "Idiotic fools," she mutters as she pushes them away from me and gently grips my upper arm. I follow her easily into the farthest cell. The one closest to the pools I'd so enjoyed with Kari just days ago.

Back when I was a guest here and not a prisoner.

Oh, who am I kidding? I was always a prisoner. Just with a few more luxuries.

"Didn't expect to see you here again, shadow fae," the

purple-eyed guard mutters. Again? Does that mean she was here the last time I'd been taken prisoner under the High Court? Were more of these guards here? I hadn't even considered that.

"Why not? Everyone else did," I say as she latches my manacles to a chain on the wall.

"My princess trusts you," she mutters.

Her princess? The purple eyes tell me she's from the Crystal Court, but she wears the High Court emblem, the High Court Guard's uniform. She would have sworn herself to the High Court, over her home court, many years ago. Does she still see Kari as her princess?

I don't question her, though. Those questions are the last on my list.

Instead, I file it away. "What is your name?" I ask because I realize this is the second time this guard has shown me kindness. Well, at least basic respect. It seems significant given the circumstances.

"Rameria."

I nod and slide against the damp stone until my lovely dress becomes soiled by the soiled ground.

With a sad expression, the fae backs out of the cell and again faces the other guards. "Leave, now," she commands. There's a pause, a few grumbles of annoyance, and then boots shuffling away.

Well, at least I'll have a little bit of reprieve from their hatred.

The truth is, I didn't mind the attacks. They couldn't really hurt me, not yet. Not there. Instead, it acted as a distraction. The scraping pain and annoyance, the mental stimulation of figuring out how to fight back in some small way... it stopped me from dropping into the despair I knew was just on the horizon.

The memories of the last time I found myself in these dungeons press on the edges of my mind and it's an effort to stop tears from welling.

I was able to avoid those thoughts, that darkness clawing at me, until now.

Now, I'm alone. And it's all I can do to stop myself from examining every inch of my prison. The mildew dripping from the ceiling. The soot piling in the corners. The hole on the far side—my new bathroom, isn't it lovely?

I swallow. I've used a hole like that before. I've eaten the gruel from the iron plate slid under the metal rungs. Though, if I remember correctly, I only got a few bites down before giving up.

I'd been okay with death back then.

I didn't *desire* it, but I didn't have any hope left for life. So, what did it matter?

The last time, I hated myself because I was here due to my own actions. I look down at my hands. Fingers, longer and leaner now but still the same hands that tore the life from a fae. The hands that broke the heart of my fated mate. Hands that destroyed my entire future.

My lips tremble. I may have been forced into the bargain, into that choice, but I still did it. The act will forever haunt me.

I had a glimpse this week, of the life I could have. And I had moments, foolish moments, where I believed it was possible. I laid eyes on the palace—my palace. In ruins, but still a bright light of hope for me.

I believed I could stand there. I could pour my power into those lands and fuel it, give back some of what was stolen from it. I could begin to undo it all.

Those hands, that tore it all away, begin to shake as I stare at them.

A fool's hope.

43
REV

Rage is like a fire in my lungs. My power flares, palms burning, but there is no one to fight. Helplessness is heavy in my chest. I can't—I can't stop this.

I could fight to stop the guards from taking Caelynn, but what would that serve? Maybe I should have argued more and made it clear to the crowd that I do not believe Caelynn is guilty.

But they already believe me under her spell, so maybe that would have backfired too.

No, I need the queen on my side. She's supposed to be. She's now my mentor. I am her heir. Her chosen.

And right now, she's my enemy.

I close my eyes, willing my heart and magic to calm. This is a battle that must be waged with mind and tongue. And so, with shaking limbs, I turn and march down the steps, not bothering to hide my anger.

"Reveln," the queen warns as I pass her. I don't know what she thinks I'll do. But then again, I don't know what I'll do either. But at the sound of her voice, I stop and turn on my heel. I cast my damning gaze to her. No one disrespects the queen the way I know my eyes do now. She sneers for only one instant, and then her expression softens.

"We have not yet condemned her, Reveln. We will discuss her fate."

"The council may not have condemned her, but your actions have solidified their condemnation." I point to the crowd. "It doesn't matter what your judgment says now. They all have theirs." All the work I'd done to shift their perception of Caelynn gone in only minutes.

Her eyes cast over the crowd, her facial features carefully controlled. She recognizes my point, I realize, though she won't dare admit it.

Before I allow my emotions to overwhelm me, I continue my march out of the ballroom. I enter the main hall and stop beside the portrait of Caelynn's ancestor. Her friend. As strange as that seems, considering he died nearly five hundred years before she was born.

Tears well in my eyes as I consider all this night may have cost her. I rub my burning eyes with my palms. I was supposed to give her life *back*. I was supposed to ensure her happiness. Instead, I cost it.

This wasn't my fault, I realize that. But it still tastes like bitter failure.

"It's not over yet," a soft voice says from behind me.

I don't move. Don't turn to the two fae that joined me in the empty shadowed hall.

I pull in three deep breaths. Maybe Kari is right. It's not over yet. "It feels like it," I admit.

"I know." Her voice is gentle. Feet shuffle closer, and a heavy hand rests on my shoulder.

"We're going to fight for her, Rev," a rumbling deep voice says.

My lips tremble at Tyadin's words.

"But this will require patience."

"They're calling a council meeting in an hour," Kari tells me.

I bark out a bitter laugh. "Those are the people who hate her the most."

"Maybe it's time we start using politics to our advantage. Who do you have on your side?"

I bite my lip and turn to face Kari. "For Caelynn? No one. You. But you're not even part of the council yet."

"My mother respects my opinion. It's not perfect, but I will urge her to be lenient with Caelynn. I believe her whole-heartedly."

Not enough. Not near enough but... "It's a start."

"Until then..." Ty begins slowly.

"I'm going to go see her." I decide quickly. "They took her to the dungeons, right?" My stomach sinks to picture it. Her in that place.

"Yes, but Rev..."

"But what? What could I possibly do for the next hour?"

"There are injured fae," Ty says. "You could use your healing power—"

I spit out a bitter laugh. "I need *her* to heal. Do they not realize that? The scourge isn't even gone entirely, and if they think I can do this, any of it, while she's fucking chained to the wall in a dungeon—" Power is connected to emotions and healing requires a very clear mind. I've only been able to do more than minor injuries with her help, and the anger in my blood right now will not dissolve until she's freed. I couldn't heal a stubbed toe right now.

"It would give you favor with the council."

I curl my lip. "I couldn't if I tried. I'd look like a damned fool."

Sharp steps echo down the hall, and a new form joins us.

"Then, you will not heal," the queen says. Her red and gold dress swishes as she approaches.

My stomach clenches, and I curl my hands into fists

"But you will make an appearance," she continues, "and hold yourself together. Today, you chose the realm. Remember your duty. Our loyalty is to the realm first, justice second."

"The realm is better with her in it," I demand.

"Perhaps. Or perhaps not. We will make that decision at the council meeting. I'm sorry that we arrested her publicly. You are right that it wasn't the best choice given her reputation."

I scoff but hold back any more words.

"You will pull yourself together now," she demands softly. "You will fight for your realm and then for Caelynn."

Expressions as varied as their eye colors stare up at me as I march into the council meeting. Some are angry, others sympathetic. Many, though, look at me like a puzzle to be solved.

I'd waited until after the meeting had begun to enter because I couldn't stand the thought of small talk as the kings and queens of the ruling courts casually entered the chamber.

All eyes are on me as I take my seat beside the queen. It's my first meeting as the High Heir, and this is not how I'd expected it to be. I'm angry at every single one of them. I have a mission for this meeting that does not align with any of their desires. I may make enemies on a day I should begin building strong relationships, but I couldn't possibly care less.

They have my mate chained to a wall in the dungeons.

I don't even try to hide the anger, and it's clear based on the expressions of the high fae kings and queens that they're unsure how to approach the conversation.

All except my father.

"So that whore of yours is finally where she belongs."

My nails dig into the wood of the table. If it were anyone else, I may have exploded at that comment. But the King of the Luminescent Court has well prepared me to handle his goading. And this time, I have the power. I pull in a long breath.

"Enough," the queen commands, her gaze rising with fire. "If you intend to make a mockery of this meeting, I will dismiss you now."

His lip curls in disgust, but then he clenches his jaw tightly.

"What the hell happened today?" the Frost Court Queen is the first to ask the question plaguing us all. Several voices ring out at once, making it impossible to comprehend any of them.

"Enough," the queen commands a second time. "I will begin with the basics and explain what we must decide today. First, welcome your new High Heir, Reveln."

She leaves off my court, which isn't very customary, making me wonder if it were purposeful. There is a lackluster round of polite applause from the twelve fae.

"You all knew this was coming, and it is unfortunate that we must move past this occasion so quickly. We will all welcome our prince with respect and dignity. Today, though, we have a heavy set of events to discuss."

The room stills.

"We received a message from the culprit tonight." The queen holds up an obsidian dagger and a sheet of parchment.

"*The ally of my enemy is my enemy,*" the queen reads the messages scrawled in blood.

"What does it mean?" one of the fae whispers, but I don't pay attention to who. I simply stare down at the writing, blood chilling.

"I do not know the details behind today's attack, but I am certain it was a message. We must remove the cause of this conflict."

My eyebrows pinch. How much does she know? How much do the rest of them know?

"They will seek our destruction no matter what we do," I say, perhaps not as firmly as I should.

"They've named an enemy." The queen holds her chin high. " They made a demand. And if we refuse, we will face a war we cannot win instead of a dangerous enemy in the distance."

"Caelynn must be disposed of," the Flicker Court King says.

"No," I growl, my breath shallow.

"We know what risks this enemy poses to us. All of us." The queen eyes me, but I stare past her at the golden wall covered in the red of the Flicker Court. Soon, they will be covered by white and silver of my own. She knows the message came from the Night Bringer. She knows who is behind all of it.

She always did. Desperate hopelessness fills my chest, suffocating me.

"This is a one step at a time process," the queen says. "Our first step is to avoid outright conflict with them."

"By sacrificing Caelynn," I say, my voice void of life.

"Sacrifice is a harsh term, child." The Frost Court Queen blinks rapidly.

"So, Caelynn," Raijin, the king of the Crackling Court says, "is not guilty." It's a question and my eyebrows furrow.

"Define *guilty*," the Luminescent Court King drawls.

"Caelynn has played many parts in this conflict. She is the center of it all," the queen says in answer.

"But she is not guilty," I growl, rage simmering again. Tears threaten to well in my eyes, but I force it down. I cannot show that kind of weakness now. Even if I'm drowning in it.

"Reveln does have a point," Rai says. "Is it truly appropriate to punish an innocent fae out of fear?"

I meet Rai's golden eyes with desperate hope. His smile is sad. He knows what is at stake for me.

The bastard that acted as my father my entire life, who made my life hell every moment he could, even now, stands. "I propose Reveln leave this meeting."

I gasp. "What? I'm the High Heir."

"You've been the heir for two hours," he drawls. Then, he turns his gaze to the queen. "The stakes of this decision are astronomically high, and he is biased. He does not have his emotions under control. He cannot think past his lust for the shadow fae."

My chest rumbles in warning, but the queen places a hand on my forearm. I mentally promise to destroy that fae king one day. I will kill him.

"I think you may be right."

"No," I whisper. "No."

The queen twists to face me. "You hurt your case more than you help when you react as you do. We will choose what is best for the realm tonight. We all understand the depth of trust you have for Caelynn, and that will play a role in our decision."

"All in favor," my father calls out, and my heart sinks again. Several hands rise immediately, a few more lag behind only a few beats. Only the Crackling Court and the Crystal Court vote in my favor. It's far too little.

I stand, hands trembling, throat bobbing. "Let me give you one piece of information before I go." My voice is dry and lifeless as I speak, but I force the words out. I pull back the sleeve from my right hand, exposing the thorn tattoo. No one speaks, and I don't know how many are aware of what the tattoo means. "Those beings are magically bound not to touch me or Caelynn. They will find every way possible to get around that bargain, loopholes will exist, including using *mutual enemies* against us." I eye the Whirling Court King who exposes nothing with his stony expression. "But I guarantee they want Caelynn out of the way for more than just petty revenge. She has power over them, much more than you realize. She is the owner of the spell book. She wields it. I don't even know if I can complete the spell on the scourge if she is gone." That's a slight exaggeration, but it may remain true considering how even my healing magic acts in response to her. Without her, I don't know what I'll be capable of. "And if you cave to their wishes, they will still come for you. Only when they come, you will have lost your only weapon against them."

Those words hang in the air as I exit the hall, leaving the fate of the love of my life with fae who hate her. As soon as the doors close behind me, that hopelessness I'd barely staved off floods me and I fall to my knees.

44

CAELYNN

My heavy lids flutter as darkness settles over the cold cell. I've been here for barely more than an hour and my behind is already numb. I've become too accustomed to luxury.

It's been barely a week in the High Court. A week since the Schorchedlands.

I knew it would be short-lived. Just not quite in the way I'd expected.

Boots stomp down the stairs, and I inch forward as far as I can before pressure on my wrists restricts my movement. *Stupid chains.* I lean in, trying to get any vantage at all. I can't see who's coming down. More guards to taunt me?

I'd welcome the pain. And if they tried more, I'd rip them to shreds, manacles or not.

But then, a familiar silhouette stands before the metal bars, and I shiver.

Rev.

"Caelynn." His voice is barely a hoarse whisper. "My God, Caelynn. I'm so sorry."

I try to force a smile, but I can't seem to command my lips

to obey. I can only stare at him. The reminder of the one thing that is so very different from the last time I was held here.

The reminder of what I held in my hands and let slip away like smoke between my fingers. I knew I couldn't keep him. Always knew he was temporary.

I just hadn't realized it was *all* temporary.

How foolish of me it was to hope for any of it to last.

I should have known the Night Bringer would ensure it was all ripped away once again. My punishment for trying to defeat him.

I lost.

My fingers find the place on my chest where the dagger pressed in. The wound is long gone, but I can still feel it. An echo of the destiny I somehow missed.

I wish he'd done it. It's a sad thought, but this reality is worse. The Night Bringer is free, reunited with his mate. And I'm here, in chains—again. Just waiting to find out if I'll be sentenced to death or banishment.

My eyes rest on the pin on Rev's lapel, the High Court crest. My heart lifts ever so slightly. Rev is the High Heir, and that's the thought that pulls me back to reality.

My life might be in shambles, but his is not. And that was the point of it all, wasn't it?

My sore heart swells.

"In the Schorchedlands," I whisper slowly. His breath catches at the sound of my voice. "In my darkest of moments, I had one wish. I knew my life was over, that my hope was long gone, but you—*you could still live.*"

"Caelynn." Rev's voice is strained. He pulls at the bars, like he intends to come curl up beside me in my cell.

"That's still true," I say. "I succeeded in that one thing."

Rev's lips tremble.

"Ever since the day I met you, my life had centered

around you. Saving you. I had other goals, but none of them were ever really a possibility. So, this—" I shake my head.

"Caelynn, stop!" he shouts. "This isn't over." But his tone tells me he knows it is.

"I need to say this, Rev. Please."

He presses his forehead to the bars, breath shaking.

"No matter what happens, I need you to know that you are my one single success. I *need* you to live. I need you to find happiness. I need you to be the best fucking ruler this world has ever seen. For me. Do it for me."

Through the thick silence, Rev's breaths continue to shake. He pulls at the bars again. His magic flickers in his palm.

"Rev," I warn, "that's a bad idea."

"I don't care," he growls. "I need to hold you." *One last time,* he doesn't add.

Another set of footsteps echo through the hall. "No need to break in. I think I can justify opening the door for the *High Prince*." It's the voice of the female guard from earlier. "But I can only let you stay for a little while," she warns. "My shift ends in one hour. And you'll need to be back on this side of the door by then."

Rev nods, accepting the terms.

She unlocks the door, and Rev rushes in. He falls to his knees, his arms around me, his face buried in my hair around my neck. "Caelynn," he breathes. After another minute, he shifts, but my chained wrist pulls. He grumbles. There's a flash of light, and then metal clinks to the floor and my arm is free.

Then, in one fluid motion, he lifts me into his lap. I curl up against his chest, without comment to his crime, and we sit there in the dark, breathing as one.

"I told you not to leave me alone tonight, angel," he whispers.

I bark out a bitter laugh. "Sorry, guess I shouldn't have been accused of a wraith attack tonight. I messed with your sleeping arrangements."

He doesn't respond to that.

"Why do you call me angel?" I ask, not for the first time.

He stills beneath me. "Just after we escaped the Schorchedlands," his voice is soft, gentle, "I carried you from the ruins, all the way back to my home. You were unconscious for most of the trip."

That couldn't have been an easy feat. We spent a week in fae hell, fighting terrible beasts on little food and sleep. Rev was tortured and imprisoned for hours. Then, after all of that, he had to carry my limp form all the way out of the Schorchedlands, through the forest to the portal, and another mile to the palace. All in one night.

"You began to wake just as we were walking through the Iridescent forest. You asked if we were in heaven."

My stomach twists pleasantly, and I close my eyes, allowing his soft voice to fill me with fleeting comfort. "Maybe I was on to something," I mutter. "These moments— maybe these small moments are our heaven."

I can hear the smile in his voice. "And you're my angel."

"With how much misery follows me, I couldn't possibly be an angel. The opposite seems more appropriate."

He chuckles lightly, lips brushing against my neck. "You may be an angel of destruction, but you're my angel none- theless."

I accept those words and curl into his warmth, knowing they very well may be my last moments with him.

45

REV

"Times up," a soft voice announces from the hall. "I've got to lock the door." The purple-eyed guard's expression is full of pity as she watches us, still clinging to each other.

My chest is tight as Caelynn stirs. I desperately fear the moment I have to let her go. "I brought you a couple things," I whisper. "I'll make it quick," I tell the guard.

I scramble to retrieve the backpack I left in the hall and unzip it to expose a leather-bound book.

Caelynn sucks in a breath. "Now that is a really bad idea."

I shrug. "It belongs to you. You should keep it."

"They won't let me keep it, Rev. Even without knowing its true power."

"Until they take it back, it's yours."

She takes her bottom lip between her teeth. I know she has a thirst for answers, and last night gave us many new questions.

"And one more thing." The stone warms my palm the moment I grip it. I hold out the glowing lumistone. "This, they definitely can't take from you. It's yours."

She blinks. "The soul stone?"

"It's just a lumistone." I give her a knowing grin. We know it's much more than that, but no one else will. They're common stones in my culture. I've never heard of a lumistone holding any value or power outside of sentimentality. "I have plenty more where that came from." I wink.

I have a few more sitting in my room upstairs in a bowl Caelynn never paid attention to. I'm going to harvest another hundred if I ever get the chance. Even if they never hold the power this one does. I don't know how or why this one is special. Somehow, this stone connects our magic.

She plucks the stone from my hand and spins it idly between her fingers. "Thank you."

Even if the book stays here, without the stone I can't use it, at all. No one can. It'll be a dormant piece of leather and parchment. But I need her to take a piece of me with her, wherever she goes.

The guard clears her throat, and I smile an apology. I face Caelynn one last time, and on a whim, I lean down to press my lips to hers. "I'm in love with you, Caelynn," I murmur against her lips.

She stops breathing, every muscle still. "How is that possible?" she whispers.

My trembling lips curl into a sad smile. "I don't know. But it's true. I love you and that will not change for as long as I live. I swear it." Our relationship has been so complex and confusing and painful. Logically, maybe it makes no sense. But my heart tells me another story.

I don't wait for another response. I release her and march from the cell, trying to hide my trembling limbs. My shattering heart.

The purple-eyed fae relocks the cell, resealing the barrier keeping me from Caelynn.

Though her cell is relocked, her shackles remain broken

and she is able to shift closer. I lower to the floor and sit with my back against the cold iron bars. I can't leave her yet. I don't know if I'll ever truly have the strength to leave.

Caelynn scoots nearer and flips open the spell book.

～

After what feels like a full hour, Caelynn closes the book with a thud. I'd remained quiet as she read, knowing I'd only distract her from her studies. The book doesn't like me anyway.

"Did you learn anything?" I ask, nodding to the book beside her.

"The Night Bringer was behind it," she whispers.

We knew that, but… "But *how*? They can't attack us."

"*They* didn't attack us," she says. "But they did choose a fae they knew desired power. Desired revenge. And they gave him the power and means to attack us. They didn't control the wraiths. Drake did."

Drake made a bargain—we also knew that. I run my fingers through my hair. "Fool," I mutter.

She shrugs. "They're good at forcing fae into picking their side. We don't know what he was threatened with."

I swallow. "But for this bargain to work without betraying mine, Drake would have needed to desire our downfall first. He probably would have needed a plan first. They couldn't *demand* Drake attack us. Drake had to choose to do so by his own free will."

She nods, but her expression tells me that truth means little to her.

"He told me this was only the beginning," she whispers.

I frown at that. Perfect, just what we need. "What did the book have to say about that?"

She sighs. "Not much. He can tell me what they've spoken aloud or written down, but not what is in their minds, and they're very careful about that."

She gently glides the book into its protective pouch and then takes in a long breath.

"Everything we learned is what we already knew," I complain.

"Yes, but it's confirmed. Drake was given dominion over an army of mindless wraiths. He was also given a large amount of power—he's stronger than before."

"The Night Bringer gave him some of his power?"

She nods.

I purse my lips, considering that. "Will he be able to shadow walk?"

"Possibly. His natural element is wind, so you should take a bit of time to research the different abilities of the most powerful Whirling Court fae in history. He'll be something like that."

Extra-powerful Drake will be a formidable opponent, even as the High Prince, which will soon allow my own increase in power. The High Rulers have access to the Source Sea, they lend their power and gain more, a symbiotic relationship.

"It also means he'll have a piece of the Night Bringer's soul inside of him." She pauses, her voice low. "Like me."

46

CAELYNN

Sunlight streams through the small square window near the top wall of the cell, and I grumble, sleep still clinging to my mind. I push my head under the only soft spot near me, hiding from the harsh light.

My arm aches from having it in a weird position, but I don't dare move.

Someone clears their throat, and I blink, groaning as I pull my face from its hiding place behind Rev's back. Consciousness returns, and I realize that Rev stayed. The whole night, his back rested against the bars of my cell. I'd curled up against him as much as I could, my arm snaked out through the bars and over his shoulder to his chest where both of his hands hold mine.

I straighten and eye the newcomer. Tyadin.

"What?" Rev mumbles as bleary-eyed as me. His fingers begin a lazy trail of circles over my forearm.

"The queen wants to see you," he says. "She's been looking for you."

"She should have known," Rev says. "I wouldn't leave her alone."

Ty shrugs, and Rev forces himself to his feet awkwardly. He faces me one more time, his eyes a dull gray. Then, he turns and passes Tyadin up the stairs.

Ty stands there for a few minutes. Silence stretches between us.

"The queen is said to have made a decision."

I bite my lip. "I doubt it's in my favor."

He nods slowly. "Everything I said before you entered the Schorchedlands remains true, Cae. You're incredibly strong. I'm glad Rev was able to see you for what you really are before —" He swallows.

"I'll miss you too," I whisper.

"You can find happiness in the human world, right?"

I bite my lip, thinking of Raven. Raven, who may not even be safe now because of me. My stomach twists, but I force a nod.

"Do you need anything?"

"No. Thank you. But Ty?"

His eyebrows rise.

"You should find your own form of happiness. Okay? Find a way to cross the sea and rejoin the dwarves if that's what you really want."

He shrugs. "I don't know. I see a lot of hope here now. Kari... well, she's open to helping dwarves in her court. We've already begun mapping out a few new laws to help. She wants to make us a part of her court's culture for real."

I smile, hoping that's true. Progression takes time, and it's hard, but it's worth the fight.

"Good luck, friend."

"Same to you, Cae."

～

I spend another few minutes dozing against the cold wall, but my mind is no longer at ease. I don't have Rev to keep away those dangerous thoughts of hopelessness.

I am not left alone for long, though.

My eyes remain closed as footsteps approach my cell.

Finally, I look up to find the High Queen standing before me. I cough, not at all what I'd been expecting. She eyes me, her red eyes scrutinizing. Behind her, there are three guards watching me with even harsher expressions.

"What gave me this honor?" I say stiffly. "That the queen of all fae would come to visit me in the dungeons?"

She purses her lips. "We need to have a conversation."

My eyebrows rise. "I just assumed you'd announce my punishment in front of a crowd like the last time."

"I don't believe you're guilty of yesterday's attacks."

My head lifts. "You don't?" I say slowly. Based on her severe expression and dragging body language, I don't suspect that's the end of our conversation. No one moves to unlock the doors. The guards still sneer in my direction.

"No, but that only makes this more complicated."

I bite my lip, unsure what that means. She rubs at the sleeve of her dress over her wrist. I narrow my eyes. She had been in on some of the Night Bringer's previous plans. Is she in on this too? She no longer bears the bargain tattoo, but I am certain she once did. Is she still bound to them in some way and we just hadn't realized, or is she just fearful?

She notices my attention snagged on her arm, and she swiftly moves her hands behind her back. "Leave us," she announces to her guards. They pause, eyeing each other, but then finally march from the dungeon without comment.

"You sealed our world's fate the moment you entered the Schorchedlands, Caelynn."

I suck in a long breath.

"I did have some hope that they'd be content with their freedom and not actively attack our court systems. I knew they wouldn't disappear completely, but... well, when I learned of Rev's bargain, my hope only increased. If he was our king, they couldn't attack us. After tonight, I no longer believe that."

"It was a foolish hope," I say, not allowing myself to fear offending the High Queen. I ignore the surprise that she'd known about Rev's bargain. When did he tell her? Or did she have spies for that sort of thing? She seems to know a lot more than she ever lets on.

"Perhaps. But what is the alternative?"

"We fight," I say, my voice quieter than I meant it to be, but I force my body to my feet. "We take what leverage we have and use it to our advantage."

The queen's eyebrows rise then fall, her eyes shifting in a way that may have been an almost eye roll. Not a good sign. "Or we can remove the temptation. I should have known they'd never leave you be. They will not rest until they destroyed you. Or, at the very least, removed you."

I curl my lip in disgust, baring my teeth. "You are really that foolish? To think that removing me will solve anything? It will not absolve their blood lust."

"Only one way to find out." The queen sighs and nausea rises up my throat. "Don't worry, child. I didn't have the stomach to dispose of you as an adolescent, and that hasn't changed now. I won't kill you. But I will not pardon you."

I close my eyes. Her words are not a surprise, but they cut deep all the same. I'd had so much hope that I could be free in some small way. I could have it. My home. My throne. My heritage.

It wasn't everything... but it was a lot. Such a large, beautiful piece of my dream.

And now, I won't even get that.

"Drake has very successfully framed you for this attack. The people truly believe you guilty. And it is only the beginning. They will find new and creative ways to get to you. Unless we act. In the human world, those creatures cannot reach you."

I look out the tiny window casting such scant light through the dungeon. My place of punishment. I got only a glimpse of the life I should have lived. Just a taste.

"Did they contact you?" I whisper.

She doesn't respond, and I take that as confirmation. They told her that they want me gone. They want me punished for defying them.

"So, you don't intend to harm me. But you'll send me back to the human world." My voice is vacant, my body numb. If I were to feel right now, it would be my death. My heart would disintegrate into ash like a wraith.

She doesn't immediately respond, and I open my eyes to see her considering. "Nothing is ever simple, Caelynn. A lesson you should learn now."

"Meaning?"

"I'd like to make a deal with you," the queen says.

47

REV

I pace back and forth past the banquet table, waiting for the queen. Why in the world had Tyadin come to retrieve me if the queen wasn't even ready to meet? I've been waiting nearly an hour.

Sunlight streams through the large windows, so much warmer than in the dungeons. Where she is. Without me.

How in the hell am I supposed to deal with this? How am I supposed to let her be sent away? I know she meant what she said, that she wants me to stay and be a great king. To find happiness. But how? How can I do that without her?

Is this what it feels like for all mates? Is what I feel for her normal? At the beginning of our quest in the Schorchedlands, I was concerned that my feelings for Caelynn had been the magic of the bond. It didn't take long for me to stop caring whether it was magic or real; I'd do anything to keep her safe.

But now—now, those previous emotions seem shallow. This ache I feel without her, the sense of fulfillment I feel with her, it's so intense I don't know what to do with it.

If this is how all mates feel, how could a mate ever leave

another? How could they ever choose someone else? A different life?

Does Caelynn even feel this same level of devotion? Or is it just me spinning out of control?

Finally, the queen marches into the room without any warning at all. I jump, eyes flying to her severe expression. She looks tired. Did she not sleep at all?

She walks right past me without meeting my gaze and takes her seat at the end of the table. "I'm sorry, Reveln. I know these last hours have been very trying for you."

I swallow, waiting to hear my mate's sentencing. I don't care for small talk or apologies.

Then, someone else enters the hall. I spin to face the newcomer, and my whole world comes to a halt.

The breath rushes from my lungs as I behold Caelynn. She still wears her black gown, now scraped and frayed, splotches of darkness here and there. But she's still so incredibly beautiful.

I blink, swearing it must be an illusion. She couldn't be free just like that.

When another beat passes and the illusion has not yet shattered, I give in to it. Forgetting everything else, I rush forward, wrapping her into my arms.

"My God, Caelynn. What happened?" I whisper in her ear.

Caelynn's laugh is strained, but I relish it anyway. "The queen and I... came to an agreement."

I turn to find the queen smiling at me. A real smile.

I barely hold back a sob of relief as I pull Caelynn back in. "It's not over," she whispers. "Just... put off."

I nod, allowing myself that small bit of hope. But I know she's right. The people still hate Caelynn. They'll still blame her for yesterday's attack. And if the Night Bringer acts again... I don't know what will happen.

But I can hardly breathe with the relief that Caelynn is out of that prison.

"We'll be leaving for the Crackling Court in less than an hour," The queen announces. "Be ready."

My lips part. The Crackling Court? We had the final healing planned for tomorrow.

"They moved the healing up to help settle the discontent in the courts after last night." Caelynn smiles, stress lines still obvious.

My fingertips glide across her cheek.

"Think we can snag a drink?" she asks, waving over a passing fae. "Do you have any sparkling wine?"

The queen pretends to be busy reading some parchment.

My mind still spins, wondering if this can be real. Caelynn is free? I really thought it was over last night, and that council meeting... I shake my head.

A moment later, we each have a glass of sparkling wine in our hands and Caelynn pulls me out into the main hall. "Any plans for tonight?" Caelynn asks casually, almost sheepishly.

"I hope not. I'm thoroughly exhausted."

Her lips curl up, and my eyes catch on them. Caelynn swallows. "Not too exhausted, I hope," she whispers.

"Did you have something in mind?" I ask, my voice huskier than I'd intended, but as usual, my mind spins down a fantasy realm. Even though I know that's not in the cards for me, I still occasionally indulge in the image of me slamming Caelynn against the wall and ripping her clothes off.

Caelynn shrugs, her eyes cast to the floor. Is she nervous? "I've been thinking a bit about regret."

I pause, watching her, but she refuses to meet my gaze. "Like?"

She takes a too-long drink of her wine.

"I did have something in mind," she murmurs, her eyes

finally meeting mine. They glitter with molten gold, even though the pupils are larger than usual. Those words have my head spinning and stomach squirming with incredible want. Desire so palpable it's hard not to act on it.

"Would you regret not having your way with me while you had the chance, angel?" I say it as a joke, but Caelynn's eyes flare, and I honestly, for the first time, consider that is really where her mind is.

Did her night in prison change her perspective on this?

"Everything I said in the past all remains true," she tells me. She wants me. But she's too afraid to act on it because she doesn't believe it will last. I would have thought her time in prison would only solidify that belief. "But..."

My eyebrows rise.

Her lips curl into a wicked smile, all sheepishness gone, and I swear my knees nearly buckle at that look. "Would you like to bargain with me, Prince Reveln?"

My fingers curl into fists at the effort to stop myself from groaning. God, please let her be saying what I think she is.

"What sort of bargain?" I force out, my mouth dry.

She presses her lips into a thin line, that nervousness returning for only a moment. "You've made it clear you'll take any inch I give you, even if it's temporary. Even if it shatters us later. That's still true?"

"Yes," I pant.

"What if I gave you the chance to take every inch you want... with a time limit."

I suck in a breath and consider. "Are you saying..."

"I'll let you do anything you want with me. For one night."

I close my eyes, shivers blazing over my body. The images of all of the things I desperately want to do to her flood my mind until it's on overload.

"The deal would begin at sundown and end at sunrise. Just one night." Her eyes dim at these words, her face serious.

It's not a change in who we are, what we are. This won't change our future. But that doesn't even remotely settle my pulsing eagerness.

I step forward, everything else in the world falling away. I don't think about who's behind me, who's watching.

"What do you get out of this deal?" I purr.

Caelynn blinks. I surprised her. But she said this was a bargain. One night together—that's the part that I want. And though, of course I fully intend to ensure she gets plenty of pleasure tonight, I assume there's more to this.

She recovers quickly, her lashes fluttering. "A favor."

I chuckle. "An unnamed favor from the High Prince. That's a hefty prize." And it is. Giving a favor as part of a bargain, without that favor being *explicitly* defined, is terribly dangerous. It's one of the first things young fae are warned against. And yet...

"Are you saying it's not worth it?" She licks her lips.

My fingers curl around her hips. "I would give so much more for just a taste of you, Caelynn."

She shivers in my arms. "We have a job to do today." Her eyes flicker over my shoulder to the queen behind me, and her expression dims.

My fingers dig deeper into her skin. "It's going to be hard to focus."

"Deal only stands if you complete your work today." Her laugh is such a glorious sound.

Just one night of heaven. I'll take it.

48

CAELYNN

My whole body throbs as I wait in Rev's bedroom, staring out the massive opening, toward the roaring Source Sea. My toes fidget and I cross my arms tightly as I wait on his bed.

I'd almost lost my nerve. Almost didn't ask Rev what I'd mentally practiced since my conversation with the queen. What I'd considered since my conversation with Kari the day before.

She was right, I realized. I would regret not having those moments with Rev. Especially now that I know tomorrow... everything will change.

But tonight will be a world all to ourselves. Tonight, we'll create the moments we can cherish, to get us through the rest of our lives. The images I'll reminisce over every night before bed, no matter where that happens to be.

Our final healing today was as simple as the last. Rev didn't even really need my help, though he told me otherwise in the carriage ride over, and the queen had expressed her concern in our brief conversation in the dungeons. This was part of our deal.

I needed to ensure the scourge was gone entirely.

We had dinner with the same group as usual. Tyadin, Kari, the queen, and her king. But I swear Rev's heated gaze never left mine.

No one else seemed to notice. Kari didn't grin at me as I would have expected. She only stared down at her food.

But now, our duties are finished. The scourge is gone. Wiped from our world entirely. We achieved what we set out to do from the beginning. And I earned the small bits of redemption I could.

The sweet fantasy I will live tonight is the most selfish thing I've ever taken, and even that is too much. But I'm going to take it anyway.

Heaven knows the world has taken its fair share from me, ravaging my hopes until I was too afraid to develop new ones. So, I refuse to feel guilty for this. For this one night. It's more than I ever would have dared to hope for before all of this started.

To have Rev look at me like this.

He stands in the doorway, his eyes such bright silver, his stance eager but he waits. He watches.

He closes the door to his bedroom softly and then approaches with smooth even steps, his eyes pinned to me.

I stand before he reaches me, and his hands rest on my hips.

We stay like that, only barely touching but saying so much more with our eyes. The wind gushes from the opening, tossing my hair around us both. Rev's gaze never falters and so I keep mine steady too.

Then, finally, he leans down and presses his lips to mine, so soft and delicate.

Such a sweet aching agony.

I close my eyes and allow myself to live this moment. This

destiny that will only last for a few hours before it's ripped away again.

Rev's kiss is slow and methodical. Sweet and gentle.

It's beautiful, and even as his tongue finds mine, it's slow and smooth and full of pure adoration.

It takes my breath away.

No one has ever kissed me like this before. I've had few lovers in my life, mostly college human boys. Never someone I've spent any significant time with, before or after. So, I suppose I shouldn't be surprised that kissing Rev is different.

"Is that what you want to do to me, Rev?" I tease. "Kiss me like an old married couple?"

"One of many things, yes." His tone is serious. He runs his thumb over my cheek and down to my jaw. More sweet touches. "And not like an old couple. Like... a desperately in love couple. Like true mates."

He takes a small step back, and I sit on the silky silver sheets.

"We didn't finish our conversation before," he says.

"Didn't we?"

He licks his lips. "I need to know, Caelynn..." His eyes flash to my legs, then take their time wandering up my body.

My chest heaves, desire flaming my skin.

"I need to know that this is really what you want."

I pause. "Why wouldn't it be?"

At that, he smiles. "I don't know why. But desire and fear don't always make sense. So I just need to hear it."

"Yes. I want this." I grip his shirt in tight fists and tug.

A low growl escapes his throat, but still, he doesn't move. Finally, his fingers dance along the sides of my legs, running over the silky-smooth nightdress.

He closes his eyes and his fingers halt their movement. "I

meant what I said last night," he says, his voice hoarse, his breathing labored.

"What?"

His eyes fly open, a blazing silver. "I'm in love with you, Caelynn."

A chill washes over me. I don't know what to say, what to feel.

"And I know there may never be a way for us to really be together," he continues. "But I want you to know that what I want isn't just sex. It isn't just your body. I want all of it. I want your heart and your soul to be mine."

My hand flies to my mouth. It's a struggle to keep tears from falling.

"Do you still have the lumistone?" he asks.

I lick my lips and then nod toward the table by the door. Next to the spell book, the stone glows softly in the dim light. Rev retrieves the stone and holds it out in front of him. "If you don't want to, that's alright. It wasn't exactly part of the bargain."

"Want to what?" I ask, heart pounding, throbbing so hard it's near pain.

"Lumistones don't hold power or value in my culture," he comments casually.

He's mentioned that before. "They're sentimental," I say, echoing his previous statement.

He nods. "They're a marriage symbol. A tool for bonding."

The breath rushes from my lungs. My limbs go numb and I swear even my heart stops beating for that one instant.

"When they're plucked, they're fruit," he continues. "But they turn to stone over time. It's part of an engagement ceremony for a fae to pluck several fruits and hold them in their pocket for a few weeks until they grow hard as stone. Then, the stones are fashioned into jewelry for their love."

I swallow. "When..." the words take effort, my throat is so dry. "Why did you have this stone, then?"

He tilts his head, and finally meets my gaze. "I only plucked one, at first. It was after you promised to help me enter the Schorchedlands, just before we traveled to the Crumbling Court. I didn't intend to ever give it to you. It was more... a symbol of what we would never have. I knew you well enough to know it was an immense loss."

My eyebrows pull down.

"I didn't think I could love you, after everything. But I've come to realize that I was wrong." His smile shakes my very soul. "It's not easy to love you, but I do. It doesn't even make much sense, but sense or not, I'm desperately in love with you, Caelynn. I want more than your body. I want all of you."

My lips part, wanting to say so much but I don't even know where to start. It's too much.

It's... "It's too much," I whisper.

His eyebrows pull down.

"I don't deserve this much," I whisper, staring at the stone. This night with him was already selfish but to take this from him... to bond ourselves knowing we'll never be truly together—

He grips my chin sharply, forcing my gaze to meet his. "Yes, you do," he growls and I swallow.

My voice is hoarse when I tell him one more thing I've done, the final thing that will probably push him away again. "I promised the queen I wouldn't be married to you while you were High King."

Rev blinks and drops my chin. "Wh—" He shakes his head. "Why?"

I swallow again, throat dry. "She made me swear it before she'd name you High Heir."

Rev closes his eyes and drops his head back, facing the

ceiling. After a few long breaths, he looks back down at me, still sitting on the bed between his legs. I watch and wait for him to reject me. To realize what I am, and what I'll always be.

"You are so selfless, Caelynn."

I blink. "What?"

His fingers find my jaw again, gentle. "Next time you make a decision like that, tell me. Please. You and me, we're a team. I don't blame you for caving to her will but..."

"Okay," I whisper. I don't want him to be mad at me and that promise will cost me nothing very soon.

He takes another long breath. "Tell me, what were the exact parameters of this vow?"

I press my lips together, then pull in my strength once again. Hope, is such a very dangerous thing. "Only that I would not marry you while you are High Heir, or High King. We cannot be publicly bound."

"Publicly bound was her wording?"

I nod. She made it clear she did not disapprove of a secret relationship, only how it was seen to the rest of the realm. "She wouldn't allow me to belong to the High Court, except as its prisoner."

"Well, then that will not preclude a mate's bonding, then."

I close my eyes and sniff, another wave of emotion floods me. The salty wind caresses my back. It's too much. "Rev—"

"You can say no," Rev says firmly. "It will not change the way I feel, or the rest of the night. I swear it."

I let out a long breath through my nose. "Would you still want this," I begin slowly, taking in his adoring expression. This is the look I want to freeze in time, the image I'll hold forever. This is love I do not deserve, but he gives it freely anyway. " Even if fate pulls us apart again. Even if we're separated permanently.

"Yes," he says firmly. "Even if we are worlds apart— I want you to be mine. I want to be yours, forever."

This time, there is no stopping the tears from falling.

"The stone is yours, whether you want to give me a claim to your heart or not. But if you do…"

A radical desire takes over my soul. "I've loved you since I was seventeen," I tell him, tears streaming down my cheeks now. This wasn't what I'd expected from this night. "And it's only grown, stronger and stronger every moment I'm with you. It's so strong it scares me. It takes over everything else. I've been so afraid that if I let you have it, have all of me, that I'll never be able to live without you. And I know I'm going to have to." I sniff, more tears falling.

He presses his forehead to mine. "I don't know about you, angel, but it's too late for me. I'm already so deeply entrenched in you. I don't even really know when it happened. Maybe it was inside the flames, when I saw that little ember of your soul and knew I had to protect it. Maybe it was when I held you in my arms, the Night Bringer killing you from the inside and I pulled you back. Or maybe it was when I chose you, over the rest of the realm. When I made that bargain to save you from that terrible fate. If we're separated again, no matter what, it will destroy me. But it will be easier for me, to be honest, to live without you if I know that our bond is real and forever, no matter what the worlds do to us. All I know is that I want you to be mine, here and now."

I close my eyes and let his adoration wash over me. I let myself feel it, believe it.

Then, lips trembling, I hold out my forearm to him. "Reveln," I whisper, "today I give you my heart and my soul."

He clenches a fist in my hair, his breaths desperate. Then

his other arm snakes out and his bared forearm crosses over mine, the lumistone sitting in his open palm. "Caelynn," he whispers. "Today, I give you my heart and my soul."

From the lumistone, little shining wisps of magic swirl. They twist and dance over the stone, and then circle our crossed forearms, examining our bond like little sprites of light. They extend and pull into a silverly thread that weaves itself over our skin, binding us together.

The magic imbeds in our skin, a straight line over our wrists and then crossing over and back around, a loose weave all the way down our arms.

When it's done, I examine the string of silvery magic on my skin, barely noticeable but there all the same. A new bargain tattoo. Only this time, the only promise we made is to love each other for all time.

Chest still heaving, I meet Rev's intense gaze. "Now, are you going to have your way with me, or what?"

He barks out a quick laugh. "My angel is so eager."

I lick my lips, my palm rising over his thigh. Hunger flaring in his gaze. "Now that you're mine, Caelynn of the Shadow Court," his voice rumbles like a growl, "I'm going to make sure neither of us forget this night as long as we live."

My grin spreads, knowing full well that's already true, but I still like the sound of it.

His hands find their way to my thighs once again, rising so achingly slowly. I grind my teeth together. I fist his tunic and tug him closer but he resists.

"You told me," he chides, "I could do whatever I want with you." He runs his tongue along the tips of his teeth, sending another throb of desire through me. Now, I understand what he meant by sweet torture. He bends down, kneeling before me. "Do you remember the other night when you told me not to move while your hands explored all the muscles on my chest and stomach and arms?"

"Not sure I recall," I tease.

He chuckles. "Well, I'd like that chance. I want to memorize every single inch of you, angel." His fingers find the hem of my dress and then the skin beneath. He glides his hands slowly up my thighs. I shift forward, hips rising off the bed to allow him to pull it up over my shoulders and head. The cool air hits my bare skin and my breath shudders.

He takes me in, eyeing my exposed body. His fingertips glide down my forearms, following the curling path of the silver bond magic. "Mine," he whispers.

I shiver.

His palms rest on my shoulders, and he presses me back until I'm lying on the bed. My heart pounds, my pulse throbbing in places I didn't even know could ache like this.

His lips begin a slow descent over my stomach, to my hip. The first moment I feel his tongue, I press my head into the cushions and let out a small whimper.

He murmurs his approval at the sound.

His hot kisses travel down my left thigh until he reaches the knee, and then he crosses to the other knee and back up my right. His teeth graze over my hip bone. I squirm and gasp.

He chuckles then continues his slow exploration. His hands join the mission, gliding gently over my sides and down as his lips press lower. His nose nuzzles my panties. Then, his tongue slides up the center of me, and I groan.

"That is not fair," I breathe as he takes another quick sweep.

Another chuckle and he gently removes the cloth barrier, shifting them down my hips. I close my eyes in the moment between. And then, his tongue finds the place I'd been near ready to beg him to touch, and my whole body ignites. His tongue slides, slick and warm over me. My hips move with his motion.

I've never felt anything like this. Like him.

It overwhelms every sense. Pulses of pleasure, desire for more. Desperate want, rising. Building. I move my hips with his soft rhythm, and he growls.

My breaths are shallow, my mind lost in the depth of feeling. Soft and yet strong. Sexy and carnal, and yet... loving.

I whimper again, and his fingers begin exploring a new place, swirling and pushing.

Before long, I'm crying out as pleasure explodes behind my eyes and I buck against him, pushing harder. His tongue and fingers ride out the waves of pleasure. When the bliss recedes, Rev looks up, his expression full of arrogance, and he licks his lips. Then, his fingers.

"What's next?" I ask breathlessly.

"So many options," he murmurs, his finger dancing along my stomach. "Would you like a say?"

"Yes," I say between breaths, desire rising anew. "I want your clothes off. All of them."

Rev's eyebrows rise, his dark locks falling into his eyes, and his lips curl into a smoky smile. I bite my lip. How is it possible a smile could be that damn sexy?

Without breaking eye contact, Rev pulls his tunic over his head. I'm reminded of the time I'd accidentally walked in on him showering. How I'd desperately wanted to join him. To touch him. To have him.

Slowly, he unbuckles his belt, and I watch, memorizing every inch as he drops his pants and undergarments at the same time.

"Now what?" he asks.

I lick my lips and consider. I want him to fuck me up

against the wall, but as I take him in, a new desire crosses my mind. I stand and approach him slowly.

His eyebrow flicks up just as I drop down to my knees and take him in my mouth. He groans, deep and desperate. "Fuck, Caelynn," he breathes and runs his hands through his hair, fisting it. I slide my mouth over him slowly. In and out. Then, I stop and look up at him with a devilish grin.

"That's not what I expected."

"Do you want more?" I ask.

He growls low in his chest. "Yes," he says. And I take him again, relishing the power of it. How he comes undone under my touch.

"Wait," he begs. "Stand up," he commands me. My eyes shine, but I obey. This night is his, after all. I gave it to him. I want to know every fantasy he's ever had about me. I want to live it out.

I rise slowly. I have only one moment to take in his wild eyes before he grabs my waist and thrusts me against the wall. I give him a wicked grin. I like that, a lot.

He prowls forward and presses his body against mine, his teeth at my neck. "Do you know how many times I've thought about doing that?" he admits, and I arch my back against him, a groan low in my chest.

"What else?" I ask breathlessly.

All traces of Rev's sweet expressions are gone, filled instead by that of a predator with its prey in its sight. I may not be anyone's prey, but damn if I don't really like when he looks at me that way. His fingers clench the underside of my thighs as he lifts me up.

I hook my feet behind his back, and he guides me down over him. We both groan as he slowly slides inside of me. There's pressure, the small sting of pain, and then bursts of pleasure as he fills me.

He rocks me against him, lifting me up and down, again and again until I'm panting so hard I can barely breathe. Pleasure builds with every pulse. In and out, in and out. I join the rhythm, matching his stride with my hips, pushing him deeper. My nails dig into the back of his neck as I kiss him, deep and ferocious.

"Harder," I beg him.

His thrusts go deeper, smooth even strides pounding into me.

"Shit, Caelynn." He groans then slows his motion. He pulls nearly all the way out and then thrusts in, hard. I moan as he pulls out. In again.

"More," I pant.

He chuckles, even as a growl rumbles from him. His teeth graze my neck. "My greedy angel," he purrs.

He pauses, taunting me. His hands slide slowly up my waist, the sides of my chest, and he gently tugs at my arms. Mischief shines in his eyes, and I buck against his still hips. I need more. More. Somehow, I manage not to voice the pleas, but based on his wicked smile, he knows regardless.

He pulls my hands up over my head and clenches both wrists with his right hand, holding them firmly against the wall. Then, still holding me tightly in place, he pulls back and slams into me. I cry out, arching my back, head pressing into the wall. Sounds I'd never thought I'd make rip from my body as Rev keeps my arms pinned above me and pounds into me.

I can't think, can't see. "Rev," I cry as the wave of blissful agony explodes. I am lost in the rush. All I know is Rev, his body, his magic, mingling with mine until I can't tell where I end and he begins.

As I writhe, so does Rev, and he crests into heaven right along with me.

49
REV

I wake after only a short while and find the sun leaking through the windows. My body is warm and comfortable beneath the sheets, but my arms are empty.

I pull myself into a sitting position and blink groggily.

"Caelynn?"

We spent hours together last night. I took my time exploring every inch of her body with my hands and my lips and my tongue, tasting every inch. Memorizing because I knew I may never get another chance.

Caelynn and I are so complicated, and I know being with her publicly could cost me a lot. Could cost the realm a lot. And while I'm willing to risk it, Caelynn is not.

And then there's the queen...

The room is empty, and I lie back with a sigh. I allow my mind one more replay, thinking over every detail of last night.

She'd run her fingers over my tattoo, memorizing it. Catching every tiny detail and the way our new bonding marking intertwined with the black ink, barely noticeable. Then, she rode me into oblivion.

I groan just thinking about the way her hips moved over me. And her desperate demand to fuck her harder. I close my eyes.

At some point in the early morning, I gave in to blissful exhaustion and fell asleep with her in my arms, but now they are empty. The bed is cold.

I know the deal was only one night, but that didn't mean she had to leave the room. Maybe I could have one more taste before we go back to pretending we're not mates. Pretending were not perfect for each other. Pretending we're not already devoted so deeply it's impossible not to be biased toward her.

I pull my heavy body out of the bed and cross to where a canister of steaming liquid sits. Still fresh. I frown. I must have been sleeping like a damn rock.

Next to the beverage is a folded piece of parchment with my name on it.

My breathing quickens before I even open it. I unfold the note with shaking fingers.

I cannot stay

"No," I whisper. *She left*, I think before my world falls away. Gravity sucks at me, and I drop to the chair.

We always knew this would be temporary. I cannot possibly express what my time with you has meant. My whole world, whole life is different now. Even though I'm going back to the human world, back to where I was before, nothing is at all the same.

I am not the same.

And I swear, you'll be with me for all of time. The world isn't what we want it to be, but I believe in you. I believe the future of our world is in the right hands.

I'll think of you, my mate, every moment of every day.
Love, Caelynn

• • •

I crumple the note in my fist. "No," I yell and slam my fist into the ground.

Not now. Not like this.

I bow my head, limbs trembling. I still taste her, still feel her on my skin. And yet, she's gone. Forever.

I bite through the pain and reread her words, trying to make sense of it. Any of it. All of it.

Back to the human world. I know she felt obligated to find Raven, to protect her, so I understand why she'd choose that direction in her first moments of freedom... But she doesn't mention taking her place in the fae world after. This letter is a goodbye. I can feel it.

She doesn't intend to come back to the fae realm.

Why? It was her dream to take back the Shadow Court. For herself and for her people.

Did she just skip that part in her note? Why does the note read like a permanent farewell, like she'll never even see me again? If Caelynn was truly free, pardoned, she wouldn't remain in the human world.

I clench my jaw and dress quickly. The queen and I are going to have a conversation.

I march past the guards into the hall. The queen is at her usual place at the head of the table, several papers spread out before her as she chats casually to her husband.

"Where is Caelynn?" I demand.

The queen looks up, eyebrows high.

"Where did she go?" I ask again as I reach her, hands clenching the back of the chair beside the king.

"Why don't you sit?" She takes a small sip of her steaming beverage.

"No," I say, keeping my voice low but with plenty of force. "I cannot sit right now."

"We can have this conversation, Reveln. But you need to be calm."

I press my lips together. Generally, I trust the queen. But with this? With Caelynn? I don't know what to make of it.

"Please," I say, pressing my eyes shut. "Tell me what happened." Desperation leaks into my tone. Pathetic. But I don't care.

"She left, though I suspect you know that. What you don't know, I'm sure, is that it's for the best."

I slam my palm against the chair, and the king rises, his eyes blazing. Guards press forward, hands on their weapons. The queen holds up one hand, that small motion a clear command to stand down.

"Any fae in existence would be upset to learn their mate left them," the queen says cooly. My stomach twists, nausea roiling. "I don't blame Reveln for his outburst."

The king narrows his eyes at me but then sits slowly. A warning in his continued glare.

"She went back to the human world," I say, both statement and question.

"Did she?" the queen asks so casually, voice high pitched. I grind my teeth together.

"You didn't know that?" I ask.

"I don't much care where she went, Reveln. Nor did how she leave have anything to do with me. I simply know she could not stay here any longer."

"Did you pardon her?" I ask. As the anger fades, the cracks in my heart spread, splintering. Pain rises until it's hard to breathe.

It was always temporary, I tell myself. But even so, something isn't right.

"No one forced Caelynn to leave. I swear." The queen holds out her palm. I stare at it and I flinch. At first, I think she's showing me her bonding marks. There is also a small flame tattoo on the underside of her wrist.

She pulls back her sleeve slightly to make her intention clear.

It's an offer to test her vow.

"Caelynn left by her own fruition. She was given a choice, and she chose to leave." It's not a common custom, for a fae to test another's truthfulness, particularly for the High Queen. I'd have to draw blood in order to test her vow magically.

The king stiffens beside her but remains silent, bowing to his wife's dominance. Just the offer to allow me to test her is a major deal. To take her up on it, though, is also serious. I could, but I know the king would not be pleased.

Besides, I do believe her.

My racing heart slows, though the pain is still immense. I know what I would get if I tested her words. She wouldn't have offered if she weren't being truthful. Her words were distinctly measured, however.

I pull in a long breath and give her a short shake of my head. She drops her arm and takes another sip of her beverage. The tension in the king's shoulders loosen.

"The scourge is destroyed," the queen says softly. "Your work is done. Take some time, Reveln, to cope with your new reality. I will give you a week to rest. A week to mourn if that is what you need. Then, you must become the prince the realm expects—without the shadow fae by your side."

My stomach twists, heart falling.

Caelynn is gone.

It's the first time I've allowed myself to really think that thought.

"Is she going to come back to the fae realm?" I whisper.

"I don't know. But she is not barred from it."

I pull in a long breath and nod. One week to fall apart and put myself back together. After that, I will live my dream as the High Prince, forever hiding my shattered heart.

50

CAELYNN

I sit inside the cafe and stare at the white top of the plastic cup. Humans chatter around me, the barista huffs at a needy customer at the counter, a blender buzzes. My mind is quiet, still, ignoring the world around me as I stare mindlessly at the beverage I refuse to drink.

A delicious chai latte. Both mine and Raven's favorite. But I can't bring myself to taste it. I desire the small bit of pleasure the creamy drink brings. But somehow, at the same time, I don't want to feel it.

I'm a failure. Why should I feel any comfort at all?

I left the fae realm four days ago, and I've achieved nothing. I'm still alone. Everyone I love is somewhere far, far away, dealing with conflicts I cannot help them with.

I lost Raven and abandoned my mate—and my vow to Darren.

The queen laid out two options in front of me.

I could stay in prison another day and force the council to convene a second time to make my banishment official. It would be public and permanent. I'd be magically barred from entering the fae realm ever again.

Rev would go crazy and do something rash. He'd likely walk away from his position as High Heir or lose it doing something stupid. And the last remaining scourge infection would remain. For how long, I don't know. But Rev wouldn't have been in the right mind to heal it, so it would likely remain for a long time.

Or I could take her deal.

The queen offered me one day. If I was willing to help cure the final piece of the scourge, I could remain in the High Court for one full day and night.

Then, I'd leave the fae realm on my own.

I sniff, hands curled around my warm drink.

My banishment is not *officially* reinstated. It will remain in that state of limbo, maybe forever. Forgotten. Neither innocent nor guilty.

I am simply not welcome there anymore. And if I return, they will make it official and place a permanent mark on my skin to ensure I can never pass through a portal to Faerie without detection.

The queen offered me this deal because she recognized that we have one goal in common: we want Reveln to succeed. And this was the only way we could ensure that while also achieving what she decided was necessary—me out of the fae realm forever.

So long as we played it right, Rev would believe I chose to leave. It's not outside of the realm of reason. I told him I never intended to stay in the High Court. So, I took the deal, made use of my last night with Rev, and then broke his heart as gently as I could manage.

I stand and march out of the coffee shop without even sipping the drink in my hands. It's cooling now. Warmth never lingers long enough.

Out the door, I eye the stone structure down the block.

A few months ago, I spent a long time researching schools in the state that would be a good fit for Raven. There were only a couple boarding schools around, and this one apparently looks really good on college resumes.

I had set up an interview for Raven and then tagged along to glamour the dean into believing she has an incredible amount of potential. That's true, whether he would have seen it on his own or not.

He offered her a full scholarship. Raven had one year in this school before she'd be out in the real world, and I needed to make sure she'd be okay. She'd have the chance to live a good, full life with or without me.

But, as with everything I try, I failed. I failed Raven.

Raven was at school here for two weeks and then disappeared. She has not been back to campus for eleven days. Since the day we escaped the Schorchedlands.

I know from the spell book that she wound up in the fae realm but then returned. So, if she's back in the human world, where is she? Why is she not back at her school?

My heart aches for so many reasons at once as I march back toward the school to question more students. My welcome has long since passed—the teachers and students are no longer amused at my questioning—so, at this point, I've resorted to glamouring the truth out of them.

I still haven't gotten much.

I've learned that there was a hot new guy in school that took interest in Raven—though a few students admitted she didn't seem to reciprocate that interest—and then they disappeared. Both of them. Raven's roommate has been the most helpful as she's the only one in the school that seems to even really care about her absence, but even so, I am no closer to finding my friend than I was in the fae realm.

I spent a full day tracking the scent of the fae who infiltrated her school, but it led to a dead-end at the fae portal. Shocker.

The fae is definitely wind element, also not new information. Though, I did find the lingering magic of a Wicked Court female along with them. Still not enough information to go by.

The thing that plagues me the most is that I don't understand their motives. If the Night Bringer is behind this and he so desperately wanted me gone from the fae realm, why take her? They got what they wanted.

Unless this was all another ploy to punish me. To torture me.

Now, I find myself anticipating I'll stumble onto her rotting remains somewhere.

If they wanted to hurt me, killing her would certainly do it. But four days have passed and still nothing.

My pocket warms suddenly, and I flinch. The cool fall wind wisps through my hair, and I shiver. I pull Rev's lumistone from my pocket. It flickers white light, pulsing comforting warmth. Like a reminder that Rev is still here with me.

All of my regrets well up inside of me as I stare at the stone.

I miss him greatly. But it's the loss of Raven that hurts the most right now.

Because Rev is going to be fine without me. Raven—I don't know.

I should have done a better job of hiding her from the fae realm. I should have taken her somewhere different once the first assassins came. I was so wrapped up in everything else going on I forgot to ensure she was okay, and now, she very well may be paying the price.

I swallow and put the stone back in my pocket.

Three more days, I decide. Three more days, and if I don't find anything else, I'm going to risk whatever I must to find out what happened to my friend. Including reentering the fae realm and confronting Drake.

51

REV

The soft whispering of a powerful being pulls me awake. I sit up and rub my eyes.

Though I've spent far too much time in bed the last few days, I've barely slept. My heart is so heavy. Every limb aches.

The spell book, sitting on a small table by the massive windows of my room in the High Court, vibrates. Rumbling like it's trying to say something.

"Shut up," I tell it. "I'm trying to sleep." I feel stupid for talking to a book. I know Caelynn could talk to it, but it never gave me the same opportunity.

The high-pitched sounds the magical book make are so much like a hiss I nearly chuckle. "She's gone." My heart clenches. "She left us both." Our magical lumistone was gone the morning Caelynn left but the spell book remained. I assume it would hold no power in the human world, anyway. Maybe she thought I'd find a way to read the book through our bond but I've tried. Without the glowing stone, the book burns and remains empty.

I lie back against the pillow that still smells of her. I hope the smell lingers forever, but I know better.

The book rumbles again, and I leap from between the sheets and march toward the stupid, stubborn piece of junk.

"What?" I say again. "It's not like I can even read you!" I grab the binding and immediate pain radiates through my arm, sharp and cruel. I drop it and shake my hand. "See? Why do you keep badgering me if I can't do anything?"

More whispers, soft this time, drift from between the pages. If only I could understand them.

I swallow and turn to the three lumistones sitting in a bowl across the room. I grabbed the fruits quickly that morning after we arrived back from the Schorchedlands, before leaving with the queen. They sat in my pocket during that first healing, just a couple juicy white fruits. I continued to carry them in my pockets until they dried into hard as stone, just like their twin that I gave to Caelynn.

These stones don't glow or hold power the way the other did. And I hadn't expected them to. I took them because I knew I'd found my future, and it was her I thought of as I plucked them from the vine.

I grab my three lumistones and approach the book again. They are not warm, they don't hold light, and I know before I even try that they won't work to release the block on the spell book. Still, I swallow and try.

Caelynn fills my mind's eye as I hold the three tiny stones in my right hand, and my left slowly descends to the worn leather of this ancient tome. A roar of agony and rage rips from me as sharp pain shoots up my arm.

I put my stones back into my pocket and grumble. "See? There's nothing I can do. Now shut up."

Breaths still heavy, I sit back on the bed, my stones still in hand. I stare at them. They reflect light but don't hold their own. I refuse to be angry with these stones for what they can't do. I plucked them for a reason, and it wasn't for power.

So, they can still serve that same purpose now. They'll represent my adoration. My hopeless hope for the mate I lost.

Three isn't enough to do much with, not that it matters now. I could make a small pendant out of these three stones but not the elaborate set of jewelry Caelynn deserves.

I pull in a long breath through my nose. More, I want more, I decide.

I haven't left the High Court palace in the days since Caelynn left. But tomorrow, I will take a trip to my homelands and harvest a bag full of these stones. I will take every single stone I can find. There would never be enough lumistones in the world to measure my true value of Caelynn, but I'll try.

The small sense of purpose puts my aching heart at ease for the time. I curl back up in bed. I hold my three stones against my chest and fall into a restless slumber.

52

REV

With unfocused eyes and itching skin, I walk down the steps toward the packed High Court ballroom. My pocket is filled with nearly a dozen lumistones. Well, most of them are still soft and edible. It's only been two days since I plucked a bag full and they'll take more time to mature into usable stones for the jewelry I intend to make for my mate. Worlds away.

I carry as many as I can in my pockets without looking ridiculous. The rest are in a bowl in my room.

"The High Prince, Reveln of the Luminescent Court," the minotaur announces.

There is a round of polite applause, but it's reserved, as if they can tell that I am not okay. That I am not the same without her.

The air is cold. Music drifts softly, but even those sounds are harsh in my ears. Somehow, even over the music and voices, I can still hear the sound of the waters below my feet. I stop for a moment to watch the waves crest and crash against stones violently, far below the transparent floor of the grand hall. The Source Sea's violent and eager magic pulses through the room.

I swallow and continue pressing forward. My muscles are tense and sore. My body is weak. No one directly approaches me or speaks as I walk through the grand hall with magic simmering in the air.

My somber walk ends only when I reach the queen's booth and I take my seat beside her.

"You act as if someone has died," she says, her tone sharp.

I don't respond to that.

"They can see it on you. If you want to remain—"

"More threats?" I spit. "That's how you'll handle this?"

The queen's fiery eyes shift my direction. "I gave you one week to mourn. Your week is through. Pull yourself together."

"One week to mourn the loss of a fated mate is not enough." No time will ever be enough. I knew I was too attached to Caelynn, knew my soul was entwined with hers so deeply it could kill me to see her go. But this is different somehow. Because I cannot convince myself that it was truly her choice.

Caelynn remains a prisoner. Punished for simply existing.

"And a grand ball was not how I'd thought I'd be introduced back into the world."

The queen informed me yesterday that she'd be holding a second event. After the last ended in such terrible fashion, she wanted to re-establish the feeling of confidence in the High Court and in me as the heir.

"She never intended to stay," the queen says gently.

We watch the fae below, mingling and drinking and dancing. A few more are introduced and descend into the hall. The air is lighter now that I am not in the spotlight. Maybe I just want them to know how I feel. How I will never forgive them for hating the female I love.

It's their fault she was torn from me.

"Why is it so terrible now," the queen continues, "that she chose to leave? How is it different?"

I consider this. It's different for many reasons. Because if she'd simply gone to her home court, she could come back at any time. I'd invite her to events like this. I could dance with her. See her smile. Know she is okay. Know she is happy. "If I believed she truly chose the human world as her home, where she'd find real happiness, I'd cope better. But I do not."

The queen blinks. "You claim I lied?"

"No. I claim that Caelynn, once again, sacrificed everything for me."

The queen doesn't respond to that. The song shifts into a slow melodic tune. It reminds me of Caelynn, her very essence. Achingly beautiful and so very broken.

"Is it not possible for her to desire a life in the human world? If it were me, I'd have wanted to flee from the scrutiny."

"No. Caelynn did not run from the hatred."

"It sounds like your goodbye was not enough to satisfy you. Maybe we need to orchestrate one last meeting so that you can get your closure. You can see she is well. And that she chose her fate."

I shake my head but don't respond. It doesn't matter. Seeing her will not help, not like that. She'd say anything to make me believe she wanted to go to the human realm. But I know better.

One glance at Darren Shadowspell's portrait in the main hall tells me what I know without a doubt. Caelynn would not have abandoned her homeland without cause.

She did not have a choice, not really.

I don't know who took the choice from her. If it was the Night Bringer's threats or a deal she made for my sake. But I know it deep in my soul.

Caelynn is not free.

In the crowd below, a pretty blond fae in a light blue dress bows to a fae male. My stomach twists but then relaxes as they begin a waltz, spinning eloquently. For a moment, just an instant, I had thought it was Caelynn.

But as I watch the female dancing, I realize I do recognize her. She was the female that helped me to find Caelynn in the shadows at the last ball.

"Who is she?" I ask, pointing to the blond on the dance floor.

The queen leans forward. "Arianna," the queen murmurs. "A Glistening Courtier's wife. No one of real significance."

I watch her. Knowing there is most definitely something significant about her. "Where is she from?"

The queen huffs out a quiet laugh. "She reminds you of Caelynn."

I nod. "I spoke with her during the last ball. She knew how to see a fae hiding in shadow. And she does resemble her."

"She came from the Shadow Court before being married. I don't know if she had any relation to Caelynn, but I suppose it's possible."

I swallow, remembering Caelynn telling me about how strong females of her court were often married off to other courts. Inter-marrying in the court system is not uncommon, but she made it out to be some great conspiracy. She claimed they forced fae to marry in other lands to weaken the Shadow Court. She told me her parents considered forcing her to marry as well.

"Her eyes were hazel," I say more to myself than the queen. She didn't have the gold or silver flecks of the shadow fae.

"A trait that often happens when a fae leaves their home

court near the end of their adolescence, but before being formally accepted into their court."

Our magic is elemental, each portion of land holds a different magic in the soil and water and air. Young fae absorb their land's magic. Their strength and depth of magic is innate, but the type of power will alter based on where they are raised. The absorption becomes exponential in their final teen years when courts instruct young fae to enter their most magically powerful areas—their rites of passage. This solidifies their element and strengthens them.

This lovely fae that looks so much like Caelynn is not fully shadow fae, as her eyes show, because she went to another court at a young age. How young? I wonder. Was she married at seventeen? Eighteen? For a fae that's... sickeningly young.

"Why do we arrange marriages in fae that young?"

The queen opens her mouth to respond but then reconsiders. "There are a few reasons—a mated pair, for example. Mostly, it is frowned upon but has become a common occurrence in the case of the Shadow Court."

My stomach sinks. "To keep them weak."

She blinks slowly. "It is more complicated than you think. As High Heir, you will be privy to deep-seeded secrets of our world. There is purpose behind many things others would consider great injustices. But it will take time to understand them all, and now is not the time to delve into those issues. If these questions still plague you, come find me tomorrow and I will give you what I can. Otherwise, they will be revealed to you in the coming years before your crowning."

I suck in a long breath. "It was because of the Night Terror. Because of Darren Shadowspell."

The queen freezes.

As the descendent of the fae who completed the spell that trapped the Night Terror, Caelynn had the ability to break the curse on the Schorchedlands. I knew that fact, but now that I know Caelynn is of the royal line—her great, great, great something grandfather was the final Shadow Court High Ruler—it all makes sense. The royal bloodline was hidden away and somehow survived, lost in the common fae of the Shadow Court.

But even with the right blood, it wasn't enough, because the Shadow Court had become so weak the royal fae did not have enough magic to complete the spell. That's the real reason the court system suppressed them. Not because the Shadow Court was hated. Not because we feared them.

But because we feared the creatures that needed them.

It was a backup plan. A way to stop the Night Bringer from using the lost line to break the spell.

But he even found a way around that by giving Caelynn some of his own power.

"We can stop it now. The curse is broken. The Shadow Court can rise again without any worry."

"Perhaps," the queen whispers.

We sit quietly in our booth for another ten songs, watching the crowd. I put my hand in my pocket and cling to the cold stones. There is no warmth to comfort me.

"You should dance," the queen says. "Just one."

My stomach sinks. I don't want to because it'll only make me think of her.

"Kari would be an apt choice," the queen prompts.

She would. I know she would be considerate and would not presume anything from the act.

But do I want to perpetuate the idea of us marrying? The crowd is already so eager for the drama of a powerful match. Of finding someone to place on my arm. Just the thought of those rumors sends another ache through my stomach.

I want it to be Caelynn. No one else. I clench my cold stone tighter.

In the corner of the hall, a young girl with dull eyes and brown hair talks with a Whirling Court male. I blink and lean in, my stomach rising to my throat.

"Raven," I whisper. Then, I leap to my feet and march into the crowd. *Raven is here, in the High Court.*

I leap down the steps and rush into the crowd. Fae gasp and grumble as I push past them. What the hell would Raven be here for? Was it just my imagination?

I find her dim brown hair through the crowd, only a few sets of bodies between us. "Raven!" I call.

She turns, mouth open in surprise. It's her, I know it is. But there is something in her eyes—the flicker of light.

Magic.

I flinch, and in one quick blink, Raven is gone.

What the hell? I rush forward, pushing fae out of the way as necessary, but when I reach the place she stood, I find nothing. No one. Not the young human girl or the Whirling Court fae she was with.

I spin, searching for her or anyone from the Whirling Court. I don't find the young fae male or the girl, but I do meet the gaze of Drake near the dancing couples. He smirks, and I imagine strangling him.

Doing that here would be a bad idea. But soon. He will feel my wrath for what he did to Caelynn. Very soon.

His smile grows.

Then, the ground begins to shake.

I blink and stare down at the glass floor exposing the crashing waves below the palace and watch in horror as a crack streaks across it.

53

CAELYNN

Light flickers in the tiny stone sitting in my palm. I shake my head and sit on the bed of my shitty motel room, staring at Rev's soul stone. It flickers with a dim light. Its shine is dulled by this magicless world.

I want to contact Rev, tell him that I love him, and wish things were different, but what would that achieve?

I want to ask him to help me find Raven.

I want him to forget I ever existed.

The ache in my chest is overwhelming. I hold the stone between my palms and close my eyes, picturing him. My mate. A flicker of warmth enters my chest.

Caelynn. His voice seems to whisper through me. I jerk, dropping the stone on the starchy orange bedspread. I stare at the stone, dull just like before.

Did I imagine that?

Gripping the stone between my fingers again, I twist it around. We know that, somehow, this stone connects us. But across worlds? Is that even possible?

I try again, focusing on Rev just to see what might happen. Tomorrow morning, I'm planning to head back into the fae realm, probably walking right into a trap. The Night Bringer has to know I know Raven is gone. Will he be waiting for me?

Was that what all of this was about? Just getting me away from the protection of the High Court, away from Rev, to meet him on his terms?

I don't even care. Let him destroy me.

I focus on the stone again. "Rev?" I whisper.

A taste, sharp on my tongue, explodes in my mouth. Shock. I'd felt shock coming from the stone. How?

The stone falls silent and nothing else comes from it. I breathe deeply, staring at my hope flickering dimly.

Maybe tomorrow will be my last day alive, but I'd rather die tomorrow than live the rest of my life not knowing what happened to my friend who I selfishly dragged into all of this. Or live the rest of my life with the regret if something happens to her.

Raven is here, in the High Court.

I drop the stone on the bedspread a second time, a breath stuck in my throat. What the hell?

Pulse racing, lungs desperate for breath, I stand and pick the stone back up.

It's more likely a trap or me hallucinating than it could possibly be real, right?

I don't know what to think or do, but my heart is screaming at me to move. To go. To save them. Save them both.

"From what?" I ask my own soul. What a stupid thing to do—more evidence it's really me just losing my mind. But I throw my few belongings into my ratty bag and toss it over my shoulder.

54

REV

Screams pierce the air as the glass floor of the ballroom splinters. The whole palace sways and shudders with the rumbling of a great earthquake.

Roars of grinding stone fill my ears, covering the desperate screams.

This ballroom was built very specifically to hang over the most violent spot of the Source Sea, where massive waves crash against stone, making quite a beautiful spectacle for events.

But as the floor falls away and horrified high fae grasp at the sharp edges to stop from falling, it has created a different sort of spectacle.

Those that are able, scramble to the edges of the room, away from the shattering glass, but those in the middle drop to the ground, barely hanging on as fragments of the floor fall away. Massive shards of glass soar a hundred feet toward the merciless waves below.

A female's scream echoes through my soul as she falls, her red dress flutters and ripples until she crashes into the waters below.

He requires sacrifice.

I suck in a breath, but I don't know where the voice had come from.

Another male follows next, falling to his death. Then another. The screams are a cacophony of sound.

I tear my eyes away from the horror and push the fae near me toward the stairs, toward the closest exit. "Go!" I yell. "Get out of here!"

It's chaos as fae scramble and push and claw their way up the massive marble staircase.

Another blast sounds somewhere in the distance, and the roaring of massive beasts shake me to my bones. Panic sucks the life from my lungs, and my eyes go unfocused.

For a moment, all I can see is the Night Terror. Her ancient voice rattling the very stone of the mountains in the Schorchedlands. Her rows of slimy teeth and roots stretching out like tentacles to strangle me.

With a roar of pain, I force my mind back to reality.

That is not the Night Terror. She cannot touch you, I remind myself.

Unfortunately, that is only a minor reassurance because if it's not the Night Terror, it means it's something else.

Something worse.

55

REV

The groaning of cracking stone rises in a crescendo, and I turn, horrified, expecting to find the entire palace plunging into the depths of the Source Sea but instead find purple crystals and brown stone intertwining to cover the still shattering glass.

Kari and Tyadin stand on each end of the room their hands outstretched.

Fae scramble, screaming in terror over the bridge that Kari and Ty have created.

My heart swells with pride for my two friends as they save countless lives. I am powerless in this situation. My magic is light, with no physical substance. I can't stop the wreckage.

But they can.

I run up the stairs and out into the fresh air among the mingling refugees. Salt and ancient magic sting my tongue as I breathe.

"What is happening?" I whisper.

There's a large gathering of panting fae standing in a large group. The ground rumbles again, shaking so violently that many of the fae fall to their knees. Pebbles begin falling from the tops of the High Court palace.

"Go through the portals!" I yell. I don't know what's happening right now, but I don't think it's a simple earthquake. No one is safe here.

As if on cue, the ground rumbles again. The stone atop the High Court palace topples, crashing down on itself.

Finally, fae follow my instruction and piles of them flee through the three still-standing portals. Another falling boulder lands right atop the next portal. Then another.

Only one left. "Go!" I scream at them. As the solid ground beside the palace cracks and groans and then slides off into the sea.

Swirling waters pour into the massive hole, and the entire palace tilts in toward it.

My blood turns cold. *The whole High Court is going to be destroyed*, I realize. It's going to be at the bottom of the Source Sea in minutes.

"What is happening?"

I turn to find the queen, her eyes glowing with angry fiery power.

"I don't know," I admit. "It's them, it has to be."

"But why?" she roars. "I obeyed them. I...."

Sent Caelynn away. And yet, they still attacked.

"Wraiths are searching the palace," she tells me through her panting. "Fae in black suits with them. What do they want?"

"The spell book is inside," I whisper.

Her eyes widen. "We need to get it first. Maybe it's the key to stopping this."

I nod and without delay, I race through the trembling halls, rubble raining down on my head, even as I realize the flaw in my plan.

We cannot use the spell book to save anything. We can't use it without Caelynn.

Even with the terror of that realization, I make it my life's purpose to get that spell book because at least it's something. At least I can stop them from getting their hands on it.

I shove my way into my bedroom.

The book whispers fervently at me in a language I don't know, couldn't understand no matter how hard I tried. And I did try this week. The book continued to badger me so often that I continued to try using it, even when the burns left marks on my skin.

It was trying to tell me something. It was trying to warn me about this.

And if Caelynn had been here, we would have known this attack was coming.

I clench my teeth as I lift the book and press it against my chest. Agony blasts through my whole body but I force myself to cling to it. My vision peppers with black as the pain shoots through my limbs.

The ground shakes, and I stumble back against the bedpost.

I run away, pretending I haven't already decided my efforts will be worthless. Larger pieces of stone fall now as I run down steps, tilted off to the side, and into the main hall. The portraits of all the past High Kings and Queens have fallen. Shattered glass covers the ground, their images scattered everywhere, lying helpless.

I crunch over the glass, stepping on their outcasted faces but find the end of the hall is blocked, walls caved in. Heart throbbing, I stop, holding the still burning book against my chest. I turn back and run the other way, back over the fallen fae rulers, and finally find a window to crawl out of. Glass bites into my skin, but I ignore the pain.

Bodies of crushed fae sprinkle the courtyard, and I press my trembling lips together as I leap over and around them to meet with the queen and the rest of the council who cower helplessly surrounded by guards. They tremble, huddled together and barking arguments at each other.

Their eyes perk up as I enter holding the ancient book. I drop it on the ground at their feet.

It buzzes and hisses, shaking in rage.

"The spell book," the Frost Queen says in a hushed tone.

"We can use it," the Wicked Court king says eagerly, "to stop this. Right?"

"Prince Reveln can use it," someone whispers, I don't know who.

The book trembles on the ground and flips open to its blank pages.

"Use it. Clearly, it has something to say," my father shouts. "Something it wants."

The queen's desperate eyes find mine. Has she realized her mistake?

"I can't use it," I tell them, my voice hoarse. The ground shudders in response, and I shiver.

"Why?" my father commands.

"The book always belonged to Caelynn. I need her to use it."

56

CAELYNN

Panic radiates from the stone in my hands, and I slide my motorcycle to a stop at the beginning of the pathway leading into the forest. Moss covers the stones and trees like a spongy green blanket. Fae magic swirls here gently. Subtly.

Pixies dart here and there. Birds with souls and minds of the fae soar overhead.

I shadow leap to the trees intertwined into an archway, and I stop, staring at the rippling magic. Magic humans wouldn't be able to see. Feel, maybe. But definitely not see.

I hold my mate's soul stone in my open palm, and I close my eyes, focusing on him.

Horrific images flash through my mind. Fae falling to their demise into crashing waves that devour them in an instant. The stone of the High Court palace crumbling. A monster rising from the waves.

I almost let the panic overtake me, almost stumble back, but I need to do the opposite.

He's rising, I remember the shadow sprites telling us. Maybe they didn't mean the Night Bringer. Maybe they meant someone worse.

Magic washes over me as I step through the portal.

I blink when the purple sky of the Crystal Court comes into view, stars twinkling. The massive purple stone tower sparks against the night light.

The peace is short-lived, though, as screams pierce the air. I shadow leap several times until I'm close enough to see the cause of the chaos. Several fae dressed in gorgeous gowns and tailored suits cower before the portal to the High Court. My stomach sinks again. More fae appear out of nowhere, joining the panicked group.

If there were guards watching this portal, they are distracted now. I shadow leap the rest of the way and push through the throng of terrified fae and into the chaos. Magic whips over me, and I fall to my knees on the gravel of the High Court island as chaos reigns.

Fae scream and run past me, scrambling into the portal I just left.

My heart is in my throat as I examine the carnage. Many fae are on the ground, blood-splattered, smashed by falling stone. The palace itself is off-kilter, tipping toward the sea where there is a swirling hole, sucking in everything nearby.

The stone in my pocket burns so urgently I flinch and grab at it. "Ow!"

"You must try, child!"

I blink at the sounds reverberating through the stone. Pain and fear. Rev's. My heart clenches. But then, the stone pulls at me and I follow. Across the island, toward the rocky bank on the east side.

I follow the pull slowly, unsure. Past the faces of panicked fae. Injured fae. Dying fae. I step over several limbs strewn across the lawn.

The ground rocks again, a massive crack forming in the center of the island. More screams, cries of pure fear, but I follow the pull until I find a crowd of High Court Guards.

Come to me, Caelynn.

Power whispers to me. That's not the stone. Not Rev.

That's the spell book.

"Move!" I yell at the guards. "Let me in!" I holler, but they don't move. I close my eyes for one moment, calm centers me, and I leap past them into the midst of the highest fae of the realm, bloodied and pained.

They jerk back as I appear before them.

"Caelynn?" the queen whispers.

"Move," I tell them all. And they shift to reveal Rev, leaning over the spell book. Welts pepper his forearms, making his tattoos rise oddly.

Rev's eyes are full of pain and fear and relief all mixed into a storm to match the one raging now.

"How?" he whispers. Then, his arms around me. "Don't you dare ever leave me like that again."

My breath shudders, but I return his embrace, his magic reaches into me, and mine answers. A song of shadows and light pours from us, and I laugh through my tears.

His teeth chatter as he releases me, I pull out the lumistone. "You were calling me."

A roar of ancient power cracks through the sky. Lightning flashes.

"That can't be good," I whisper.

"Well, if you can use the book, then do it, child!" one of the queens behind me yells. I bite my lip and look down at the trembling book, whispers reaching out to me like fingers, begging me to use it.

I drop to my knees and swallow just as another tremor shakes the ground. The palace slips closer to its demise in the swirling waves.

"It's coming this way," someone whispers. "We have to leave. Get out of here somehow."

"All of the portals have been destroyed," Queen Zanterleisha says. "It's too late for that." I look over my shoulder to find even the Crystal Court portal in ruins now. It seems rather suspect, that every single portal has been destroyed, even before the rest of the palace.

The arguing continues behind me, but I instead focus on the ancient magic pulling at me from the yellowed parchment.

"What is happening?" I ask frantically. "How is the Night Bringer doing this?"

"*It's not the Night Bringer,*" the book tells me.

"Then, what is it?" I yell now, even though I think I already know. Wind rushes at us like a raging scream ripped from some ancient beast.

"*He released him.*" The book's voice is in awe. "*He is awake.*"

"Now is not the time to be vague, book!" I'm screaming, barely able to hear my own voice over the raging winds and crashing waters devouring stone as the palace falls away piece by piece.

The spell book's power pulses over me, a spell rising on the pages.

The King of ancient Kings, the text reads at the top of the page. I close my eyes for a moment. The key to killing the Night Bringer and his mate, and yet the ancient spell book most fears.

It wasn't us that raised the powerful being, our enemies did. That can't be a good sign.

"The Night Bringer and his mate are not the only ancient beings still living in your world," I tell Rev, remembering the story the book told me days ago. "The King of all Kings was slumbering." Ice fills my veins.

"Who?" Rev asks.

But I don't get the chance to answer. Instead, ancient magic rushes into me, and my hair whips back in the darkness. I obey the book's silent orders.

Instructions blast through my mind. "Kari," I command, and she rushes forward. "The foundation of the island itself is crumbling. I need you and Ty and anyone else you can find to use your magic to support it." She nods, though her expression remains unsure.

"I need someone from the Glistening Court," I say. Two kings step forward proudly. The High Queen's mate and the Glistening Court King. "Water is filling the sinkhole; we can't support it without the water being removed."

They blink and look to the hole that the palace sits precariously over. "I'm unsure we can," the High King admits.

"You must. Get more help if needed. There are other powerful fae here."

They nod in unison and march from the group.

"Rev." My voice is hoarse. He leans closer. "This is going to take all of my power. I... might need help."

"Anything you need," he says, holding out a hand to me. I take it.

I give myself three seconds of preparation before I place my other hand onto the pages of the book and open myself to its power.

My vision goes black in an instant. This power so much stronger than anything I've ever used before. The magic blasts out of me, fueled and guided by him, the spirit inside.

Shadows flow from me in a wave, knocking the kings and

queens back. Even Rev loses his balance, but I pull him back with a quick tug. His warm magic swells into me. My shadows and his light twist together. His supporting mine.

I'm on my feet suddenly, and Rev follows. My back arches as more power pulses, and then my feet are off the ground. My skin stretches, pulling, power pulsing, and taking over every inch of me. Rev's hand still squeezes mine tightly, keeping me grounded.

"*Whose power calls to me?*" a thunderous voice cries over the waves.

Another roar of power booms. Kari and Ty scream, hands held tightly as they fight against the pull, keeping the island from falling into the greedy waters.

A wave rises up from the sea, pouring ancient power. White light flares from beneath the ancient giant form.

The answer almost releases from my lips, but the books prompts me to stop. *Don't tell him who you are. Don't show him your magic.*

I suck in a breath, more fear, more terror. *He won't listen,* the book had told me. *He will hate you. He will kill you.*

"Rev," I whisper. "I need you to call out to him."

Rev frowns but then puffs out his chest. "I ask you to stand down," he calls out to the beast.

"Stand down?" the ancient creature cries out, followed by laughter that shatters the ground.

Hail begins raining down. Another strike of lightning flashes. "I was called upon. Awoken. By whom?" His baritone voice is so powerful the world quakes along with it. The palace slips closer into the sinkhole with a shudder and more ricocheting screams.

"Other ancients," I answer, "who wish to use you against your own creations." Fear spikes in my chest. "They seek your power only to create more destruction."

A new desire overwhelms me. Rage and revenge, bitter on my tongue.

"Destroy them for us. You are the only one that can," I call out.

His eyes are black holes in blinding white light. I tremble beneath his power.

"Who are you?" The monster pauses, looking down at me.

"No one," I say. "But I wield the Book of All—"

"You are shadow fae," the ancient yells, and his voice is so powerful it rattles my bones.

In a flash, so much faster than a beast that large should ever be able to move, a hand of light streaks out and grabs me.

My body is swallowed in his palm of burning light. Even my scream is sucked away from me.

"Caelynn!" Rev screams, his hand torn from mine. We are so small, next to this monster. So insignificant.

"You wish to call on me to destroy your enemies," the god of light rumbles smoothly, to me. I curl up into a ball in his own palm. Roaring agony tears through me. Melting my bones, my flesh, my soul. "Yet you do not even know who I am. You do not realize that I am the enemy of all shadow fae."

No, I whisper in my mind, but I can barely think. I can feel nothing but the boiling rage.

"Please!" someone calls. Begs. "Don't take her from me."

The ancient pauses and the pain halts for a moment. "Who are you?" his voice is softer, curious, and the burning halts. I pant, my vision flickering red and black.

"Reveln of the Luminescent Court. She is my mate!" Reveln calls. "Please. Give her back to me, and slumber once more."

"You are a child of light. And she is a child of darkness,"

the ancient king murmurs. Another wave of shock rocks through my body, still in his open palm far above the raging sea. "And you are mates." His chest rumbles, a curious sound. Neither angry nor pleased.

"Yes," Rev says, so soft I don't know how I could hear it.

"I pity you, mortal," the ancient says to Rev. "To be linked to one with a soul so dark. But you choose her anyway?"

"Yes," he answers.

His black eyes narrow on me. "And you wish for me to slumber again?"

"I wish for you to stop destroying our island," I say pathetically, through clenched teeth. I tremble, clinging to my knees.

He stares down at the carnage below. "I see." And suddenly I can feel as he feels. His disappointment. He wanted to be used. To reign once again.

"Only those worthy, will wield my power. Only those willing to give all will receive it."

My vision blinks in and out, and then my body slams back to hard ground.

The ancient king's ominous message rings over the island. Waves wash over me, cooling my burned skin but I am held by caring arms. Anchored to solid ground by my mate.

His magic rocks through my body the moment the waves recede. He's healing me.

I groan, barely able to register what's happening until the clouds above clear, exposing a bright full moon and glittering stars.

The ancient king's body of blinding light crashes back into the dark waters.

57

REV

I cling to Caelynn's too-hot body, my magic circling us both as the ancient beast crashes back into the sea and disappears.

The ground has stopped trembling, the hail has stopped pouring. The world is quiet in those moments.

No waves crash against the remaining stones. No ripples appear in the blackened water.

"Will you ever stop saving me?" I ask Caelynn, my lips at her ear.

"Never," she whispers. "But I think it was you who saved me, this time."

I chuckle. "If you hadn't come, we'd all have been doomed."

Kari and Tyadin and several other earth element fae yell to each other, their motivation renewed to support the palace. To save the High Court.

The two Glistening Court kings work together and a massive river of water rushes out of the hole in the middle of the island, pouring back out into the sea. Stones fill it, every able fae aids, building stone upon stone.

"What the hell was that?" one of the king's demands.

"An ancient king of power," Caelynn answers. "The Night Bringer tried to raise him."

The council is quiet.

"It nearly destroyed the High Court," The queen says, finally.

I nod. "They'll continue to find ways around their bargain. They *wanted* to drown the High Court and the spell book along with it." It all fits. The spell book is our greatest advantage against the night ancients. Without Caelynn we cannot use it, but they likely wanted to ensure that. And punish us all for thinking we could resist their reign.

Either that, or they thought they could convince the ancient king to fight for them.

The queen's eyes are distant as she watches the water and ground fae work together to save the palace.

"And they wanted Caelynn banished because she is the only one that could stop it," I tell them.

"It needed to be both of us," Caelynn mutters. I blink down at her. Why had that beast hated her? A question for another time.

"This book only bows to her?" the Frost Court Queen asks. That was fairly well established in the midst of the chaos, but if they want it clearly stated, I will oblige.

I nod. "Only Caelynn's power unlocks the ancient tome."

"That is a lot of power for one fae to wield."

"And yet," I tell them, "It is significantly less than what our enemies hold."

They frown collectively.

I release Caelynn's hand and turn to face the council and the queen. "The Night Bringer and Night Terror are free and at full power." I let my voice carry, unconcerned with who hears. I need these ruling fae to understand. To see what I see. "We have very few elements in our favor in a battle against them. My bargain with them is one of them. The spell book is another, which we can only use with Caelynn's help."

The kings and queens of the council remain quiet, their eyes wide. This time, it was so much more than politics.

"We only have two choices. We can fight and find a way to destroy them before they destroy us. Or we bow to all of their requests and accept their reign over all fae. If you choose the latter, then you will do it without my help."

Panicked whispers scatter through the small group.

"What are you saying?" the High Queen asks. "Are you refusing your position as High Heir?"

My stomach sinks. Part of me wants to, but... "No. I intend to remain and fight. But I will step down if the council intends to pander to these creatures. They want to rule over the lands, over us. And they will do whatever they must to achieve it. I will fight for you, with you, as your High Heir. But that will mean pardoning Caelynn. I need her in order to fight. *We* need her. The realm needs her. As you all witnessed tonight."

I can feel Caelynn bristle behind me, tense, waiting for her sentencing.

"She refused my order and came back here without permission," the queen says, her voice low.

I glare at the queen, anger rising to the brim. Magic flares in my palms and I bare my teeth... "You told me she chose to leave by her own free will. And now you admit she was ordered to never return?"

The queen takes a step back. No one rushes in to protect her.

I curl my lip in disgust. "She came back to save our damn asses."

"You disrespect your queen," my father grumbles, eagerness in his eyes. He wants me to be rejected by the queen and council, and if just one thing goes wrong here, I will be.

"You have a choice now," I announce to the council. "Choose my side in this conflict and allow me to fight—with my mate at my side."

The kings and queens gasp at my admission that Caelynn is my mate. I don't care. Let it be one more secret they hold from the rest of the world or shout it to every corner of our continent. I don't care.

"Or tell me now," I continue, "and I will walk away and allow you to rule how you see fit and hope those creatures are sated by my dismissal. But if you really believe that petty revenge is all they are after, then you are all fools."

Rai steps forward immediately. "I am with Prince Reveln."

The Frost Court Queen steps forward also. "Me as well."

Three more kings and queens step forward. Followed by the High Queen. "I am with High Prince Reveln as well. We were proved wrong today. We were humbled. And I will choose to right that wrong starting now."

She turns to Caelynn, whose dark eyes are wide.

"I hereby pardon you off all crimes. You are free to do as you wish, Caelynn."

58

REV

It takes a full hour of work for one of the portals to be reconstructed to allow the surviving fae to escape the half-destroyed island. Even then, the portal is haphazard and the structure flimsy, but we were able to transport the injured fae into the Glistening Court, where healers were waiting to aid.

The High Queen, Caelynn, and I didn't stay there, though. The Glistening Court is so close to the wreckage, I think we all could feel it—the hatred of the Night Bringer breathing down at us. And now that the Whirling Court is the home of our next worst enemy, remaining at a neighboring court seemed unwise.

Instead, we chose to travel to one of the kingdoms farthest from the conflict in the High Court—the Frost Court.

We could have gone to the Luminescent Court, which is nearly as far in distance, but my father was hesitant to welcome the shadow fae back into this home, even with a command from the High Queen. So, we took the Frost Court's invitation.

The High Court is still being worked on and will be for

weeks, I imagine, before the structure is rebuilt and its luxury reestablished. For now, we'll remain as guests here.

Snow falls gently past the windows, piling on the grounds.

The fire ripples softly in the fireplace, warmth radiating from the hearth. Caelynn sits on my lap, my arms tucked around her, and I breathe in her scent. "I missed you," I tell her.

"Me too." She lays her head against mine.

"I'm sorry I didn't come after you," I admit.

She snorts. "That would have made no sense."

"I want us to be together," I whisper. "It makes all the sense in the world."

"Me too. And we are, for now."

"For now?" My heart squeezes and so do my arms around her. We both know our next step is to find a way to destroy the night ancients. They've proven that they will not leave us be, bargain or no. But I want her to know that *we* are forever. "We can be together forever if we want."

Caelynn freezes in my arms, muscles tense.

"You want that, don't you?" My voice breaks, suddenly unsure. She bound her soul to mine, when she believed she'd be leaving the realm for good. Maybe it isn't really what she wants.

She crawls off my lap and stands before the fire, watching it pop and flicker.

My stomach sinks. "Caelynn?"

"There are a lot of things I want. Things I need. Killing the Night Bringer is my first priority."

I stand and approach her slowly. "I agree."

"I need you to understand something, Rev." She turns to face me, her eyes void of the golden light I've come to adore.

I wait for her to continue, fear like a knife pressed to my chest.

"I know nothing has been easy for either of us, but you... you have reached all of your goals," she tells me. "You're the High Heir. You're going to be the High King. Having your mate by your side, even one hated the way I am, doesn't seem like such a far stretch. But for me—"

My stomach drops to my feet, for the first time understanding what she's been saying all along. "You don't have the things you want," I say. It's not a question. It's a realization.

She's pardoned. She's free. And yet— that's not enough. It's not nearly enough. Not even close to what she deserves.

She shakes her head. "I want to be with you. But it's not all I want."

How had I not seen that? Caelynn still has to claw and fight for anything.

We could help the Shadow Court, together, through the High Court. She could remain with me, even despite the queen's bargain for us to never marry. But what will that earn Caelynn? A luxurious life in my arms far from the lands she adores. And nothing more.

If she chooses me, she's choosing *only* me.

I've been saying for weeks that I want to give something back to her. I know Caelynn doesn't expect anything from anyone. She learned long ago that she wasn't deserving of those things.

And for the first time, she's fighting for something for *her*.

"You deserve the choice," I say softly, even as my heart aches. I reach out, wrapping my arm around her waist and pulling her close. "I just want you to know that I'll help you. I'll help you gain all of the things you want. Even if it means we'll never be together the way I want."

Caelynn's shocked expression only remains for a few seconds before it crumbles, tears welling in her eyes. She grips my shirt in her tight fist and presses her face into my neck.

For a moment, I think I've said the wrong thing, but then, between her desperate, tear-filled breaths, she says, "Thank you."

It shouldn't be expected for Caelynn to give up her dreams for me.

She is the true Shadow Court heir, and if she wants to rule her kingdom, then I will not stop her.

It isn't what I'd wanted for us. It's not what I'd planned or hoped for.

But love, I've realized, is more than just kisses and sweet words. It's hard choices and sacrifices. It's choosing someone over yourself.

So, it hurts, telling Caelynn—my soulmate—that I'll help her choose a destiny that separates us. But I do it because her happiness matters more than mine.

A Note from the Author

Thank you so much for following Caelynn and Rev's story. I've become so invested in these characters and I'm hoping the same can be said for my readers! As I was writing Shadow of Thorns I wasn't sure if it would be the final book in the series or, but turns out—there's a lot left to say. I didn't want to skimp on any part of Caelynn and Rev's story and so this part of the series grew longer and longer! So, there will be one more book in the WICKED FAE series!

If you love this series, PLEASE PLEASE PLEASE leave a review. Reviews get harder and harder to come by when you get this deep into a series and they make a major difference to indie authors. I want to keep writing and to do that I need people like you to continue to support me.

The best way to support authors you love is to talk about them!

Find me, and my newsletter at www.StaceyTrombley.com

And be my friend on Facebook, Instagram and Tiktok @StaceyTrombleyAuthor

ABOUT THE AUTHOR

Stacey Trombley is a casino pit boss by night, indie author by day. She lives in Ohio with her husband, son, and GSD Riley. When she's not writing or reading her husband is probably dragging her along on one of his crazy adventures for this travel vlog or competing against him about who can pick the most Survivor winners in the first episode (hint: she's winning). But mostly, she's probably reading.